Ruth Gogoll's
Taxi to Paris

Ruth Gogoll's

Taxi to Paris

Newly revised edition
Translated from the German by
Susan Way

© 2010

édition elles

www.elles-books.com

Translation by Susan Way

Cover Photo:

© Sandor Jackal – Fotolia.com

ISBN 978-3-941598-08-9

—— 1 ——

I like it when my women defend themselves!"
Her eyes blazed with anticipation again – of the fight, the conquest, the siege.

I did not want to give myself to her. Even so, everything in me longed to touch her, to be touched by her.

"Come on, tell me again that you don't want it! That you hate me!" She laughed, cynical, provocative.

"I hate you!" I screamed. It was the truth, but that didn't stop the desire burning inside me. And I hated myself for that, for obeying her wish. That was what I wanted least of all, to please her. I could see her arousal climbing. Her eyes flashed. She came closer. Her lips parted. I saw her teeth gleaming and thrashed my head from side to side, trying to escape. She pressed me against the wall and held my wrists with an iron grip.

"No, I don't want to! Not like this!"

She did not let me go, but threw her head back and laughed. "Yes, defend yourself. That's how I like it best." Her voice was hoarse with excitement.

I stiffened. She took advantage of the opportunity and, like lightning, pressed her mouth against mine. Her tongue thrust hard against my tightly clenched teeth. She pressed me against the wall with her whole body. I had to take a breath. She penetrated me, took possession of me. The passion and excitement almost left me unconscious. At the same time, revulsion crept up my throat; I bit down. Her head flew back, but she still held my wrists as tightly as manacles. I had the impression she wasn't doing this for the first time. She was used to it . . .

She looked at me wildly. A drop of blood hung from her lip. She ran her tongue over it to wipe it away. My eyes never escaped her stare. "You little wildcat! So I had you figured wrong all along! I thought you'd be boring and bourgeois, the type to just lie down and spread her legs."

A shimmer of hope flashed in me. "Yes, yes, that's exactly what I am, boring and bourgeois." Maybe that would stop her.

"No, no!" She laughed again, ragged with excitement. "It's too late now. I've seen through you. You want it. You want the fear; you want the pain. That turns you on, admit it!"

Her fingers kept tightening around my wrists. It hurt, and I cried out.

"Yes! Scream, scream as loudly as you can!" Her voice was now just a raw, excited whisper.

I was startled. The pain hadn't sobered me, as I'd expected. Instead, I felt it right between my legs, just as she'd said. Was this really what I wanted?

She noticed my indecision. Her mouth fell upon mine again, and this time I didn't refuse. With brutal force, she plunged in, almost to the back of my throat. I thought I was going to vomit, but just before it went that far, she pulled her tongue back. She really was experienced at this! How many women had she already done this with? Perhaps there were more who wanted this than I would have imagined. And I? Was I one of them? Did I want it?

She began again. I felt the need overcome me, to kick back, to join in, and not to let myself be passively used anymore. But that was just what she wanted! I had to defend myself against that! At least, that's what my head demanded. My body betrayed me. I could no longer hold back the ever-stronger desire building in me. My knees weakened. She noticed and loosened her grip a little.

My tongue sought hers. She pulled back for an instant, a look of astonishment on her face. Then, she sank into my mouth again, probing and demanding, almost smothering me. Suddenly, she let go of my hands and laid hers on my waist. I stiffened in anticipation of fresh pain. She tore my shirt from my pants and raced across my back. Everything tingled.

Unhindered, she dug her fingernails into my shoulders. I moaned in exquisite pain. Slowly, she raked them across my entire back, down to my waist. It was as if my skin was being torn away, but still not quite such that I couldn't stand it. I moaned, louder, out of pain or growing arousal I didn't know which.

"Yes, come on, tell me you want it," she murmured against my mouth. Her hips still held me, pressing and trapping me against the wall. I tried to arch against them, to push, to rub against her. No, this wasn't me! This was my pelvis, which had declared its independence from me. *Traitor*, screamed something inside me. The desire kept growing stronger.

"You want it – say it!" she insisted, hot across my mouth.

"No!" I threw my head to the side and tried to push myself away from her.

She pressed against me again, leaned back a little, and tore off my shirt. I was boiling inside. I could not allow that! She threw the shirt on the floor next to me and bent over me once more. I thought she wanted to start kissing me again. *Kissing? Was this kissing, this thrusting, this throttling?* She threw my head to the other side. She did not follow. Her head sank down upon my shoulder. A piercing pain ran through me. I cried out again, although I'd pressed my lips together and resolved not to.

"Yes – scream, scream!" she insisted. Her head descended again.

"No – please," I implored her. She bit down. The pain ripped through me even more sharply than the first time. Now my knees could finally hold me no longer. She held me tightly and pressed me against the wall as before. Her hand moved over my breast. She stroked the rock-hard nipple with her palm. I moaned – this time out of lust.

"It's quite sensitive," she said, grinning noticeably.

Panic rose in me again. "Please, don't do that," I whispered, trembling in fear. Defensively, I lifted my hands and tried to push her away from me. She laughed, aroused again, and fought playfully with me. Her iron grip damned my hands to inactivity. Slowly, she lowered her mouth onto my breast. She ran her tongue over her lips. I stiffened, trembling even more; my whole body was a single, tightly strung bow, arming itself against the pain. I pressed my head against the wall and closed my eyes. They were so sensitive — I couldn't bear it!

She sucked my breast in, flicking her tongue across my nipple, over and over. All my fear could not keep down the arousal this triggered. My hips began to push up against her again, but a cold sweat broke out across my skin.

She looked up at me and grinned. "You're afraid," she remarked, pleased.

"Yes." There was no sense in denying it, anyway. "You're going to hurt me." I tried to make my voice as quiet as possible.

Completely unexpectedly, she let go of me. While her eyes held mine, she took a small step back, grabbed my waistband, and unbuttoned my pants. Then, with one swift movement, she pulled the zipper down. I leaned against the wall as if paralyzed. She saw that I wouldn't defend myself anymore. An expression of disappointment spread across her face.

"Come on, don't spoil the fun."

"Fun!" I flared. "For you, maybe!" Dammit, that was the exact opposite of the truth! Her eyes blazed again with repressed excitement.

"Yes, it's better this way." She came closer and placed one hand on either side of my head without touching me. "You little wildcat," she whispered into my ear. She nibbled on my earlobe. I expected her to bite down at any moment and stiffened again. Her lips ran down my neck and sent waves of shivering arousal mixed with fearful anticipation through my body. She laughed softly, pleased. I felt her breath moving across my skin. "Yes, it's best this way. You're afraid. But you want it anyway."

Fury rose and made me careless. "Yes, I want it." I pushed her away with suddenly regained strength. Agilely, she moved one step back. I blazed at her furiously. "But I don't want you to force it on me. I don't want pain, I want desire, I want tenderness, passion, excitement, all of that, but no brutal force. That's ..." I searched for a word for what I felt.

She raised her eyebrows and said, smirking, "Perverse?"

"Yes – yes! Perverse!" I yelled, full of rage at her, myself and this word I'd never used before. I'd always hated it when the smug bourgeoisie asserted their own "normality" and discredited others with that word. Everyone who was different was defamed indiscriminately, regardless of the reason: homosexuality, communism, or whatever else. But my furious tension lasted only a moment – it gave way to a feeling of senselessness.

I folded my arms behind my back and leaned against the wall. "And now, as far as I'm concerned, you can go get your whip – or whatever else you use – and beat me."

Her eyes glided over my face.

"You're beautiful when you're furious," she said softly. I wanted to protest this platitude – straight out of a bad 70s porn film – but her mouth had already descended upon mine and closed it. I waited for the pushing, demanding penetration, but she just ran her tongue gently along my closed lips. The tingling grew unbearable. When I opened my mouth, she began to play lovingly with my tongue. She teased the tip of my tongue with hers until I nearly cried out with desire. Her mouth was still the only thing touching me. The air between us crackled.

I raised my hands. No, I didn't want to touch her! My arms began to tremble. She kept kissing me. Sighing, I let my hands fall to her shoulders and pulled her to me. The buttons on her shirt were cold against my naked skin. She sighed appreciatively in my mouth and encircled me with her arms. Everything was so gentle and tender. What had transformed her so suddenly? She pushed me against the wall again, one leg between mine. Even through the cloth, that touch made me half crazy. I moaned and began to rub against her with more intensity. Then I held back. That was again the point at which she'd inflict pain; I'd subjected myself to it again! I held still.

She noticed this. She stopped kissing me and took a step back to look at me. "You're confused." She stated it without inflection. I didn't answer. What would she do now? She reached out a hand and caressed my face. I didn't stir. She let her hand sink. It glided over my shoulder to my arm and down my side to my waist. There it stayed. She consumed me with her gaze. Then she set her eyes upon mine again with hypnotic power. "I won't hurt you," she declared emphatically. Her hand slid between cloth and skin. A shudder ran through my body. "I want you. I want you like you are." She worked her way down with unbearable slowness. My whole body cried out with desire. "I want you to moan, and I want you to scream. But not from pain."

Her fingers touched my hairline and kept moving torturously, slowly downward. She never released my eyes. I tightened my shoulders and buttressed myself with the wall. She wrapped her other arm around me and held me tight. Now her hand lay motionless between my legs. I moaned and bucked wildly against it. Heat rose in me like a volcano. I felt the wetness collecting on her hand. I flung my body back and forth with arousal.

She pulled her hand back. I let the breath I'd been holding out of my lungs and moaned. "No. You promised not to torture me. Please . . ."

She laughed heartily. "I promised not to cause you pain. And I won't. This is something entirely different." She stroked the cloth between my legs. I moaned again, demandingly, and rose against her. She placed both hands on my hips. Slowly, she slid my waistband down.

She took her time. Again and again, she ran her hands back and forth. It seemed like an eternity to me. When she had finally undressed me, she bent over and ran her lips along my breast. My skin was on fire wherever she touched it. She approached my nipple. I went stiff. She reacted immediately. "I promised," she murmured. Then she looked up. "I won't do anything that you don't want." I still could not relax. The fear lay too deep. She ran her lips across my breast again. Then, ever so gently, she took the nipple in and ran her tongue over it.

The sensations washed all my reservations away. "Yes," I moaned.

She stroked my hard, erect nipples, alternating between her hands and tongue.

I was crazy with desire by this time – I couldn't have stopped her from doing anything at this point, regardless. Her face was suddenly square in front of mine. She wandered along my lips – just lightly, without hurrying. I tried to hold onto her. She smiled and pulled away. Her hand glided over my breasts, along my stomach, and between my thighs. She stroked gently with two fingers along the insides, wandering back and forth from one side to the other, and then touched the center. I squirmed in her arm.

Now, she began stroking more intensely between my legs, seeking out with circling motions the most sensitive place. The whole time, I felt as if I were just about to explode. She pressed harder. I felt her finger. She found my opening.

"No!" I tore myself away from her mouth.

She stopped immediately. She pulled me to her. "What's wrong?"

"I . . . I don't like that." I swallowed hard. "You promised . . ."

She laughed good-naturedly. "I haven't forgotten. You don't have to keep reminding me."

"I'm sorry. I'm a little sensitive . . . in that area."

"You certainly are sensitive, I've noticed that." It seemed like she wanted to brush me off, but then her tone became concerned. "Does it hurt there?"

Now I had to answer. "Actually . . . no, not really. I . . . I don't really quite know."

"You don't know?"

I looked at the floor behind her. "No," I declared defiantly.

She stepped back and held me at arm's length. The way my face was burning, it must've been beet red. She laid a finger under my chin and lifted it up. "But I'm not the first woman you've slept with."

"No . . ."

She looked at me attentively. Obviously, she expected that would get me talking faster than direct questioning.

"I mean, I've been with lots of women . . . but not like that." With defiant emphasis I added, "I just can't!" I spun around to face the wall.

"And that's the only reason?"

The wall protected me, at least, from her direct stare. Nonetheless, I had the feeling that her eyes were boring into my back. "What else? Isn't that enough?"

"You've never been with a man —?"

I didn't let her finish. "No, I haven't!" I spun back around to face her. "Should I be ashamed of that?"

She still watched me vigilantly. "No, of course not! What were you thinking? But I also meant not against your ..." She broke off.

"Against my ...? Oh," I understood. "No, I haven't been raped."

She sighed, relieved. Now I was really furious. How could she be so concerned all of a sudden? "And until this evening, no one had tried, either," I hissed angrily.

She turned around and took a deep breath. Then she looked at me again. Not a muscle moved in her impenetrable face. "Then everything's fine," she said.

I thundered inside. She thought everything was fine now?

She sighed. "Earlier, that was ..." she paused to consider, "... a misunderstanding." As if that had settled everything, she sauntered back over to me, smiling.

Attempted rape a misunderstanding? She couldn't think I was that stupid.

She didn't, either. Attentively, she'd followed the emotions playing across my face. She sighed again. This time, she sounded resigned. "Yes, I know what you're thinking;" explaining, she continued, "but most women want it that way. That's why they choose me." She looked at me sadly. "You obviously didn't know. And I thought ..." She let out a bitter laugh. "Like I said, a misunderstanding."

By this time, I was more than confused. "Didn't know what?" Somewhere in this chaos, there had to be some key I could find to untangle this mess!

She turned to face me fully and stood with one hand on her hip. "I'm a whore, sweetheart!"

I was shocked. That was definitely one of the effects she was going for. But the other – that I should feel repulsed – she didn't get.

She stood a few steps away from me and looked out the window at a neon sign as it blinked on and off. She spoke into the empty darkness, "You can go quietly now. I won't hold you back." Her spine was straight as a board.

I took a step toward my clothes. But then I stopped. I didn't want to leave; that was perfectly clear to me. But what else did I want here? She was a hooker; she had expected me to pay for a "service" I had no idea I was getting. She conformed to my wishes when she saw that I wanted something different – as any good service is performed to suit the wishes of the client. The client? I suddenly saw myself in a very unfamiliar light.

She turned around and glared coldly at me. "Should I leave?" Her voice was icy.

I suddenly became aware of my nakedness. Embarrassed, I grabbed my shirt and threw it on. "No, that would be ludicrous."

She shrugged. "Most women want to be left alone afterwards. It's all the same to me." This icy voice somehow had a heart-softening quality. A contradiction in itself, but it seemed that way to me.

I buttoned my shirt and observed her. She had her arms crossed and stood there, legs apart, an unconquerable fortress. I went toward her. She followed my every move with her eyes, but she didn't stir. I stood in front of her and looked up. *My God. She was at least 6'2"!* "I don't want to be alone, and I don't want to go." I watched her, unshaken.

Mockingly, she screwed up her mouth and looked at me.

"Ah – the lady has developed a taste for it!"

She laughed. It sounded rather lachrymose. She bent down a bit. "Until just now you didn't know, and you were irritated. Now you know and already" – she snapped her fingers – "it turns you on, right? Until now it was just a somewhat exotic adventure. Something outside of the ordinary, am I right? But now, what an opportunity! What's it like to sleep with a woman who does it for money? You'd like to know, right? Why shouldn't you try it, now that we're already here?" She turned away from me and unbuttoned her cuffs. Over her shoulder, she added, "I hope you have your checkbook with you. I'm quite expensive."

With one jerk, she took off her shirt and tossed it on a chair. I saw her taut back and heard the scratching of her zipper. With a quick shake, she kicked off her boots, and her pants flew after her shirt. Now she was naked. With a crisp movement, she turned around and raised her arms for a moment. "There you are; I'm at your disposal."

Finally, I had the opportunity to look at her again and to establish what I had noticed at first glance, once more, she was unbelievably beautiful. I moved toward her and touched her. Her skin radiated the cold of a marble statue.

"No." I shook my head. "No, I won't do it. I won't treat you like a whore just so you can get rid of me more easily." I backed up.

"But sweetheart," she raised her eyebrows, as if to express her bemusement that I obviously didn't know the rules, "you're paying me. And I am a whore. Come!" She had put on a professional smile and came toward me. She reached behind my ear and stroked the sensitive spot under my earlobe with her thumb. I shut my eyes. "That's better," she cooed.

I wanted to forget it. I wanted to give in to the sensation of her stroking hand. But I couldn't. I opened my eyes. She was still smiling professionally. "What would you like? You can tell me, even if it's unusual. I'll fulfill all of your wishes. You needn't have any inhibitions."

She played it out like the opening credits to a movie. Suddenly, she smiled knowingly. She stopped stroking behind my ear and ran her hands down along my body until they rested on my buttocks. Then she knelt down. Only now did I realize what she had in mind. I'd been too busy with her show and my sensations. I pushed her head away. "Stop it!"

She wiped the smile from her face, stood with an indifferent expression, and looked at me coldly. "Whatever. It's your money. If you'd rather, you can abuse me for it, too."

I'd never before been in such an intimate situation with a woman who could switch herself off like that. She made me nervous; I wanted to know what she really felt. It enraged me how she took control of me in this way. And I'd never been able to conceal my anger. I blazed at her.

Promptly, she turned her smile back on and tried to pacify me. "But there must be certain things that you've never dared to ask from a woman." She laid her hand behind my ear once again. It would've been a wonderfully tender gesture if she hadn't done it so mechanically. Nevertheless, I enjoyed the moment of quiet. She bent down and kissed me gently on the lips. I wanted to believe for a minute, to imagine that she saw in me the woman, the beloved — not just the customer, the client.

She kissed me carefully, yes, that was the right word, carefully! She forgot nothing important! Her right hand ran down my body. Her left slid under my shirt and played with my nipple until it was hard. It was such an automatic routine; it almost made me sick. She must've done exactly this at least a thousand times before!

I wanted to push her away, but my hands landed right on her breasts. They were wonderfully soft. The velvet skin arched itself against my fingers. I began to stroke them. Instantly, she began to moan and pulled herself toward me. At first, I was surprised, but then it occurred to me what she was doing. Regretting that I had to give up the velvety softness of her breasts, I pushed her away. She looked at me with clear eyes. No trace of arousal.

"Didn't you like it?" she asked, professionally interested. I tried to hold her eyes, but she avoided me. She looked over my shoulder. "I'm sorry. I need some time to adjust myself to you. Most of my customers' demands aren't so . . . eccentric."

I couldn't help but smile. Her helplessness did more for me than the self-assurance she'd displayed up until now. I looked at her with loving affection. "You're beautiful."

Something flickered in her eyes, but then her face clouded over again. She asked coolly: "So why don't you want me then? You're paying for it. The others tell me what I should do, or if I shouldn't do anything . . ." She opened her hand in a gesture of helplessness.

An idea crept into my head. Under no circumstances did I wish to let myself fall into her game. But if she'd listen to me . . . She kept watching me, waiting coolly.

"Lie down," I ordered, with as much authority as I could muster. Astonishment flashed briefly across her face and disappeared again immediately. She spun around and took a step. Then she stood still.

"Where?" she asked flatly into the air. Her stiff back became even straighter.

"On the bed," I decided.

She set herself in motion. She strode gracefully to the bed. When she'd laid herself down, she stretched out her arms toward me. "Come," she said. She'd obviously decided to dispense with the professional expression. She looked honestly and deliberately indifferent.

I crossed the room and stood next to the bed. "Not like that," I contradicted. "Roll over." She hesitated. I waited. Then she turned herself over onto her stomach slowly, with an odd sidelong glance at me. I admired the soft, curving line of her back. She was really a beautiful woman. What could have caused her to ...? Well, that was a pointless thought. She'd have her reasons. My fingers tingled with the desire to touch her, but I only traced the outline of her body in the air. I bent down and kissed her between the shoulder blades. She jumped. "Don't you dare moan," I warned. "We already had the show."

"The others like it now and then," she countered, shrugging, with her cool, indifferent voice.

"But I don't. So let it be."

I couldn't see her face, but I could've sworn she was smiling. "As I said before, you're somewhat ... eccentric."

I kissed her again between the shoulder blades and noticed how she tensed up. She was trying to suppress the twitching. I smiled. That wasn't such a bad start. I began to cover her whole body with kisses. Slowly and tenderly, I wandered from her neck to her shoulders, then to her arms and back to her shoulder blades. My mouth glided along her ribcage and dawdled awhile in the hollow above her bottom. Although I took full advantage of this activity, I tried to observe her at the same time. At first, her hands lay next to her head. She seemed peaceful and relaxed. After the first kisses, she got goose bumps. She began to dig her hands into the pillow. Her knuckles became even tighter and whiter. As I came to her lower back, fine drops of sweat beaded up on her skin and shimmered, glistening like a fine rain. She breathed heavily, but buried her head in the pillow.

Again, my fingers traced very lightly the path from her neck to her ass. She jumped at many places this time. Her breath became heavier. She couldn't get enough air through the pillow anymore; she lifted her head and turned it to the side. Gasping, she sucked in air.

Although I believed her reactions were real, a little devil suddenly appeared on my shoulder. Perhaps the particular dynamics of this game I'd never played before, had taken hold of my brain and knocked out my normally attentive control mechanisms. In any case, I didn't think any more about it. Against my better judgment, I reprimanded her: "Don't act for me . . . I warned you!" It was only supposed to be a joke. I was firmly convinced she'd notice that, but she stiffened immediately. She was still gasping. After a few gulps of air, she began to tremble. Her hands pushed slowly under her head. "Please don't," she whispered flatly. Her voice was harsh with fear.

What was wrong? I stroked her back soothingly. She drew back as if struck by a whip and pressed her hands more tightly against her head. "No," she whispered hoarsely, almost inaudibly. "Please don't hit me," she whimpered softly, to herself.

For a moment, I was dumbstruck by such words from this big, strong woman I'd been so afraid of! Then I overcame the shock. I grabbed her shoulder. She cried out in fear. I shook her violently. "Never, do you hear me? Never! I would never hit you! Look at me, please." She lowered her hands and laid her head to the side. Her eyes drooped. She was coming out of a nightmare. As soon as she recognized me, she turned her head away.

"Please go now." She spoke to the wall. "You have no obligation to me whatsoever." She paused. "Of course, you don't have to pay." Her tone was bitter. "And of course I can't stop you from talking about this." She took a deep breath.

At first, I wanted to challenge her furiously. Then I controlled myself. That wouldn't do either of us any good. I grabbed the blanket and pulled it over her naked body. Surprised, she rolled onto her side and propped her head up on her hand. "Thank you," she said. Her voice was neutral. She let her gaze glide over me coolly. "It would really be better if you left now."

I sat carefully on the edge of the bed. "I don't think so," I really just contradicted her because everything had flown by me so quickly, and because I don't like to leave a theater without understanding the plot, but her reaction was violent.

Her eyes narrowed to slits. They glistened like pure ice. "I see," she said, drawing it out, "you're not one to be satisfied with half a cookie when someone's promised you the whole thing." With a swift motion, she grabbed me and pulled me onto the wide bed. "You'll get the other half. I always keep my promises. And now, since I've let you out of paying, it's even free." She laughed scornfully. "You'll never get a hooker as classy as I am this cheaply again."

I granted her that. The desperation I felt in her made me helpless. I only hoped that she wouldn't hurt me too much; I'd never been very good at tolerating pain. And today, I'd already established that my ability to do so had not improved.

She detected my fear. "Ah, now you're afraid?" She emphasized her words with a dismissive hand gesture. "I told you I keep all my promises, didn't I?" I nodded, to avoid making her angry again. It seemed doubtful to me that I would be able to guarantee such a promise in her condition.

She grabbed my arm. I held back a cry of pain. That was going to leave a nice bruise. She pushed me backwards onto the bed and laid herself half across me. Ruthlessly, like at first, she penetrated my mouth with her tongue. But she only went as far as she'd promised, and she didn't hold my hands down. I lifted them slowly and ran them along her back. She moaned deep in her throat. Now I knew for sure that her reaction earlier had been genuine. I stroked her back some more, and she gasped even more heavily in my mouth. I noticed that she was definitely ready to lose control. But first, she abandoned my mouth. With a violent movement, she tore my legs apart. At least two more bruises!

She let herself fall between my legs and lifted them up. She kept pushing them even farther apart and higher up. It hurt, but it was bearable. With the same severity that she'd shown in penetrating my mouth, she now entered between my legs. No foreplay, no preparation, not even a quick caress. Instead, the movements of her tongue were even heavier and more demanding, as she forced my legs even wider apart. My God, soon I'd have to scream in pain! I clenched my teeth and waited for her to be satisfied with me. On its wild hunt, her tongue found the center of all sensation. I moaned aloud. Had it not been for the pain in my thighs, this might've felt rather nice. I sighed.

She'd taken a brief recess and rested up. Then she began again, carefully, circling my clit with her tongue. She flew back and forth across it like a butterfly. I jumped every time. Gradually, my sensations grew more intense. Surely, she'd stop soon. All she wanted was her own satisfaction, which I was to bring to her. As I began to lift my pelvis against her, moaning, she stopped. Ah, that was it. I tried to hold back my excitement. Suddenly, I cried out. She penetrated me deeply with her tongue, like no woman had done before. This long tongue, which had caused me so many problems in my mouth, brought me here only pure, ecstatic pleasure. She pushed back and forth, and in between played briefly behind the entrance. She really knew every spot! I suddenly didn't care that my legs hurt, that with every thrust of my hips I felt red-hot needles all the way down to my tiptoes.

"Come," she murmured, barely audibly, between my thighs. She thrust the full length of her tongue into me once more. Then, she pulled it out and resumed her butterfly dance against the erect pearl. "Come," she whispered again, demanding.

I exploded in long, raging waves. I heard myself screaming, but it was as if the cry would not stop while the waves came and went, came and went. I tried to count them, but there were too many. After an eternity, I collapsed and struggled, exhausted, for breath. I'd never be able to breathe normally again! She came up and nipped at my breasts.

I still hadn't caught my breath when she propped herself up next to my shoulders and pushed her legs between mine. After they'd been ripped apart like that, everything hurt. I groaned in pain before I could stop myself. Immediately, she lay quietly. I raised a hand and brushed the sweaty hair from her forehead. She gave me a strained smile.

"Go on," I said softly. "You're not hurting me."

"I'm not, really?" she asked, confused.

"No." I brushed the hair tenderly from her face once more. "You really aren't."

She began to move again, carefully. Then she began to speed up. After a short while, she was again gasping with excitement. I could feel all of her muscles straining. I felt a vibration between my legs. She came in quick thrusts, moaning. Her eyes were closed. I thrust my hand between her legs. When she noticed that, her eyes flew open. "I don't want to . . ."

"Yes, you do." With my other hand, I held her tightly against me. It didn't take much, in any case, to change her mind. She began to moan as soon as I touched her. I entered her carefully. "Yes." A primitive sound forced its way from her throat. She bucked against my hand as if she wanted to take the whole thing into her. She stiffened. A small cry left her lips. Completely exhausted, she let herself fall back onto the bed. Still breathing heavily, she lay next to me.

"That was ... not ... necessary," she managed raggedly. I propped myself up on my elbow and smiled at her.

"Yes, it was. And actually, I believe you need some more yet."

She pressed her lips together and shook her head. It most likely had been a long time since she'd been so free of resistance. I slid on top of her quickly. She protested weakly. She tried to hold her legs together, but she hadn't yet regained her strength. With both hands, I pushed them apart and laid myself between them.

She was as beautiful down there as she was as a whole. I said so loudly enough that she could hear me.

"Get back up here right now!" she hissed in answer.

"Not a chance!" I laughed at her irritation. Slowly, I began to sweep a wide circle with my tongue. She sighed, and I noticed her thighs tightening. I twirled the circle smaller and tighter. She chased my tongue with her hips.

"You're driving me crazy," she whispered, so softly that I could barely understand her. I continued. She dug her hands into my hair and held on. "I can't take any more ... please." I didn't let her out of my mouth. "I can't stand it anymore! Please ... let me ..." Her voice was hoarse and demanding as it reached down to me. I took all of her into me and let her find her own rhythm. This time, she came with a long, steady scream and innumerable twitches. When her orgasm had ebbed, she lay as if dead. I slid on top of her and kissed her. She was covered in sweat.

When she could speak again, she smiled easily. "Whatever did you do?"

"I? Do? Not a thing." The innocence of a country girl was nothing compared to me.

She laughed, amused. "That's not at all what it felt like." She groped at the nightstand and pulled a long, narrow cigarette from its long, narrow package. She lit it with a beautifully decorated silver lighter and took a deep drag. Cliché, at its purest.

She looked at me. "Oh, pardon me, would you like one also?" Her hand wandered back to the nightstand.

"No, thank you," I pouted. "I hate to get lost in a cloud of smoke right afterwards."

"I usually don't either, right afterwards. But today ... it's your own fault. If you hadn't worn me out like that ..." She reached one hand tenderly under one of my breasts, leaned over, and kissed it. "Mmm," she hummed appreciatively. "Sweet as champagne." She looked at me again, closely. "Like the rest of you," she said then. She leaned back onto her pillow and smoked.

So, she had decided, at least for the moment, to like me – or perhaps just to tolerate me? I observed her from the side. She sat there, relaxed, an incredibly beautiful woman, holding her cigarette with an elegance I'd never imagined possible. The smoke circled up just as elegantly, as if it felt obligated by her manner to do so, toward the ceiling.

She ignored me. At least, she acted as if I weren't there. What did she expect from me now? Our business relationship was clearly over. I scolded myself silently. I didn't want to think about it, but I had to. What should I do in this situation? Should I just leave? But that was exactly what I didn't want to do. I wanted to stay with her; I wanted to get to know her. She had touched me deeply – her vulnerability, which she tried to hide behind miles of protective walls – her fear, and that she had chosen this in particular as a career ...

I looked at her, searching. She crushed out her cigarette and looked over at me. When she noticed my expression, she twisted her mouth a bit.

"Don't bother holding back."

"From what?" I asked, somewhat irritated.

She pulled the blanket up over herself and covered her breasts. "You want to know how and why I got here, to what I am, right?" In another situation, those cold, flashing eyes would've driven me right out of the room. As she'd inflected it, it was really an obscene question that I'd never dare ask. I kept silent.

She raised her eyebrows. If she did that one more time, I'd have to kiss her, even if I had to pay for it!

"Everybody wants to know that. I'm sure you're no exception." She looked out the window. "Almost every time I'm with a new client, she asks the same question."

I stiffened. I didn't actually want to be a "new client". And I didn't feel like one, either.

She looked at me indifferently. "You really don't want to know?" I shook my head. "Well, I don't suppose it makes any difference; I never answer the question."

I could tell that she wanted to be rid of me. She began to get restless. Any minute now, the fastest way to get me to leave would occur to her. And here it came already!

"So, did you get what you expected?" She looked at me very professionally. I almost expected her to add, "Will there be anything else, ma'am?"

I had to smile to myself. Instinctively – or perhaps completely rehearsed – she had chosen the topic that would, under normal circumstances, scare me off the fastest. But what were "normal circumstances" in a relationship with her? This whole evening and the entire night up to this point could not be compared with anything in my experience. And this woman was not going to get rid of me so easily.

She became impatient. "Were you satisfied?" She gave me a scrutinizing look. "Or did I do something wrong?" My silence made her nervous. "I know it didn't all go as you had imagined it would." She made a remorseful face. She was good at it! I bet most women melted right down when she pulled this one. She grabbed an appointment calendar from the nightstand. "We can make an appointment that's convenient for you, and you can tell me what you didn't like." She unfastened the black leather band and flipped through the pages.

This was truly unbelievable – she was offering me an improvement!

"What are you afraid of?" I asked.

She froze. Her eyes told me, more clearly than her reaction or any words could, that I had hit a sore spot. She retreated to her own mental terrain in order to steady herself.

"Should we not make an appointment, then?" she asked, leafing aimlessly through the calendar. She turned to face me once more. Her eyes had this I-have-no-idea-what-you-want-now look. They reminded me of the big luxury cars with wipers on the headlights. One moment dirtied – one wipe, and they were clear again.

Now she smiled knowingly. "If you have a reason to complain, that's bad publicity. And bad publicity is bad for business."

I was reminded of a conversation I'd had recently with a car salesman. He'd presented himself in much the same way. In that case, though, he'd wanted to sell me a car and not his body.

"You can call me." She pulled out a card.

"Oh, no!" I groaned. "Don't give me your business card now, too!"

She laughed, pleased. It seemed authentic. "I knew you'd hate that," she said. She took a pencil and wrote something on the card, then handed it to me. It was an elegant, white, handmade card, completely empty except for the large, curving figures in the middle. No name, no address, just the numbers. That was really the extreme in discretion.

I looked at her. Tiny laugh lines crinkled at the corners of her eyes. "Business cards are not typical in my line of work," she explained, even more amused. "Sorry to disappoint you."

There we sat, two naked women in one bed who had just slept together, as if we were sitting together having coffee at an upscale café.

"Would you like some more sugar?"

"Oh, no, I'd rather have another small orgasm. But not too strong; I'm having my hair done this afternoon."

The scene occurred surreal to me.

I had no more reason to stay, much as I didn't want to admit it. But I wanted to see her again. How could I do that? As her client? Never! Did I have the slightest chance, then? I kept looking down at the card in my hand. Slowly, I was growing uncomfortable in this bed. And it could have been so comfortable. Fall asleep together, wake up together, a little cuddling, a little sex … I felt the tingling begin again.

She watched me. I glanced at her out of the corner of my eye. No, I decided, she'd never do that. And I needed to get out of here as quickly as possible.

She continued to scrutinize me. Before I could think of my next move, she said, "I'm going to take a shower now. Would you rather go first ...?" Her polite, professional, obliging manner hid it badly; this was my final dismissal. I shook my head mutely, without looking at her. She rose. I watched her go. That graceful walk ... I relished every one of her movements.

When she had shut the door behind her, I leapt out of the bed. I dressed quickly. At the door, I spun around one last time. I heard water running and looked back on the bed. I wasn't going to forget this night anytime soon.

—— 2 ——

My office was waiting for me at eight o'clock the next morning, as always. "Project Manager" was under my name on the door, together with the names of my two male colleagues. We were the so-called "project leader pool." My work was a bigger part of my life than I often wanted to admit. I didn't feel right when I was away from it for any length of time, like for vacation or sick leave. After that, I was usually really happy to get back behind my desk again. And often, work alone had gotten me through my personal crises.

"Where on earth should I start? Look at all this!" My colleague Mark let out his usual lament as soon as he saw me. I smiled involuntarily. Even though I had next to nothing to do with my colleagues on a personal level, I couldn't help but like them. This made working together a lot easier.

"Oh, Mark, you're not the only one with a lot to do. We're all up to our eyeballs in work." My answer met his expectations, just like the rest of my normal behavior. This was our daily ritual. He was only half listening to me, just like I would half ignore or automatically answer his usual running commentary on the day. This gave us a sense of belonging together, and didn't distract us too much. Professionally, we were busy with two completely different projects, such that we rarely had a substantive conversation.

My other colleague came through the door in his usual quiet manner and saw me. "Good morning," he said, which I knew had to be the beginning of a business conversation. I wasn't disappointed. "Have you looked over what I left on your desk yet?" I turned around and saw his report lying on top of the mountain of other paperwork on my desk. I shook my head.

"No, I haven't. I just got here myself." I went over to the desk and flipped quickly through the pages. "You adapted the plan, like we discussed yesterday?"

He nodded. "And I made the changes you wanted to the draft. I think that will shorten your project by as much as 200 man-hours. That you'll see in the project plan. I printed a copy of the new version."

"Okay." I smiled at him a bit absent-mindedly, as my gaze had already shifted to the next report that was positioned under his. My thoughts wandered on to alternative proposals and solutions. I was in work mode.

Throughout the day, work proved an effective distraction from the previous night's experiences. The evening, on the other hand, was only torture. Wherever I looked, I saw her face. *Her eyes, the way they'd flashed at me, and sometimes her hands, the way they ... try not to think about it!* I longed for her; I could not forget her. My body felt like an addict going through withdrawal. I wouldn't have been surprised if someone had tried to sell me some dope on my way home. In love with a hooker – wonderful!

I'd planned our next encounter so nicely. In a couple of weeks, I'd go for a walk through town. Coincidentally, I'd run into her. We'd greet each other cordially, share a banana split in an ice cream shop, chat about our common experiences – *Remember the incredible sex we had that night?* – and make another coffee date. A really nice, uncomplicated friendship. Well, I could toss that to the breeze! In a couple of weeks, I'd be dead!

I'd hardly slept that last night, even after I'd gotten home. With the intensity of my work that day, I hadn't noticed that my appetite had also fallen off considerably – but now it registered that I hadn't even gone with my colleagues for our usual lunch together. No food, no sleep – how long could a person live like this? In the insane hope of meeting her "coincidentally" this evening already, I left at five o'clock to run aimlessly through the streets. I ate the banana split as well – even fate must be given an opportunity.

When the sun went down, I gave up. At home in bed, I tossed restlessly. It seemed like I'd only just shut my eyes, but suddenly it was morning. I made coffee, drank it, made more coffee, and drank that too. My nerves thanked me with uncontrollable shaking. Since the day before yesterday, I'd had nothing but the banana split to eat. I picked up the phone and called in sick. In this condition, I'd never get any work done. I didn't want to go out; that would induce me to go looking for her again. So I paced in my apartment like a caged wild tiger – from the balcony to the window, from the window to the balcony.

I looked at the clock. It was eight o'clock in the morning. Much too early to call someone like her. I held out until nine. Then I got out the card with her phone number. At a quarter after nine, I called her. She was probably still asleep, with long nights like those ... She answered with her number. She sounded wide-awake. I announced myself with my name, somewhat less wide-awake.

"Yes?" she said, expectantly.

"I'd like to ..." What should I say now? "Can I ...?" I didn't want to make an appointment with her, at least not officially.

"You want to come over?" she asked quietly.

"Yes." That was the hardest part; I exhaled heavily.

"When?" she asked, in the same quiet tone.

Preferably, right now! But of course, I couldn't say it like that.

"Today?" I asked for that reason, trying to imitate her tone of voice. But she could do it much better.

"Yes, that's fine. At eleven o'clock?" She awaited my answer.

"Actually, I was heading into town just now ..."

"No," she declined firmly. "I don't have time before that."

That meant she probably had a customer with her, or was waiting for one! Can one be jealous over a prostitute? I could! To be able to answer, I swallowed the lump in my throat. With a halfway normal voice or, at least with what I hoped was one, I said, "Good, then. Eleven o'clock."

She hung up. Without a word. She was definitely not alone! My imagination tortured me with scenes of her room. While she was talking to me, perhaps another woman had undressed her, caressed her, and kissed her. But wouldn't I have noticed that? Her voice had sounded so calm. *That doesn't mean anything! She's a whore; she doesn't feel anything during ... Really?* I remembered it much differently!

The minute hand on the clock seemed to be counting hours instead. Every time I looked up, it seemed hardly to have moved at all. I changed clothes at least five times, although there weren't all that many possible combinations in my closet. Shirts and pants in different varieties. I didn't have any skirts or dresses. First, the jeans seemed too casual; then the pleated pants too formal. The plaid flannel shirt was too rustic and the silk too sensitive to sweat spots.

What do you think this is that you're going to? Really, now! You act as if you were headed for some sort of rendezvous. Oh, yeah? I couldn't decide how I should categorize this meeting. I seemed to be behaving as if I were anticipating a romantic rendezvous, and I felt like it as well, but my head was correct, this was no such thing. This was an appointment for paid sex.

Finally, it was quarter to eleven. She wouldn't particularly like it if I got there too early, and she lived right around the corner from me. So I waited another five minutes. When I arrived at her door, it was one minute before eleven. I rang the doorbell. For one brief, horrible moment, I thought she'd stood me up and wasn't home. Then I heard footsteps. What if that was another customer that she was saying goodbye to? No, she wouldn't do that! Or would she?

The door opened. She stood before me. She held the door for me and stepped aside. "Come in."

I walked in past her. A heavy waft of perfume struck me. She seemed even taller than the last time. No wonder, with the spike heels she was wearing! She was obviously dressed for her clients.

She wore a black leather miniskirt, shoes that made her almost four inches taller, and a leather vest, under which she appeared to have nothing else on. The outfit wasn't definitively that of a prostitute. Lots of women went out dressed like this, but I could picture how the woman who must've just been here had found these clothes exciting, how she'd unbuttoned the vest ...

She took a few steps forward – she could actually walk in those shoes! – and gestured to the sofa. "Take a seat and have something to drink." She smiled. "I think you'd like it better if I changed my clothes."

I watched her disappear through a door off to the left. I realized that, until now, I'd assumed that this was a one-room apartment. That was because the bed was in here. But of course – that was professionally necessary. She had a bedroom in which she really slept ... alone.

What would her change of clothes bring to light? A see-through negligee and garters? What did she think I was expecting? I had clearly made this appointment as a client, and she would treat me as such. The hell with it! What else could I have done?

The door opened and she came back into the room. I'd guessed wrong about the negligee, she wore a floor-length white robe, something that every good housewife might have in her closet, if not in such luxurious a silk as this one.

She looked at me. "Didn't you find anything?" At first, I didn't know what she meant. Then I noticed she was looking in the direction of the bar.

"I don't drink much," I said quickly.

She smiled and walked over to the bar. "Neither do I, but I have non-alcoholic things, too." She poured something into a glass, came over to the sofa, and stood in front of me. "Would you like to try some?" She offered me the glass. I looked up at her. I wanted to try something entirely different! She saw that I didn't want any and took a drink herself. Then she set the glass on the coffee table and sat down next to me on the sofa. She crossed her legs. Her robe slid open a bit.

I saw her long legs. They were naked. The robe didn't reveal anything indecent, but I assumed that she wasn't wearing anything underneath it. My mouth went dry. I wanted her so badly I could've torn the cloth from her body. I reached for the glass and took a long drink. It was apple juice. I had to smile. My first time – at least officially – with a hooker and I was drinking apple juice!

She sat there, calmly, and smiled at me. It was the smile she'd put on the last time to show me how well she could do her job. It was a friendly, almost loving smile. If it weren't for the heat building inside my body, I might've imagined her as an old friend. I wanted to touch her so badly I could already feel the softness of her skin on my fingertips. But I didn't want to be a client!

She noticed that I wasn't getting down to business, as it were. "Do you like music?" she asked.

Oh, no, not that too! Some kind of sleazy mood music? Oh, well, why not? That was, after all, what I was here for. I had to agree. "Yes." I didn't manage to say more.

She stood up and went over to a small stereo. She put in a CD, pressed the play button, and turned around. The Four Seasons. I'm sure I looked quite dumbfounded.

"I believe you like classical," she said, "but I can put something else on, if you'd rather." She stayed there, waiting for my answer.

"No, no – that's exactly right. I like Vivaldi." Even if she'd put on heavy metal, I probably couldn't have complained, but in this case, it was actually true.

She came back over and sat down next to me. So now, we'd have the great seduction scene. But she did nothing of the sort. She just sat there. I stared at her legs, which she'd crossed again. The president of the garden club couldn't have looked better bred. Just a breath of luxury and eroticism. I felt compelled . . . I simply had to ask her. "Do you have . . ." my voice cracked. I tried it again. "Are you wearing anything under that?"

This seemed to cheer her up.

Visibly amused, she remarked, "No. What would be the point of that?"

I sat there, paralyzed. It was a game. She drew me in, behaved in an unmistakably seductive manner, and invited me to seduce her. *But with how many women has she done this before me? That doesn't matter – you're enjoying it! Yes, I like it, but* I'd *like it even more if she'd just do it for me, if she were seductive for me alone. You'll never have a woman like this to yourself. Even if she weren't a hooker. She's too beautiful for that.*

My dark thoughts must've been apparent. When I looked at her, a shadow fell over her face and replaced the look of amusement.

"Should I undress?" She reached for her belt.

"No, please don't." I raised my hand. I couldn't stand it, this look. This waiting for instructions.

She looked at me. "Would you like to ...?" She nodded toward the bed.

Oh, yes, I wanted to ... and how I wanted to! But not like this, not in this professional manner. And how much time did we have? Perhaps we should clear up that point to start. I cleared my throat. "How long ...?"

She laughed out loud. She sounded relieved. "Oh, you're worried about the time!" She leaned over me and laid her hand, as if by accident, on my thigh. Her touch ran through me like lightning.

Her face came closer. "You needn't think about that for the moment." She spoke very softly. She nuzzled her cheek against mine. Her hand moved higher up my thigh. She whispered in my ear, "I have lots of time for you. A client canceled." I threw myself back against the arm of the sofa. There it was again!

"My God!" She jumped up and shoved her hands in the pockets of her silk bathrobe. "Don't do that!" Her eyes flashed in my direction. "That's just how it is! You know what I am!" She spun around on her heels, stared in the opposite direction, and then turned to face me once more. "And you're my client today, no?"

I sat on my hands and rocked back and forth. "Yes, I know."

She looked at me a bit more gently. She came to the sofa, propped a knee up on it, and took my head in her hands. "Would it help if I told you that I really like you?" She looked me right in the eyes.

I nodded mutely. I swallowed. "You don't say that to ...?"

"No, I don't say that to everyone." She laughed mockingly. "I really don't." She still held my face between her hands. "So, I like you." She gave me a little kiss on the left cheek. "I really like you." The same on the right. Now she laughed seductively. "I even like you a lot." She plunged me into a boiling volcanic sea with her sensuous whispers. Then she let herself sink forward and kissed me. She could kiss unbelievably well, and as had happened in our first meeting, she set me completely on fire.

She slid down beside me and pulled me to her. I wrapped my arms around her. The silk was wonderfully smooth and cool. I didn't know whether I would've liked better to hold her with or without this piece of clothing. I freed myself from her kiss and said, "I don't want you to undress."

She laughed very softly and said, "I think that can be arranged."

She touched her lips to my throat and ran them along its length. I moaned. The leather upholstery was soft and inviting. She let herself sink down until she lay under me, but kept her mouth on my neck. She began to unbutton my shirt. With every button that she opened, she ran her lips across the skin she'd laid bare. Finally, she let herself fall all the way back and looked up at me. She didn't smile. I looked down at her and knew that I was in love with her. And that I could never tell her that, just like I could never expect to hear it from her.

"Wouldn't you like to make yourself a little more comfortable?"

I emerged from my thoughts. I still had my boots on. How embarrassing! I leapt up. I took off my boots and unbuttoned my pants. I saw her lying on the sofa. Her white robe contrasted stunningly with the deep black of the leather. It was unbelievable how she completed the sequence, lying there so perfectly arranged. I looked at her, crestfallen.

"Should I do it?"

"What?" I was quite irritated. I'd forgotten why I'd stood up.

"Undress you." It sounded absolutely self-evident. She seemed expectant. *Of course – the wishes of her clients …* I shook my head roughly to chase away the uncomfortable thoughts.

"No," I fought loudly against the voice in my head. Too loudly. "I can do that myself," I added, my voice deflating.

"I'm convinced of that," she stated, slightly amused once more.

The silk of the robe she wore made clear the contours of her body – her straight shoulders, her breasts, the sweeping line of her hips. Slowly, I took off my pants. She watched me. I was embarrassed. "Could you maybe look somewhere else?"

"Yes, of course." She agreed to my wish immediately. Nonetheless, I had the feeling that she looked away against her will.

That's unfair of you. You look at her with such longing, and when she does the same . . . Yes, I know; but she's so beautiful — and she's used to it! My conscience was starting to bother me. *Is that an excuse for bad behavior?* It scolded from the recesses of my mind. I ignored it haughtily.

I went back over to the sofa. My arousal climbed. I could feel my pulse beating in my neck. She was still looking out the window. I kneeled next to the sofa and laid my hand on her stomach. She didn't react. After a second, I understood. "Look at me, please," I said. She turned her face toward me. If she just wouldn't do everything I asked!

Her belly rose and fell regularly beneath my hand. I went deeper and slid it under the cloth. My hand lay on her upper thigh. She still breathed quietly and evenly. My thoughts from early that morning occurred to me. *Perhaps she really didn't feel anything from that. But last time . . .? So much was different then from today.* I pulled my hand back.

She said nothing. She propped herself up on one elbow and laid the other hand on the nape of my neck. Her lips parted. She pulled me a little closer and kissed me. She tickled my neck a little; her kiss was careful and exploratory. Was this Technique No. 324? Despite her experienced tongue, my arousal fell to zero.

She noticed. "Am I doing something wrong?" This friendly willingness in her voice, this striving to make everything satisfactory for me. There it was again, the professionalism. But it was her job, after all! Why couldn't I accept that?

"No, no," I denied quickly. "It's my fault. I guess I'm just not in the mood today." I knew that was a flat-out lie, and she knew it too. I stood up. I couldn't do it and I'd never be able to. That was clear to me now. The last time we'd seen each other, everything had been a surprise. This time it was planned — and that was the difference. She looked up at me, waiting, but — so it seemed to me anyhow — without any particular interest. "I'll leave right away," I said. "Please excuse me."

She stood up anyhow, with one of her elegant movements that made me look like a bull in a china shop. "Oh, that's all right. An unanticipated free afternoon." She smiled. Like a neighbor. A very cursorily known neighbor. She made no attempt to hold me back. Of course not, why should she? I didn't matter to her. The facade had crumbled a bit during our first meeting for whatever reason. Now, at any rate, there was nothing left of that to notice. I felt the tears begin to well in my eyes. Only now did I realize how much I had wanted her reaction to be different.

I forced the lump in my throat back down and turned around. In a matter of seconds, I was dressed. She still stood there with that neighborly, well-wishing smile on her face. "I – what do I owe you?" It was awful. I hoped it wouldn't take her long to figure that. Soon, tears would start pouring down my cheek.

Something about her smile had changed ever so slightly. Now, she raised her hand. "Nothing. Your kisses were worth it."

Her smile drove me crazy. Her unconcerned demeanor made it very clear to me how much I'd been kidding myself. Love didn't occur to her. And I obviously was not the woman who could change that. That the opposite was the case for me was obviously my problem. She couldn't afford love in her profession. That should've been clear to me from the beginning. And only an old, macho, sucker of a woman like me could've expected anything else. I could turn anyone my way, couldn't I? Yes, a "normal" woman perhaps, but her? She'd had more women in bed than I could even imagine.

I saw myself as if in a mirror. An average-looking female manager with the typical short lesbian-cut dark hair. *That'd be a nice contrast to her blonde* – . Stop it already! One doesn't make jokes in that situation! But the objective attitude that the intellectual in me insisted upon at that moment helped me back down to earth for now, and helped hold back the tears I already felt pressing on my eyeballs. I had to laugh involuntarily, even if it seemed a little out of place. "Well, then," I said, just to say something at all. And she reached out her hand to shake! Automatically, I laid my hand in hers.

How unbelievable this moment seemed – an eternity of five seconds. She stayed perfectly in character. She was still smiling. I couldn't any more. I turned quickly and ran for the door. As I closed it behind me, I saw from the corner of my eye that she'd already turned around and gone to the bedroom. She would enjoy her unexpectedly free day.

I pushed the button for the elevator – and then took the stairs anyway. I went down so slowly I could feel each individual step under my feet. I would've liked most to be going the other direction. It was all so senseless. I'd been in my office for years, I could lead projects and head a project team, make decisions, spend or earn millions for the firm, and what was I doing here? I was agonizing over a woman who wasn't worth it, who didn't want me at all.

The path home was a blur of tearful glances. My surroundings passed me in a dismal flood. Hopeful and then resigned thoughts shot through my head. Maybe she'd still ... maybe not ... She'd probably long forgotten me by now. She'd take a little ride through the neighborhood – I could easily imagine her in a chic little sports car. Well, maybe in a bigger car, with her long legs. Oh, what did it matter to me? What had I expected? This wasn't the first time I'd fallen for a woman who didn't feel the same way about me. And it certainly wasn't the first time I'd suffered for it. And had I grown one bit wiser from the experience? No!

I remembered one of my "great loves" from back in my college dormitory. She'd looked similar to her. Actually, they all looked something like that. And as soon as I saw such a blonde, blue-eyed Madonna, I was gone. That was it! My studies suffered – every woman cost me at least a semester – and I suffered. What did I want with that? Now I had a good job, I'd been single for a while, and everything was going pretty well, wasn't it? But with her ... with her, there was something else. An extra feeling. Mother of God! You've imagined that to be there every time. Every time, the woman was something special. Just be happy that all your colleagues are men, or there'd be imminent chaos there, too. Then you'd never have lasted six years with the company.

I had to realize that things always returned to normal. And I hadn't learned a thing. A pretty woman, if she was blonde, could have anything from me. And I fell in love with her almost automatically. One of my grandmothers had prophesied that I wouldn't have it easy in life. It had annoyed me at the time. But hadn't it happened just that way? Why did I have to make it so unnecessarily difficult for myself? I went home with the understanding that it just had to be that way. Even that was nothing new. Hadn't I already thought that about the previous woman, and about the one before her?

The short walk had at least let me calm down a bit. I thought. I lay down on my ottoman, and the desire came back immediately. I smelled her, I felt her, I saw her before me. Not as she'd been most of the time, but as I wanted her to be. As the woman who loved me and allowed me to love her. My body yearned for her touch so strongly that I suddenly felt very hot. Maybe it was just the unresolved arousal from earlier. I jumped up and tried to shake it off. But my body wouldn't be deceived. At least not with such insignificant movement. So, I grabbed my gym bag and headed for my health club.

I ran through my usual two-hour program, which I normally did two or three times a week, and then moved on to the bodybuilding machines. When I couldn't force myself to push or pull one more thing because my muscles were twitching, I went for the stationary bikes. I chose the "race" option and picked out the most difficult opponent. I knew I wasn't up for it, but I wouldn't have managed to win against a weaker opponent either. Today, I saw myself as the absolute loser. When the little red light on the control panel reached the finish line half a mile ahead of me and confirmed my estimation of myself, I was finally satisfied. Exhausted, I hit the showers. I barely managed to drive home and crawl up the stairs to my apartment. I let myself fall into bed in my sweatsuit and fell asleep immediately.

A wild dream woke me. A person was standing next to me in the room. Things moved on their own. The door opened slowly and cast a shadow on the wall. Something seemed to be hiding behind there. I grabbed for the bedside lamp and groped for the switch. When the light came on, I saw that it had all been my imagination.

A psychologist explained to me once after a similar experience that such fears are the reversal of a wish. One doesn't really want to be alone, but one is. So one imagines that someone is there. Unfortunately, that causes just as much anxiety as being alone, because it's not real.

This did not, unfortunately, allay my fears even though I believed the explanation. So, I left the light on, and after my eyes had flown open a few more times in half-asleep panic, my over-stimulated synapses finally let me have the restorative sleep I needed. I even fell asleep with a smile on my lips, because the last thing I thought about was a similar experience in the second dormitory I'd lived in.

That time, I'd just moved in and had a nightmare that drove me out of my room. As it is in student housing, I only had the one room. So I sat in the hallway, unable to force myself back in with the terrible ghosts of my imagination. Early the next morning, after I was already half frozen (I couldn't, of course, go into my room to get a blanket), a fellow student came home. Naturally, he was totally unaffected by my ghosts and just saw me sitting there in the hallway in my pajamas, shivering. I'd only seen him once before, so we didn't know each other at all, but his remark of "Do you have mice in your room?" finally tore me from my dismal thoughts, because I had to laugh. After that, I could go back into my room and go back to sleep. Such a remark, such an unknown and unexpected friend (or better yet a girlfriend) was just what I needed right now. But this time, I'd obviously have to handle things alone.

—— 3 ——

The next day, I went to the office even though I knew I'd hardly be able to concentrate on work. Staying home, however, seemed to me to be a worse prospect. Like the mice in the room. And during the day, I didn't even have that excuse. So, I tried to keep my work to the essentials. I was surely not the best worker that day, and definitely not the best boss. My co-workers on the project team were certainly used to my not always being in a wonderful mood, but most of them had never seen me like this. Instead of making decisions, I put them off. I delegated what I could, but so badly that I constantly had to answer questions and make clarifications. And those who had the bad luck to need to ask me a question also had to put up with my temper.

It went like that until I couldn't even stand myself any longer. I tried the health club again. Afterwards, I returned to the office somewhat relaxed and was tolerable for the rest of the day.

At any rate, my inability to control the situation didn't please me at all. I knew from experience that this had only two possible outcomes. Either I could convince her to behave toward me as I wanted her to, at least in part, or I was damned to think about her for a very long time, always swaying between joy and hope, disappointment and resignation. Although I couldn't imagine how I might accomplish the first, I knew from repeated practice that the second possibility was so exhausting and nerve-racking, I'd rather avoid her altogether. I concluded that I'd have to give up one thing, namely, sex, if I wanted to have the other, namely, inner peace and satisfaction. Basically, irreconcilable. In connection with her, completely unimaginable.

All of our previous meetings had had only to do with sex. How could I possibly reach her on another level? Our whole relationship – if we even had one – was based on that. What would I suggest to a woman I'd just met, a woman I hadn't slept with and didn't even know yet if it would ever come to that? That was pretty clear. I'd suggest something very ordinary, a movie or dinner for example. Sure, why not? The worst thing she could do, is say no; and then I could just deal with the disappointment.

I noticed how enthusiastic my masochistic streak was about this decision. I'd get plenty of sleep tonight, and tomorrow was another day. Perhaps a day to call someone . . .

——— 4 ———

"That's a rather unusual appointment," she said.

Now that was really strange. She found it entirely acceptable to make an appointment for sex, but she called a simple invitation to dinner "unusual." Until now, I'd thought of going out to eat as a relatively ordinary activity. When work didn't prevent it by sabotaging my social life – some did call me a workaholic – I went out to dinner with a friend or girlfriend two or three times a week. Cooking wasn't always possible with my workload, and it wasn't much fun to cook just for myself. When I had time, which, granted, didn't happen very often, I'd ask a couple of friends over and cook for them. In contrast to my outer appearance, which didn't always seem to fit with such "feminine" activities, I actually cooked quite well. My soufflés are famous.

"Too unusual to accept?" I asked directly. There didn't seem to be any reason to beat around the bush. Her decision probably depended on criteria I knew nothing about – as little as I knew about her. In my head, a few ideas buzzed around about what I'd do if she turned me down. Tie balloons outside her window with "Happy Birthday" printed on them? I didn't even know when her birthday was. Whatever I did, I was going to get turned down. I loved to be frustrated by a woman with whom I was haplessly in love!

"Too unusual not to think about it first," she said right away. She wouldn't let herself be surprised. Neither professionally nor personally. I could understand that. But her cool manner annoyed me. I wanted to know what was beneath it.

"So I can't give you an answer right now," she proceeded rather indifferently. I could've kicked myself for calling her at all. She had no reason to want to meet with me. Other than, perhaps, professionally, but that wasn't what I'd offered. Or was that what was holding her up? Did she first have to decide in which category I belonged: client or – *Yes, or what?*

"Can you call me again next week?" *What? Next week?* Damn it all, what was I doing here? She didn't want to!

"Yeah, sure. When – when's the best time to reach you?" The thought of disturbing her "at work" was unbearable.

"You'll know," she said.

Of course – either she answered the phone or she was "occupied." Why did I torment myself like this? *Because you always do. Because you find those women most desirable who reject you.* It angered me, but I couldn't contradict my own head. It was simply right. And to be honest, that was probably the only reason we'd ever come together in the first place. Her cool look-right-past-you attitude, her indifference, pretended or real, had attracted me. In the meantime, I probably should have noticed that it was real. I would have liked to suppose otherwise.

"Fine, but do you prefer a particular day?" I'm sure my voice sounded rather sarcastic. I didn't feel like calling her every day and not reaching her until the end of the week. My masochism didn't go that far after all.

She laughed, honestly, she laughed! "You're mad," she remarked.

"Does that surprise you?" Now I was really ticked. She'd laughed at me! I definitely would not put up with that. And ordinarily, my dinner invitations were taken with a little more enthusiasm! I grumbled under my breath. She didn't even notice!

"I won't be reachable before Wednesday, if that helps you."

"Oh, yes, that helps a lot. Thank you very much!" I slammed the receiver down into the cradle. What did she take me for? Probably precisely that which I was: a dog scratching at the door. I was embarrassing myself, but I couldn't give up yet. She still hadn't said no.

I buried myself in my work and tried not to think about her constantly. The project hadn't made such rapid progress in a long time. With regard to not thinking about her, I had less success. Every free minute was filled with thoughts of her. In the middle of filling out a form to request a half-million-dollar budget increase, I saw her there in her silk robe, smiling at me. I wanted to undress her, to press myself against her, but that couldn't be. I simply couldn't imagine her naked. I knew why. She'd willingly put her body at my disposal. There, she hid nothing. Until now, only a tiny piece of her soul had shown itself, when she wasn't looking. What interested me was the rest of what belonged to that tiny piece. It was, no doubt, very well hidden. And she'd hardly show it willingly.

During the course of the week, I came to the decision to try one last time. I couldn't, after all, make a complete fool of myself! Whether or not I could stick to my decision I didn't know. She occupied my thoughts completely. The worst part was that I imagined she wouldn't waste a single thought on me. She probably amused herself with some other woman who had more to offer than I did.

— **5** —

The days slid past like scenes from a bad movie. I remembered our first encounter, in a women's café called Bella Donna. How appropriate. That's exactly what she was, a pretty woman and – so it seemed to me now – a slow, deadly poison.

How she'd turned me on! She came in, a majestic appearance, seeming to know no one or everyone. She could've been there for the first time or the thousandth time. I couldn't tell whether the women who spoke to her did so because they found her as riveting as I did or because they already knew her. She treated them all with the same noncommittal nonchalance and didn't join anyone for a drink. She sat alone, and the others came to her – truly, like a queen holding court. I observed her from a distance and, after a while, decided to get her attention. She didn't look my way at all. That intrigued me even more. Perhaps it was just my mild frustration that drove me to the determination I felt to meet her. She seemed completely disinterested.

To be honest, I couldn't really reconstruct how it happened after the fact. I'd just found myself suddenly in the middle of a situation without knowing quite how or why I'd gotten there. And this was the outcome of that!

By force of will, I managed not to spend the whole day thinking about her. I did, after all, have other things to do – a little work, for instance. This forced distraction was to my advantage. Otherwise, the day would have dragged on forever. After a truly dreary weekend spent in self-imposed isolation – why did I do this to myself –? Wednesday had at last rolled around. No, no, no! I forbade myself to call her all afternoon. Who knew what awaited me?

It occurred to me that she was probably "booked up" more often in the mornings. One went to the hairdresser, another grocery shopping ... I wondered how the other women felt about that, about fitting her in between the butcher and the greengrocer. Did that kind of frivolity hold a special attraction for them? Or was it just more of what they always did, passing the time? The more I thought about it, the more I became aware that this was not part of my world. And yet I'd fallen in love with her!

Ha, ha, ha! You're making a fool of yourself! You're making a fool of yourself! Like jumping rope in grade school, when the rope cuts through the air, before it clatters and scrapes across the floor, the singsong chant turned in my head. Angry disappointment surged in me. Was I not my own master? Couldn't I decide what was good for me and what wasn't?

Is this good for you? No, probably not. So, why are you doing it?

Exactly.

So it was. I had to come to terms with it. I yearned for her; I wanted more than just to have dinner with her. I decided something. *Special women require special plans, you idiot!*

So I called her that afternoon. It was almost like the first time. She answered quietly, without announcing a name.

I couldn't think of a good opening line, so I asked her directly, after I'd said who it was, "Have you considered my suggestion?"

"Which suggestion?" she asked.

I should have known! A week was, after all, a good stretch of time. How could I expect her to remember my invitation? She had certainly been busy with entirely unrelated things.

I was afraid to speak, because I knew my anger would be plainly audible. "Are you still there?" she asked after a bit.

"Yes," I said, carefully controlled, hoping that wasn't obvious over the telephone. "I had asked you if you'd go out to eat with me."

"Oh, yeah," she said, as if she could vaguely remember that. "I've considered it." That was a feat! She'd forgotten it, but still managed to think about it. Someone should do that to her sometime!

"And?" *Biting* might just begin to describe my tone of voice. "To what conclusion have you come?" I really didn't know how much longer I could control myself. She was definitely going to decline, I was sure of that. And that forecast calmed me. A short, painless *(yeah, right!)* end could, after all, only be good for me.

"I'm not sure yet," she answered softly.

"You've had an entire week to think about it!" The outburst came more from surprise than from irritation. But, of course, she hadn't had a week to think about it, she'd just now been reminded of it by my phone call.

Why were so much anger and so much desire building inside me at the same time? Had she stood before me, I wouldn't have left as I had the last time – that much was clear, regardless of whether or not she meant to charge me. I wouldn't have gotten what I really wanted from her, but at least I would've gotten great sex. Even I knew that much!

"A week is short," she remarked, more as an excuse than as a statement of fact.

Oh, yes! I was convinced that the time had passed much more quickly for her than it had for me. In a busy life like hers, time went by much faster. She made me look really old. But my rage slowly faded away. It was pointless, after all. She would put me off for another week if I let her, then another, and another . . .

"It's all right," I said, in a resigned, self-sacrificing tone. "You don't have to if you don't want to."

"I didn't say that." She surprised me yet again. Now it was turned around – I got a more positive answer than I had expected. "There's just so much to think about."

About a dinner invitation? She really did live in a wholly different world from mine. With me, there were only two things to consider: could I and did I want to. And perhaps also the type of food. But that decision couldn't possibly take a whole week – could it? "Why? Can you not decide whether you'd like Chinese or Italian?" As banal as that seemed to me, maybe it had a deeper meaning for her.

She laughed. "It's not that simple," she said. This line of reasoning was too much for me. I couldn't imagine any convincing grounds for this degree of complication. And I couldn't wait another week, I was sure of that. So it was now or never!

"Could you accept an invitation to meet at a place outside the city that's just opened, doesn't serve Chinese or Italian, and has a patio?" That truly left all possibilities open. It was neither too intimate nor too casual, and on a mild summer evening, who knew what might happen?

A sound came through the line that didn't sound too unlike a chuckle.

"You're really stubborn," she said.

"Well, yes, it's hard work to convince you to go out to eat, I'll admit that. But for —" a beautiful woman, I wanted to say, but that would surely bore her since she heard it every day, so I finished with "a good meal, I'll do almost anything." That would have to do!

"Well, then ..." she agreed good-naturedly. "But I still have to put you off. I can't today. The first I could go is tomorrow."

Immediately, the wildest of possibilities flew through my head as to why she couldn't go out tonight. There could really only be one reason: she already had another commitment. And I could imagine with whom. It was certainly with a client.

A client, who was more important to her than I was. So we were back to square one. I suppressed a new wave of anger and the impulse to contradict her. "Should I pick you up or should we meet somewhere?" I asked instead.

"Tell me where it is. Then we'll meet there." She seemed to want to avoid dependence on me, by all means possible. Although it seemed to me to be rather environmentally irresponsible to go in separate cars, it was clear that she wouldn't agree to anything else. So I told her the address.

"Oh, yes, I've heard of the place," she said in acknowledgment.

Lightning flashed through my head again. From whom, I wanted to ask. But I didn't. "When?" I asked.

"Eight o'clock," she answered without thinking. She had her schedule memorized. That must help her avoid jealousy and embarrassment.

"Then I'll see you there," I said finally.

"I'll be there," she assured me.

I hung up hesitantly. I would've liked to talk with her more, but there was absolutely no reason to go on. And I would see her the next day, or so I hoped. Would she keep this kind of date? I didn't know her well enough to predict that. Perhaps she would only come because she still saw a potential client in me, one she didn't want to turn away Did I want to know that? No, I didn't want to know, I decided. But all that would be clear to me tomorrow after dessert, at the latest.

—— **6** ——

She was already there when I arrived, although I was, contrary to my usual habit, extraordinarily punctual. I'd been staring at the clock all day long, and it took a serious discussion with myself not to come early.

She was sitting under one of the old lime trees that made the patio such a lovely and interesting place, and would certainly make it a popular and crowded meeting place soon. It was still relatively empty. I could see her from the entrance before she saw me. It seemed to me that she had dressed quite conservatively, but for my taste still very attractively. I asked myself what that meant. Did she always dress like that for dinner dates, had she had an appointment right before this one that had demanded such an outfit, or had she dressed that way for me? And if the latter were true, what had I expected?

I wasn't going to solve this mystery standing in the doorway, so I entered the cobblestone patio and walked without hurrying – something that took a considerable effort – to the table. She was looking in another direction, so I had a good view of her classic profile. Her beauty almost frightened me. The symmetry of her features was almost surreal. Never had I seen anything close in another woman.

She first noticed me when I was near enough for her to hear my footsteps on the stones. Almost startled, as if she'd been thinking about something totally unrelated and wasn't expecting me at all, she looked up.

I felt like a troublemaker. I deliberately put on a friendly smile, to take some of the uncomfortable intimacy out of the situation. "Hello. I'm sorry if I'm late."

She smiled back with the same friendliness. "You're not. I like to wait for people in peace and quiet."

"Peace and quiet" in conjunction with "waiting" was in and of itself a contradiction to me. I hated having to wait and tried to avoid it whenever possible. In this respect, we seemed to be very different. I hoped that wasn't true in other things.

"Have you been here long?" A little small talk couldn't hurt. After all, this situation was really very different from all of our previous meetings.

"Not more than half an hour." Apparently, that was quite normal to her. It seemed like an eternity to me. I probably would've died from impatience.

"I hope you haven't been too bored." I still couldn't imagine why anyone would intentionally come an hour early.

"Bored? No. I'm never bored."

I wondered at the way she took this statement for granted and sighed a little. "I could never say that about myself. Just the opposite."

She laughed softly. "I can't imagine that."

I sounded to myself like I was having a teatime chat in Queen Victoria's salon. That would definitely have bored me. I reached for the menu that lay on the table. "Have you ordered yet?"

She looked at me and grinned a little. "How could I? There's nothing Chinese or Italian here."

I got a terrible feeling in my gut. "Would you rather go somewhere else?" Damn it again, I'd picked the wrong restaurant! The evening was shot.

She looked right at me. Her eyes seemed to drill right through me. It was incredibly uncomfortable. I tried to hold up my part and not look away. "You are much too serious for your age," she finally revealed to me, conclusively.

"For my age? I just turned thirty-two!" I sputtered, because she'd surprised me so much.

She laughed, satisfied. She was obviously having a heathenishly good time. "Thank you!" she said with a little nod and a slight emphasis on the second word. "That was all I wanted to know."

At first, I had to steady myself a bit, but then it began to seem funny to me as well. "And I bet that if I ask you how old you are now, you won't answer, because it's not polite to ask a woman her age."

She winked at me. "Right."

Such a little tart! I was no longer so sure that I was ready for her. It was extremely difficult to guess her age. She could be anywhere between twenty-five and thirty-five, or so it seemed to me. I gave up. One would probably never get that secret out of a woman like her. Nevertheless, I assumed, for no apparent reason, that she was younger than I was. But why did that matter? She was flirting with me; that was all that counted. And she was an expert at flirting.

I noticed how her magic worked on me and I didn't even get the impression that she was doing it on purpose. She possessed a natural charm that was only emphasized by her impeccably good manners. I knew though, that she could also put them aside if she wanted. Maybe that was part of her attractiveness. After all the effort and nerves it had cost me to get her here, and the cool precision with which she had made the date, it surprised me how relaxed she was. She laughed at my jokes and was incredibly charming. I was captivated. When she was this loose and relaxed, the whole world seemed to revolve around her. I hadn't seen her like this before. She seemed more and more like the embodiment of my dreams. Could such a woman really exist?

I imagined what a relationship with her might be like. Our everyday lives didn't fit together very well, that was certain. When I went to work, she'd still be asleep. When I wanted to sleep, she'd be working. Working? Well, what else? Not exactly uplifting, the idea of what she did for a living. That brought me back to reality for the moment. Suddenly, something occurred to me. "Your eyes aren't blue at all!" I was truly surprised. I'd been fooled by my constant assumption that any woman I'd fall in love with had to be blonde with blue eyes.

"No, grey," she answered, somewhat put off. Until now, I'd always thought of grey as a rather dull color, but her eyes gleamed like glittering diamonds. Spellbound, I stared at her — I could barely tear myself away. "Is that a problem?" she asked, wrinkling her brow.

I had to laugh in embarrassment. "No, of course not. I just thought you had blue eyes. I have sort of a funny fixation about that. But obviously I've never really looked at you carefully before."

She laughed. "I hadn't really gotten that impression." Then she became suddenly serious. "But perhaps my eyes aren't really what interests you most about me." She poked around in her salad a little and, with extreme precision, chose a single leaf.

Damn it again, I was a regular bull in a china shop! The relaxed atmosphere was gone. I tried to save the situation. "Your eyes are beautiful." What else could I say? That was a fact. But what woman wouldn't be offended if her date didn't notice that? I, for one, always took it very poorly. "I noticed that immediately. Just – unfortunately, you're incredibly lovely all over."

She quit sorting her salad and looked in my direction without actually looking at me. "Um, thanks," she said. She probably didn't know what to do with such an unusual compliment. I didn't know how to explain it either in case she asked me. But she didn't do that. A movement by the patio entrance distracted her. She sighed. "I knew that this was a mistake," she said, more to herself than to me.

"A mistake? What?" Now I was irritated.

"Going out." She closed herself off incredibly quickly. I could make neither rhyme nor reason of her reaction. The only thing I could imagine was . . .

"I should have known," she said, while she set her fork on the table and laid her napkin next to it. It looked very final. She laughed apologetically in my general direction. "It has nothing to do with you."

That didn't reassure me much, since everything about her behavior indicated that she was about to leave. And that was a much earlier and more abrupt end to the evening than I had imagined or hoped for. As long as I didn't know what caused this sudden change in her attitude, I could hardly stop her from carrying out her present intentions. So I had to find out. "What should you have known?"

She coolly lifted an eyebrow, as if I'd asked a completely indecent question. "That isn't important," she said. She raised her hand to signal the waiter that she wanted to pay.

My God, this was going too quickly! I didn't know what I should react to first.

"Obviously it's grounds enough for you to leave," I said nervously, glancing around perhaps to learn what she had seen. I only saw a couple of people who had just come in: a middle-aged couple that was heading for a table at the other end of the gardens. The woman was very thin and petite. She walked rather stiffly behind her husband. Other than that, I saw no one. Suddenly, the woman spun around and threw an icy glare in our direction. It was only a brief moment, and then it was over.

I turned back to the table. The waiter was already standing next to her. "Wait," I protested, "I'm the one who invited you." This was all moving much too fast!

"Leave it," she insisted firmly. "I don't think you've gotten much of what you're trying to pay for."

What? What was that supposed to mean? She had completely confused me again, but before I could even reach for my billfold, the waiter was gone again. Just as suddenly, she was standing.

"Please, stay and finish your meal," she said. "I'm sorry."

What was I supposed to do here without her? She didn't seem to think about the fact that I'd hardly come here to eat alone. I jumped up as she was turning to go. "Wait," I said again quickly.

She stopped for a moment and turned halfway back to look at me. "Please, stay," she said. "I don't want to be responsible for starving you as well." She forced a small smile.

"What's the meaning of this?" Even as I was saying that, she had turned around and started for the exit. I followed her and held her back. "Can't you tell me what the problem is?" She kept walking as if I hadn't said a thing. She ignored me. I would have to provoke her if I wanted an answer. "What's with that woman? Who is she?"

She stopped abruptly. "That's none of your business," she reprimanded me irritably.

So I'd hit the nail on the head. She was the reason. "Maybe not." I wasn't prepared to fight with her. "But it is my business that I'm standing over here with you instead of sitting comfortably at our table and eating dinner with you. For that, I would like an explanation. Even if it has nothing to do with me."

She was agitated, and I was probably irritating her even more. But if she just walked away, that wouldn't do much for me. I'd rather chance the storm.

"You are really . . ." She didn't say what it was she thought of me.

Instead, she took a deep breath. "Okay. You're right. It's unfair. I admit that. Is that enough?"

She suddenly became very cool and calculating again. In that mood, I couldn't hope to get anything out of her.

"Would you like to go somewhere else?" I asked, for the second time that evening.

"No," she answered promptly. "That was the mistake. My mistake," she stressed emphatically. "I don't normally go out." That surprised me, given our first encounter. She remembered that and corrected herself. "Almost never. And when I do, I don't go places like this." She glanced around.

"Are you looking for something in particular?" I had assumed she would go to her car, but she was still standing at the edge of the parking lot – really just a wide spot in the road under a couple of trees in front of the restaurant.

"A phone booth." She sounded rather distant.

"Here? In the middle of the woods? What for?" It was beginning to get tiresome, asking all these questions. She would only give out as much information as she absolutely had to. This was incredibly tedious.

"To call a taxi."

"You didn't drive?" *She probably flew here on her invisible angel wings.* I was getting sarcastic. My patience was finally wearing out.

At least she answered me this time. "I don't have a car."

I just had to laugh. I suddenly remembered the Italian coffee commercial where a handsome man tempts his lovely neighbor with hot cappuccino until she finds out he doesn't have a car and dumps him. I saw the way she was looking at me and stopped laughing. She didn't think it was a bit funny.

"Excuse me," I said, sobered. "I just thought of something." I considered whether she might accept the offer of a ride. It was possible. Then there was always the question of where I would take her. I might've invited another woman back to my apartment for coffee. But her? And going to her place was out of the question. I chanced it. "Would you accept me as a taxi?"

"You?" She turned her head away from the tree she'd been looking at and toward me.

Perhaps I just wasn't born to be a taxi driver. In any case, she looked at me with disbelief. "Yes, me. I have a car" – just had to grin at the thought of the Italian, he did it so well – "and I even have it here. You won't believe it."

She stayed cool. "I don't want you to go out of your way for me."

Out of my way? Oh, yeah, she didn't know ... "I live right around the corner from you, if that's what you mean," I explained. She obviously wanted to go home. I could save myself the trouble of making another suggestion.

"Oh really?" It didn't seem to interest her very much. But I couldn't take this much longer. If I was going to have to let her go, I wanted to get it over with.

"My car is over there." I indicated a car on the left with my arm. Without waiting for an answer, I started for it. When I opened the driver's door, I looked over my shoulder. She was three steps behind me. I went to the other side of the car and unlocked the passenger door. She looked at me and smiled gently.

"How gallant," she remarked. At least she was starting to take me somewhat seriously again. But if she began flirting again, I was finished, I knew that much. I shut the door behind her quickly.

When I got in, I realized that I had forgotten to consider two things when extending my invitation – the unavoidable physical closeness inside an automobile and her erotic charisma. In the open air of the restaurant patio, she'd already started to have an effect on me, but here, where she sat only a few inches away so I could feel the warmth of her thighs ... I put the car in reverse and acted as if I were completely unaffected. My heart was beating in my throat. I thought about all the hot goodnight kisses I'd had in cars in my life. Would she give me one too?

In order to back up, I had to put my arm around the back of her seat. I tried not to touch her, but I could feel the heat of her body on my side. This could get interesting! Thank God the drive wasn't very long. I drove down the winding mountainside through the forest, giving my full attention to the road. It was very quiet and dark. Only the headlights cut into the night ahead of us.

When we were almost there, she cleared her throat. "Perhaps I should explain something."

"You don't have to." I wanted to appear disinterested in order to maintain the distance between us. A little closer and I would fall all over her.

"I know." Apparently, she'd brought herself to some conclusion, although it was difficult for her. "As I said, I almost never go out.

Every once in a while to the Bella, when I . . ." There it was again, something she didn't want to discuss. "But never to a public place," she continued, without really finishing the sentence. "So I should never have accepted your invitation in the first place." At least that explained why she'd taken so long to decide. At first, I thought that was all she was going to say, but then all of a sudden she added, "But you were so stubborn." I heard the smile in her voice, even though I couldn't look at her because I had to concentrate on the road.

We had come into the city and were on a relatively straight street. Another restaurant was right in front of us. This was actually a tourist area. "Please, stop here," she said. Probably she had just realized that she'd rather walk the rest of the way than to open up to me any more. It was so hard to figure her out!

I found a parking place and stopped. I'd hoped she was going to get out, but she didn't move. I didn't dare look at her. The need to touch her kept growing inside me. With great effort, I stared directly ahead through the windshield, grinding my teeth. Oh, what was the point? She could leave any time if she wanted to. "I'd like to kiss you," I mumbled at the reflection of the headlights in front of me.

Her hand appeared next to the steering wheel and turned off the headlights. "So do it," she said. I froze. She touched my thigh briefly below the steering wheel, then moved her hand away. The spot on my leg still burned. I turned toward her.

"Would you believe me if I told you that wasn't why I asked you out?"

"No." Her voice still had a bit of a smile to it. "But that doesn't matter."

Yes, it matters to me! Still, her proximity and willingness destroyed my self-control. I bent over her and found her throat with my mouth. She laid her hand on my shoulder and caressed it gently.

While enjoying the silkiness of her skin, I ran my hand slowly down her side until I found her breast. She moaned softly. My lips wandered to her mouth. She was ready for me. While my tongue sought hers, she wrapped her arms around me and pulled me as close to her as the cramped quarters would allow. Then she let an arm fall and felt around for the lever that reclined the seats. I stopped kissing her.

"You don't want to . . . here?"

"Why not?" She probably did this more often than I did. At any rate, it sounded incredibly uncomfortable to me. My lips still burned from her kisses, and I could imagine that she was quite capable of making me forget where we were. But at the same time, I realized that she hadn't believed me. So I sat back up in my own seat.

"This really isn't why I invited you," I grumbled as I started the car. Before she could react, we were back on the road.

"You don't even believe that yourself," she replied. She was right, but I wasn't about to tell her that.

Instead, I tried to learn something more about her. "Why don't you believe it? Why do you think that everyone only wants to sleep with you?" I didn't know quite where I intended to go with this conversation, but at least it would distract me from my lustful thoughts momentarily.

Her answer shook me. "Because that's the way it is," she said.

I found the calm and naturalness with which she said those words horrible. What kind of effect would it have on her self- esteem if she were convinced of this? On her idea of life? I suddenly felt very cold.

Perhaps it would've calmed me if I'd gotten the impression that she only meant that statement about her clients. In that case, such a belief would be entirely justified. A client really would come to her for that reason only. But strangely, it sounded to me like a general observation. An observation she'd made in all of her relationships, not just her professional ones. That's why it was so upsetting.

I looked away from the street and at her for a moment. "You're a very desirable woman, that's indisputable," I stated finally, "but you have other qualities."

She laughed aloud for a moment. "Yes? What are they?"

She'd taken me completely by surprise. I knew how I felt about her, but had yet to identify what exactly was behind that. So I had to think about it.

"You see," she said, "you can't think of any either." On the one hand, she seemed pleased by this. I had demonstrated what she truly believed. On the other hand, there was a hint of resignation in her diagnosis. Maybe she had hoped a little tiny bit that I would be able to show her an alternative she had yet to consider. And I had failed.

"That is absolute nonsense," I protested, more upset about my lack of presence of mind than about the confirmation of her self-assessment.

"Come, come." She seemed to want to pacify me more than herself. "Don't trouble yourself about it." She was disillusioned, in such a way that it somehow touched me deep inside. But, as with most apparently hopeless causes, the fighting spirit awoke in me.

"I would really like to trouble myself quite a bit about it," I explained carefully. I was aware of the risk that if I started this I might get too close for her comfort. That could cause her to cut me off entirely and prevent me from ever getting close again.

She let out another dry little laugh. "Why?" she asked contemptuously.

"Because I believe that you're worth it." She fell silent at that. I couldn't make out her reaction, except that she didn't answer. We drove silently through the darkness, but for the occasional dim glow of a streetlight. I would've loved to look at her, but I had to pay attention to the road.

It wasn't long before we arrived in the neighborhood of her apartment. I found a parking place right in front of the entrance to the pedestrian zone. "So." I shut off the motor. "I'm sorry, madam, but I cannot take my vehicle any farther into the pedestrian area." I kidded around to avoid sitting there in the unbearable silence for another minute. I could never tolerate that kind of tense silence. Perhaps we would have something in common after all? When she didn't say anything and made no move toward getting out of the car, I tried again. "They have such arcane customs for keeping away unauthorized vehicles." I shuddered. "The Towing Torture, for example."

"Why are you doing this?" she asked. Now that I wasn't trying to drive, I could see that she was hanging her head. She didn't look up despite my address.

I really didn't know exactly what she was referring to, and for some reason I was slowly beginning to fear for my own courage. What if I had destroyed everything with that? So I had to ask. "What do you mean?"

"You're going to leave me someday too," she said quietly.

I had to laugh at her theatrics. "Thanks for the hint, Pythia," I said so good-naturedly that it camouflaged my fear. I knew her so little, knew so little about her, that every glimpse at her inner self was a voyage into the darkness of the universe. There were so many possibilities for a catastrophe in there. And I could do no more than a child who whistles when going into a dark basement.

She didn't stir. "Would you like ..." My voice was starting to sound a little husky. I had to clear my throat. "Would you like to stay out here?"

She started a little, as though she were waking from a dream. "No ... no, of course not. Forgive me, please. I'm sure you want to get home." I wasn't so sure of that. Just the opposite. She reached for the door and opened it. I got out quickly and went around to her side of the car. "Oh," she said, freshly astonished. "I forgot how gallant you are." She smiled again, just slightly.

"Less gallant than well-reared," I said. "I can't take credit for it." I didn't actually want to start a big discussion about my manners.

She leaned against the car and looked at me. With one of her inimitably flowing motions, she separated herself from the car and came to me. I had the sudden desire to flee. Pure instinct, like a wild animal. But she'd already reached me. She let herself sink against me. I felt the suppleness of her breasts and the gentle pressure of her body against mine. "I like it anyway," she whispered in my ear, "it's been a long time since I've been spoiled this way."

I put my arms around her and felt her nestle up even closer to me. "Come with me," she breathed, right into my ear. I still didn't want to admit that I'd been hoping for this kind of ending to the evening. I would've thought she wanted something entirely different. But obviously, she could read minds. "I believe you," she whispered, ever so softly.

And I wanted to believe that she believed me! I pulled myself away from her gently and locked the car. She was already at the door to her building. It was only a few yards away. While we waited for the elevator, she put her hand on the back of my neck and gave me a suggestive little kiss. She brushed her lips against mine ever so lightly, just touching them with the tip of her tongue. Before I could part my lips and take her in, she had pulled away. "Oh, you're mean!" I moaned.

She laughed seductively. "Yes, I know. But that raises the excitement, doesn't it?" As if that were necessary!

When we got to her apartment, she took a few steps inside and then turned to face me. "I'd like to put on something a little more comfortable. Would you mind?"

It was as though a wall had suddenly gone up between us. I couldn't touch her, although she was right in front of me. What kind of an idiot was I? I should have known. As soon as she was in this room, everything that had to do with sex was work for her, even when it started out looking like play. I was sick of this cat-and-mouse game. Couldn't it work any other way?

"Why are you asking me that?" I replied. "What could my decision about whether or not I mind have to do with what you actually do?"

I couldn't have surprised her as much if I'd suddenly stripped naked. Indeed, that would have been much more logical behavior. Although she'd already heard a few things from me this evening that didn't fit her usual pattern, she had still seemed prepared to go through with her regular routine. In any case, she looked at me as if my reaction had caught her completely off guard.

"Would you rather I stayed like I am?"

Not that again! This was, in part, where our difficulties were coming from. The other part came from me; I knew that. Our sensibilities just didn't seem to fit together. That made communication very difficult.

She was wearing a summer dream of crepe de chine that went

beautifully with her – as I now knew – grey eyes, a dress that really only worked on women over six feet tall. I'd envied women of such height since grade school. Nonetheless, whether she took it off or kept it on, or even what she put on instead, or didn't, couldn't be my decision. Not at this moment, anyway. "You haven't been listening to me," I remarked.

"Yes I have." She was visibly unsettled, even though she was trying to control herself. "But you're not exactly making it easy."

"That's not the point." I'd finally found a plane on which mutual understanding seemed possible. "I'd rather things were different, believe me."

"What do you want, then?" She seemed very irritated now, maybe even a bit overtired, despite the not-so-late hour. Who knew what kind of week she'd had? Perhaps it had been more stressful than I could imagine in my wildest dreams. I softened my tone a bit. Then I remembered what kind of activities would have caused that potential stress, and my kindly manner disappeared again.

"That's a good question, and one I've asked myself often. If I knew the answer, I probably wouldn't be here." Why should I make things easier for her than she had for me?

She went over to the sofa and dropped her purse down. Then she pulled off the light summer gloves she'd been wearing and tossed them after it. As she did that, she turned halfway toward me and watched me out of the corner of her eye. It looked like a scene from a film.

"Good," she said, sitting on the sofa and crossing her legs. "What now?"

"I would like to have a conversation with you," I said, quite naturally as though I'd never intended anything else.

"Conversation." A swarm of overfed ravens at which one tossed a single grain could not have seemed more contemptuous.

"Is that so unusual?" Her reaction had unsettled me yet again. She questioned everything I took for granted. The idea that people would talk to each other before sleeping together, for example. But I didn't really want to show her how much she unsettled me. So I waited for her answer.

She didn't answer right away. "Somewhat," she said at last.

"Which brings us back to the topic at hand," I retorted rather cheerfully. I never knew I had this much talent for acting. Actually, I felt miserable. She'd put up such a solid wall around herself, there wasn't even a crack through which I might catch another glimpse of the real her.

Her forehead wrinkled. "The topic at hand?"

"Mm-hmm. You found this entire date to be unusual from the beginning. And me too, apparently. From time to time." This couldn't go on so doggedly for much longer. She would exhaust me before I even saw a light at the end of the tunnel.

"That's true. From time to time." She smiled so suggestively, the Mona Lisa would've looked like a grinning nun next to her.

"Why do you think I asked you out?"

"My God," she sighed, annoyed. "Not that again!"

"Yes, that again! That's the crux of the matter." I didn't let up. "So, what do you think?"

She sighed again. "What do you want to hear?" Her bored tone indicated that she would tell me anything I wanted to hear if I would just drop this subject.

"Something convincing," I said. "Something true."

"Christ!" Now she was almost laughing, if sarcastically. "And you have no other wish?" She leaned toward me a bit. "A wish I could fulfill for you?" She took on a seductive tone.

"You're just trying to distract me," I answered uneasily. I noticed that her method worked on me immediately, despite my careful mental defenses.

"Why not?" She'd registered my reaction immediately. She turned the seduction up another notch. She rose and started toward me. "There are plenty of nice things with which we might amuse ourselves."

I backed up against the door and held up my arm. "Watch out," I said, "if you take another step, I'm leaving. Maybe that's exactly what you want, but if not, then stay where you are." When I was in college, we'd never handled anything like this in Communication Theory. Once again, my education had failed to provide practical information! I had to learn all the important things from experience.

She laughed and stood still. "Okay. Whatever you want," she capitulated cheerfully. "But we're not going to get very far this way." She beheld my face with a derisive smile.

"That depends on where we're trying to get," I said. I tried to suppress a sigh of relief.

"I'm beginning to wonder about that myself." Her tone of voice had changed. She seemed more earnest now. She turned and walked back toward the couch, then changed her mind and chose one of the two armchairs positioned at opposite ends of the coffee table. She eased herself into it and offered me the other. "I'm not dangerous at the moment." She smiled. "Have a seat."

I wasn't quite sure whether I could believe her – her brand of "not dangerous" was rather like an unarmed atomic bomb – but all this dancing around the possibility of mutual understanding had worn me out. I was glad for the chance to sit down, and took it. The two chairs were far enough apart, and the table was between them. This way, I could look her in the eye with a bit less effort. She looked at me questioningly. She wasn't going to take control this time. At this point, she obviously didn't feel she was in charge.

"I'd really like to learn more about you," I began, somewhat haltingly. Before I could continue, she interrupted me with a dismissive gesture.

"There's nothing interesting to learn, believe me. If that's all you wanted to know . . ." She started up. "Would you care for a glass of wine? I'd like one." She waited for my reply.

"Actually . . . Yes, sure. Why not?" At least that would create another opportunity to converse with her. Although I didn't believe the alcohol would make her any more talkative. She wasn't the type for that. She would certainly have the self-control not to drink one drop too much, if it came to that.

She returned with a bottle of Cabernet Sauvignon and two particularly lovely wine goblets. After she'd poured, she handed me my glass and toasted, smiling. After that, she sat back down in her armchair. She didn't try to get any closer. She twirled her glass thoughtfully with one hand. "I don't know if you understand me," she said, "but I just don't want any trouble." She took a sip of wine and savored it on her tongue.

I felt rather overwhelmed. What did she mean by that? That I was going to cause her trouble, and because of that she'd rather have nothing to do with me? I developed an uneasy feeling in my gut. She seemed completely impenetrable to me. My intuition told me I should stay away from her, but at the same time, I knew that I didn't want to separate myself from her for a minute.

"Are you in a relationship?" she asked suddenly. She sounded amiably interested.

Would I be here if I were? I just looked at her. How could she assume such a thing?

"Oh, you don't think that makes sense?" It was as if she'd read my mind. Unperturbed, she continued, "Most of my clients," she shot me a look, as if to see how I would react to that word, "are married."

I was surprised. "I thought only lesbians . . ."

"Well, yes, that's what they are – after a fashion," she said with contempt, "but of course they'll never admit that publicly. The particularly adventurous ones call themselves 'bi.'" Her expression got a shade more contemptuous. "But even they would never admit that they go to a hooker."

As much as I fought it, I couldn't hold back the fascination I felt with her lifestyle. It was so strange, so new and unfamiliar. But what could I ask her that wouldn't make me sound like a cheap, nosy tabloid reporter?

"You don't have to talk about it," I said, embarrassed by my own curiosity.

"Oh, it's not so bad," she said, once again passionless. "Don't worry about it." She reached for her glass and took another sip.

"I'm sorry," I said, shaken by her indifference and the pain I sensed it concealed. "But you get something out of it too." *Dammit!* I bit my lip. I was confused and had groped for something pleasant to say. It just slipped out.

"You think I . . .?" She looked at me somewhat sympathetically. "I think you have the wrong impression of what it is that I do. I don't get satisfied; I satisfy others. Often I don't even bother undressing."

"I – I didn't mean . . . I'm sorry . . ." I was stumbling around in the darkness and couldn't find the way out. What a mess! "I just thought ..." *Yeah, thinking is a matter of luck, young lady. Sure, you insult me now, too!*

Apparently, she had more sympathy for me than I had for myself. She went on, "If you really want to know, last week I had my first orgasm in two years."

I stared at her, dumbfounded.

She laughed. "Incredible, isn't it?"

That was certain! "You mean with someone."

"No," she said. "At all."

Now I was truly speechless.

"Believe me," she continued, as if this were ordinary small talk for her, "when you have ten women in a row, you no longer feel like doing it yourself."

"Ten?" The idea just about bowled me over.

"Well, not every day. But some days, sure." She laughed when she noticed that my mouth was still hanging open in amazement. "You never in your wildest dreams imagined a day like that, am I right?" She sobered. "I think that's enough for today."

It sounded so final that I didn't dare contradict her, although I had the feeling that it might get interesting if she continued. I had to doubt that I would catch her in such a candid mood again soon.

She rose. "I think you'd better go now," she said.

I didn't want that at all, but I didn't seem to have a choice in the matter. I felt wretched. But wasn't that my own fault? "So I guess dinner wasn't such a good idea," I suggested.

She shook her head. "Oh, no, I wouldn't say that. Normally, my clients don't even say hello to me when they see me on the street. And I act like I've never seen them before, either. You're a big improvement."

I felt like someone had struck a giant gong right next to my ear. That's what I was to her, an improvement in the quality of her clientele!

She looked at me as if stunned and took a step in my direction. "Forgive me," she said. "I didn't mean it that way." She put her hand under my chin and lifted it gently. "I get to spend so little time with people who ...," she couldn't say it out loud, so she kissed me. She spoke that language flawlessly! It was a very cautious kiss.

It was probably only supposed to be a little goodbye kiss.

But during the course of the evening, so much had built up inside me that my desire awoke immediately and with all its might, the moment her lips brushed against mine. She freed herself from my mouth again and stepped back. *Should I leave now?* I sighed. "I admire you," I said. "How can you always stay so calm?"

"I can't." Suddenly, she got very daring. She took a quick step toward me and kissed me again, for real this time. "I want you to stay," she whispered in my ear.

She had set me completely on fire, and I couldn't imagine anything nicer. Still, I hesitated. If I stayed, that would have serious consequences.

"Only if you want to, of course," she added immediately, noticing my hesitation.

I shook myself. Who could ever really know what would become of any given situation? "I'd rather stay, too," I admitted.

She didn't show any particular reaction, except that she smiled a little. "I'll be right back," she said, as she turned and walked away from me. With that, she disappeared into her bedroom and left me alone with the all-consuming heat in my belly.

I sat down on the sofa, somewhat tense. In order to think about something else, I tried to analyze our relationship – if that's what this was – up to this point. At least from my perspective. Maybe it really was love and not just a crush? Sometimes I felt so good with her, but then . . . I just couldn't figure her out. Every time I thought I'd found a solid foothold, she slipped out from under me like a ghost. That, of course, only heightened my desire to find out who she really was. I wasn't going to give up that easily!

 — 7 —

She came back into the room. She was wearing her silk robe. With a suggestive smile, she sat down next to me on the sofa. She smelled of something new – not too strong, but enchanting.

"What is that?" I asked. I buried my face in her hair and filled my lungs with the fragrance.

"That's my own perfume," she said. "I have it made in Paris."

"In Paris?"

"It sounds more luxurious than it is. Lots of women do it. And I fly to Paris sometimes, when I ..." she searched for a word, "want to be alone." After the scene in the restaurant today, I understood what she meant.

"Come," she whispered without hesitation. She leaned over my body and sank into the sofa with me. The scent of her perfume, of her body, penetrated every pore in me. It made me dizzy, took away my breath.

"What's in it?" I asked, somewhat cloudy.

"It's a secret." She wouldn't say any more about it.

"If you want to seduce me, you don't need any help," I said, dazed. "I'm already crazy about you."

"I know that." She caressed me tenderly, gently, lovingly. "But it's even better this way."

She would certainly know that better than I would. I entrusted myself to her. Her hands were all over my body, her scent all over my skin, her mouth – I didn't know where. It excited and tormented me at the same time. I suddenly found the sofa rather narrow, and told her that when she came up for breath between two kisses.

She smiled at me and reached behind me. "That can be fixed," she said. The back of the couch leaned flat. I sucked in my breath when I started to tip backwards, but the soft upholstery caught me again.

"Heaven!" I gasped, dumbfounded.

"Mm-hmm," she promised with relish. "You'll be there soon, I hope."

She lowered herself onto me, and I felt her hands again. Her mouth followed them everywhere. I writhed in pleasure. Good thing the couch was big enough now! She undressed me quickly and skillfully. I threw my arms around her and pulled her to me. The silk was still cool and smooth. It excited me in yet another way – or was it the scent again?

After a little while, she untied her belt and lay naked on top of me. Now, the silk draped over both of us, almost like a little tent. I felt her breasts and her skin as though they were my own, only much more intensely. "Isn't this lovely!" I moaned. Her wonderful body still covered mine like a soft, warm blanket.

She arrived at my mouth and kissed me. "Yes," she murmured, "and that's how it should be. I want it to be fantastic for YOU." She kissed me with growing desire. Her tongue was like fire in my mouth. I could only breathe with great effort. Nonetheless, I wanted nothing more than for her to consume me with that fire.

Slowly and carefully, she pulled away from my mouth. "Oh, no!" I protested weakly.

Her lips wandered over to my ear and whispered sensuously, "I only have one tongue, darling." Then she moved down my body, so slowly it felt like torture. Pools of boiling lava formed everywhere on my skin.

Suddenly, something leapt into my head. *Darling?* Had she said "darling"? Before it was always – if anything – "sweetheart," and that, I was sure, she said to everyone. It hadn't sounded very loving or tender. *And now? Darling?*

I reared up, moaning loudly. Her tongue turned me into a mindless object of desire. She plunged deep into me. I couldn't wait another minute. "Please …," I said. "I can't take any more …" She stroked and kissed me in so many places at the same time. How did she do that? I gave myself completely over to her. Whatever she might have asked of me at that moment, I would've done. I was propelled into a heaven of lustful satisfactions. I couldn't tell how long it went on. As I lay there gasping for breath, I saw from behind barely-open eyelids how she observed me. I couldn't decipher her expression. It was indefinable. With another woman, I would've had some idea. But she wasn't any other woman. She was she. It was just the heat of the moment, I thought. One is always prone to such flights of fancy in such moments. It couldn't be more than that.

— **8** —

I awoke with sweet thoughts in my head. I felt the previous night's passion in every fiber of my body. My breasts burned, and I still felt a slight pulsing between my legs.

I'd heard of substances that enhanced sexual sensation, but so much! And only a scent! But that wasn't really it either. She was the cause. She had brought out all those feelings in me. I only had to think about it, and already I felt a tingle.

I rolled onto my side and stretched contentedly. I was alone on the sofa bed. She had covered me up. A bit of regret began to grow in me. Somehow, I'd hoped that she'd be lying next to me when I woke. But why should she? The sun shone brightly through the windowpanes and cast patterns on the linoleum. So it was no longer too early.

Still — where was she? The apartment was quiet. Not a sound anywhere. I glanced around the room, irritated. Did she also — I had to laugh in spite of a pang of jealousy — make "house calls"? I couldn't imagine that. And even if she did, then surely not so soon. But a small hint of uncertainty remained.

The key scraped in the lock. She came in and looked immediately toward the couch. When she saw that I was awake, she smiled softly. "Hello," she said in a silky voice that I'd heard from her only rarely. Actually, only in bed. And there, it turned me into a hopeless romantic every time with a spine made of gelatin. That is, if I wasn't that already. It worked this time, too. A great feeling of tenderness rose in me. She had a paper bag in her arms, which she carried into the kitchen. "I did a little shopping," she explained in my direction. She smiled apologetically. "I'm not much of a cook to begin with, but I really didn't have anything at all in the house."

It suddenly occurred to me that I'd never thought of her as doing such mundane activities. But of course she had to do a few "normal" things also. Even she couldn't spend the entire day lying in bed. That thought sent another current of arousal through me. That's unfair, I thought. She's not lying down most of the time anyway. *And that is a frivolous thought!* A voice chattered again from the background. *Oh, you again! I thought I'd gotten rid of you.* I got no answer.

She returned from the kitchen and stopped a few steps away from the sofa. "Can I offer you anything?" she asked, quite the good hostess. For strength? I wanted to ask, but didn't. I looked at her.

"Yes," I said, entirely harmlessly. "You."

She stared at the floor. Had I gone too far? Then I caught a glimpse of her face from below. "You're blushing!" I was so utterly surprised that it just jumped out of me.

"Yeah." She looked up. "Am I not allowed?" Her voice took on a slightly defensive tone.

"Yes, of course!" I wanted to make up for my mistake. "It's very ..." I swallowed my emotion, "charming," I said.

She smiled, reassured. "No one's said that to me in a long time," she said mildly.

The lump in my throat refused to subside. How could she just stand there and turn my world completely upside-down? I wanted her. I wanted her forever. And that was the catch. In a flash, I sobered. I threw the blanket over myself and stood up. "Could I perhaps take a shower here?" I asked.

She noticed the shift. "Of course," she said haltingly. "Everything is at your disposal." Putting it that way made it all even worse. She had said that the last time, when ... I didn't want to think about that. I pulled the blanket tighter around me. When I passed her, she smiled again, as though – if only slightly – amused. I probably just should have walked by her naked. But I couldn't do that now.

The shower did me good. Under the hot stream, I forgot, for a moment, my unrest. Reluctantly, I turned the water off after a while. I hadn't brought my clothes in with me. That meant I would have to go back out and get them. I'd make a fool of myself. But I couldn't just parade around naked in front of her now!

I wrapped myself in the blanket again and went back into the main room. She'd lit a cigarette and was standing at the window, looking out. When she heard me, she turned around. She had looked rather serious, but when she saw me wrapped up in the blanket, her smile regained a hint of amusement. I picked up my clothes and turned to go back into the bathroom.

"I could just turn around," she suggested somewhat cheerfully.

"Well, fine," I retorted dejectedly. "If you must watch, then watch."

I threw the blanket aside and began to dress myself. I didn't look at her, but I would've bet that she did in fact behave herself. When I was finished, I looked back in her direction. "Are you happy now?"

"Yes," she said. "Totally." It looked like it took great effort for her to control herself. Obviously, she was greatly amused by my behavior. Somehow, I didn't quite see it that way!

"If you're just going to make fun of me, I'd rather leave," I grumbled with irritation.

"I'm not making fun of you," she continued earnestly, "I just don't know what's going on."

And I couldn't tell her myself! Actually, I was pretty much over it myself. "Oh, forget it," I replied nonchalantly. "Sometimes I just act . . . dumb."

"I hadn't noticed that at all," she remarked a bit derisively. If I couldn't always figure out what to do with her, perhaps she felt the same way.

I went over to her, by the window. "I missed you," I said tenderly. Now that the irritation had passed, her presence once again overcame me with its unbelievable sweetness. She turned to face the window. Was I getting too close? I didn't know. She must be used to compliments in all forms, after all. Or maybe not? How could that be, with so many women? That wasn't really the topic I most wanted to think about at the moment, however. I wrapped my arms around her, and she let herself sink softly against me. We looked out the window I didn't want anything else from her – only that she was there.

I don't know how much time went by while we stood there like that. In my whole life, I'd never wanted to do anything more. At some point, I let my head fall against her back, because it was getting too heavy to hold up. "I'd like to kiss the back of your neck," I wished dreamily, "but you're just too tall."

She sighed. "Yes, that's always been a problem for me." The supple softness of her body turned into tension. I knew what was coming. If only I'd just kept my mouth shut!

"I could kneel," she offered. That's exactly what I'd expected.

She just couldn't get past that!

"Would that really be much fun for you?" I asked solemnly.

"Fun?" She seemed entirely confused. It obviously hadn't occurred to her to think about having fun with this. At least not for her.

"Yes, fun! You know, that's the silly reason why people talk to each other, why they go out together, why they sleep together. Just for fun! And for both of them, no less."

"Yeah, sure." She looked at me like a child to whom I had just suggested something it didn't quite understand.

"And? Would it have been fun for you to kneel in front of me?"

She squirmed uncomfortably. "No," she said quietly, as if she were expecting me to hit her for answering that way. Her sovereignty had disappeared.

"Then why did you offer?" I asked as gently as I could.

As if it were completely self-explanatory, she answered, "Because I thought that you . . ."

"Exactly!" I said. "Because you thought I would like it."

"But you said . . ."

"I said I'd like to kiss the nape of your neck. I still want to. I have these urges sometimes with women I . . ." I bit my tongue in the nick of time – "like. But I could stand on a chair to do it, or maybe I'm still going to grow a few more inches."

She clearly couldn't follow my train of thought. "You're still growing?"

"Yeah, I'm a genetic wonder," I sighed, exhausted. "No, of course not. I just wanted to point out that there are other ways to do this sort of thing."

"Oh, I see," she said. "Sure." She took three steps to the left, toward the other window. "Pardon me." She emphasized the meaninglessness of this error with a careless gesture. "I'm just used to this."

"That's the terrible thing!" I exclaimed. "You're so used to going along with other people's wishes that you've forgotten about your own." She'd understand that quickly, I was sure of it. More than such a quick peek behind the facade was out of the question, but I was sure of this much.

"Yeah, yeah." She tossed off my observation. "It's not quite like that, either. Don't make such a big deal of it."

Make a big deal about it? Me?

She looked back at me. "I know what you mean," she continued placidly, probably in an attempt to get this conversation over with. "But in my line of work, my own wishes are the last thing taken into consideration."

It was a simple explanation that apparently sufficed for her purposes. She had accepted it and lived by it. And her clients had as well. *A fait accompli.* Didn't she have any other desires? And her clients – was there never one among them who, like me, wanted to know more? Who wanted to know about the joys and sorrows of the woman behind the mask? And who said so? I'd come back to the place where I noticed how strange this world was to me. "Don't they ever ask ...?" The strangeness of the situation had propelled me to ask the question.

She laughed disdainfully. "Once in a while, sure. But of course they don't really want to know. And they only ever do it once, usually at the beginning."

"And you don't talk about it?"

"No, of course not. No prostitute would." Yes, exactly, that was the reason. I still didn't think of her as a prostitute.

I shrugged in a gesture of resignation. "I'm sorry," I said. "I didn't want to ..." I was just like the rest. Instead of finding the cause, I let my frustrations out on her. How was she supposed to know what I wanted from her? "I just don't understand it. It's so strange to me. They are women, after all. Don't they ever tell you something ...?" How could I put it, that which was so self-explanatory to me, without actually saying it? Expressions of love would get me nowhere. Then she'd retreat anyway.

"Encouraging?" I concluded vaguely.

"Oh, of course!" She laughed bitterly. "They do that."

Now I didn't understand anything anymore. *So they did?* "But what ...?"

"What do they say to me?" She smiled coldly. "Sometimes they just say: 'You're really good.'"

I looked at her blankly. She responded accordingly.

Ruth Gogoll's Taxi to Paris

"You don't think that's so bad? That's true." She took a few more steps away from me, crossed her arms, and looked back at me. "Do you want to hear some more?"

I didn't really want to, but that had been a rhetorical question.

She continued without pause, "Sometimes they also say, 'you made it really nice for me.'"

I didn't want to hear any more. She was making a voyeur of me. But apparently, she wasn't going to stop now.

"Sometimes they make comparisons. Then they say, 'You really fuck the best.' Or they just grab me between the legs when they pay and say, 'You're a horny –'"

"Stop it!" I couldn't bear it any longer.

She was still smiling coldly at me. "That wasn't nearly everything. Was it encouraging enough?"

"Oh, God," I said. "They're women."

"Yes," she said indifferently. "They're women. But they're paying me. And for that, they should expect a little fun, right?"

She was so bitter; it felt like physical pain. Slowly, I began to understand. Those humiliations, this contempt – and for how long had she put up with it? Actually, it didn't make much difference. I wouldn't have wanted to take it once – and I probably couldn't. That's where her hardness and indifference came from. Now she was so closed off again, she felt like a stone fortress.

And it was their fault! Anger flooded me with such furor; I almost vomited. Then I felt a sudden coldness inside. No, it wasn't their fault – it was my fault. I'd asked her to talk about it. Now I was no better than the others. Just the opposite. I was the worst one of all; she'd trusted me, at least to a degree. I could at least have done my best not to cause her more pain. But now it was too late. There was nothing left for me to do but leave. I couldn't help her; I was only making things worse by staying. The noose around my neck pulled itself tighter. I swallowed hard. I felt paralyzed.

She stood there – an icy mountain of contempt. I was afraid to leave her alone. But I had to. I was only going to keep reminding her of all the pain and insults. I forced myself to make a decision.

"I have to go now," I said. I tried to look at her. She stared blankly into space. I couldn't move her to say goodbye, nor could I say anything to her myself. I turned around and headed for the door, hesitantly putting one foot before the other. Finally, I got there. I laid a hand on the doorknob. She still didn't say anything. I opened the door and turned around. She still stood there, completely lifeless and stiff. She didn't look at me. I closed the door behind me.

— **9** —

The next few days were like a preview of the fires of hell. I went to work, came home from work, slept, went to work ... Sleep wasn't really the right word for this restless tossing and turning, nor could one really say these were nights to remember.

After a week of this, I looked like a ghost. My colleagues sent me home with good intentions, under the assumption that I would find rest there. This made it even worse. Now I didn't even have those few hours a day during which I could throw myself into a routine and forget her.

I started walking through the city, looking in shop windows, though I couldn't have said what was in any of them. I visited cafés full of old women stuffing themselves with cream pastries.

On the third day, I saw her. It gave me quite a shock. She was crossing the street – I only saw her back – but I recognized her immediately. That wasn't exactly a great feat, given her unusual height.

After she crossed the street, she walked along the main strip of the pedestrian zone's shopping area. I leapt up and threw the money for my coffee on the table. From the corner of my eye, I saw my waitress jump in confusion as I dashed out of the café like an elite sprinter. Perhaps I could still have a shot at the Olympics.

By the time I got to the pedestrian zone, I couldn't see her anymore. I sprinted some more. My lungs burned. The street forked. I raced off to the right. She wasn't there. I ran back and took the other path. I caught a glimpse of her at the end of the block, entering a supermarket. Of course she wouldn't shop at little mom-and-pop stores – those were much too personal. A supermarket provided the anonymity she required.

I was about to slow down when I realized that the supermarket had two exits. I begged the pardon of my aching lungs and sprinted off down the block. When I got to the market, I tried to decide what she would be likely to shop for. She had admitted herself that she didn't cook, so I could forget the produce as well as the usual "housewife" areas. Slowly, I began to breathe normally again. I wandered hesitantly through the aisles.

The deli section! I walked more quickly again, turned the corner and looked around. There she was.

She was putting two bottles of champagne in a cart. Those were for her clients, I assumed for no particular reason. Perhaps because she'd never offered me any. I followed her. She picked up a few more things – not many – and headed for the checkout. After paying, she put everything in a leather backpack and walked quickly to the exit. She was in quite a rush. Was it always like this when she went shopping? Hurry home quickly to get out of danger?

I only now realized how much of a gift she had given me by going out to dinner. Hopefully she flew to Paris as often as possible – no one could put up with this for long!

She had chosen the exit that was closest to her apartment. She would probably be going directly there. I was going to lose sight of her soon if I didn't hurry up. Those long legs!

As I got closer, I saw the reactions of the people who crossed her path. Some stared shamelessly at her. A couple of women ignored her so ostentatiously that I assumed they were clients of hers. She walked with a stiff back. She was getting close to home.

What should I do? As soon as she got to her building, there would be nothing left for me to do. I ducked into an alleyway that I knew intersected with the main street again several yards ahead. I ran. Panting, I rounded the corner. I'd caught up with her precisely. I almost ran into her.

Her backpack slipped. Oh, shit – the champagne! I reached for it quickly, just before it hit the ground, we both caught the bag. Only then did she recognize me. Her face went blank.

"Thank you, ma'am," she said.

Ah! She wanted to act as though she didn't know me. Like she did with her clients. *You aren't going to get rid of me that easily.*

"You're very welcome," I replied. "How are you?" She was in the middle of straightening herself out and stopped dead in her tracks. She stood rather crookedly.

"That's not good for your back," I observed helpfully.

She finally stood up straight. She looked at me as though she were rather distressed. I acted as though I didn't notice. I had to get it right this time. She wouldn't be giving me a second chance.

"Would you like to have coffee?" I offered, as if we were old friends who'd just run into each other around town. "At my place?" I added with emphasis.

She still looked quite distressed. This was the chance I'd been hoping for. I decided to act. "Fine." I exhaled. I had to collect myself first. Then I pointed in the direction of my street. "I live right over there." I turned to the left. "Are you coming?"

She actually did. She walked right behind me, mostly staring straight ahead, but once looking in my direction with the confusion of a deer caught in headlights. *If I could just get her into my apartment quickly, everything would be all right.*

What would be all right? At some point, she was going to get her wits about her again; I should just have myself lobotomized and be done with it. *Leave me in peace!* I protested silently.

She was still following me like a little lamb when I opened the front door. I turned to face her. "I'm afraid there's no elevator," I said apologetically. "It's an old building." I didn't get the impression that this interested her in the slightest. I started up the steps. Four stories! Why hadn't I decided to live on the ground floor?

By the time we got to my floor, the tension in my body was almost unbearable. I gasped for air, and not just from climbing the stairs. She was breathing quietly, as if four flights were nothing to her. She must be in great shape. *No wonder, with her job – she'd have to stay fit! Shh, be quiet!*

After I'd shut the door to my apartment behind us, I let myself exhale. We'd made it! "To the left," I directed. "In the kitchen."

She went on ahead of me. She must still be deep in shock. She still wasn't quite all there. Most likely, she'd planned on never seeing me again – and certainly not so suddenly.

I motioned to my rocking chair – the only piece of furniture that I almost never gave up for a guest. "Have a seat," I said softly. I'll make some coffee."

She sat down. I filled the kettle with water and set it on the burner. I was starting to get a little worried. She'd have to react to something eventually. I went over to her and took her bag. She just let me take it. "The champagne should probably go in the refrigerator, don't you think?" I offered congenially. Oh, damn!

Exactly – that woke her up! "Champagne?" she said. "How do you know that I bought champagne?" Her eyes, as they probed my face, were getting some life back in them.

I tried to brush it off and act harmless. "I looked in the bag."

"No, you didn't," she countered firmly. It seems she'd been with it enough to follow that much.

"Right." I was going to have to come clean. If she got up and left now, there would be nothing I could do to stop her. "I saw you at the grocery store."

"But I didn't see you." She obviously had no idea why not, and was trying to figure out how she would have missed me.

"No," I said.

Her face hardened into a mask. "You were watching me," she concluded icily.

Oh, God, I was never going to get her to open up this way! "Completely by accident," I said to pardon myself. "You were crossing the street, and I was sitting over at the café." At least she shouldn't think that I'd been watching her for any length of time. "I saw you go into the supermarket . . ."

"And so you just followed me in," she finished soberly.

I could no longer be so calm with her. "Yes, dammit!" I exploded. "I wanted to see you again! Is that so hard to understand?"

"You could've called me," she suggested, as though it were the most obvious thing in the world.

"And make an appointment with you?" *Oh no, not again! Why couldn't I just keep my big mouth shut?*

"For instance." She underlined her unequivocal coldness, even more than before, with disinterested calmness. She would not be provoked. Instead, she examined her fingernails absently.

I could've bawled. Why had I done that? I knew perfectly well how she reacted to attention. She was used to it. She walled herself off to it and became unreachable. I looked at her. I couldn't take it anymore. "I ..." *Love you,* I finished in my head. I walked over to her, bent down, and kissed her. She opened her lips automatically and let me in. It was a terrible feeling. That's how it must be when she let her clients kiss her! I pulled back and straightened.

"You could've had that, too," she said, completely unaffected. "You didn't have to ambush me on the street."

The teakettle started to whistle. I turned around and shut it off. I'd done everything wrong! Now I really would have to go to her as a client if I wanted to see her. She'd never allow me more. Assuming she'd even allow me that. I stood with my back to her. I couldn't look at her now. I leaned against the stove. "Please ...," I said. Not a sound. I turned on one heel. She was sitting exactly as before. All the feelings I had for her overwhelmed me at once. "I yearn for you," I said desperately.

"I understand," she answered unconcernedly. "Where is your bed?"

"No – please – don't do that to me!" I wanted to scream, but I could only manage a torn whisper.

"Do what to you? I thought you wanted to sleep with me." She was the cool professional again, the whore.

Yes. Yes, I wanted that. But with her, not with this soulless body. I collapsed inside. "I can't." I felt completely burned out.

"Then I can go." She took her bag, stood up, and went to the door. I followed her. She turned the knob.

"I love you," I said.

For the second time that day, she stopped dead in her tracks. I repeated, "I love you."

Slowly, she let go of the doorknob. "No," she whispered, almost inaudibly.

"Yes," I restated quietly. "I can't help it."

Now nothing mattered to me anymore. I went up to her, embraced her from behind, and pulled her tight to me. "I love you, I love you, I love you!" I was so happy that I could finally say it. Even if this had to be the last time.

"You can't do that," she said, just as softly as before.

"Yes, I can," I insisted. "Not even you can forbid me that."

She jerked. I thought she was going to cry, but I didn't hear a sound. I snuggled up against her one more time, and then let her go. If she wanted to leave, there was no way for me to stop her.

She didn't move. We stood there so completely motionless that we could hear the clock ticking all the way in the kitchen. I turned to face her.

"That's not possible." The pressure I'd brought to bear on her was apparent in her face. "I'm a —" Contrary to her usual habit, she didn't say the word aloud.

"I know what you are. And I didn't just find out today." I took a deep breath. "It doesn't bother me." Whether or not that was true wasn't something I wanted to test just now. "And it certainly won't stop me from loving you. Whether you like it or not." So, it was out! Either she'd go or she'd stay. I had to leave that up to her.

She fought with herself. She knew she'd have to leave now if she were to put an end to all of this, I didn't dare consider whether she loved me, or would ever love me. But I could be certain that she liked me. At least that was a start.

"I can't concern myself with those feelings," she explained. She'd gotten hold of herself again. She did seem somewhat discomfited, but distant at the same time. "I don't know what to do with them. Please don't ask that of me."

"I'm not asking anything of you," I assured her, as calmly as possible. I knew she wasn't being cruel on purpose. She was just trying to protect herself. "But is it so terrible to be loved?"

"It's threatening," she said, momentarily more open than I'd expected. "It scares me."

Love scared her? Why? I knew from my own experience that this kind of attention could seem oppressive coming from some women. I'd probably been guilty of that sometimes myself. But I also knew that nothing had happened between the two of us that even came close to that kind of situation. So the reason had to come from her past. Of course, I couldn't change anything about that. The only thing I could do was to treat her as gently and lovingly as I was able, in order to show her that things could go differently. But first, she'd have to let me close enough to do that!

"Am I threatening to you?" I asked directly. She was such a master of evasion, no other route seemed likely to get me anywhere. But I was afraid of the answer as well.

"You win," she said. That could mean anything in the world.

—— **10** —

The days went by like a dream. She simply stayed with me. Once, over breakfast, I asked her if she didn't need to go back to her apartment. "No," she said, "I'm officially in Paris."

"But you've never even ..." She'd neither made a telephone call nor left my apartment.

"I didn't have to tell anyone. It was already scheduled." She looked at me mischievously. "Before you kidnapped me."

The memory was embarrassing. I blushed.

She kissed me on the mouth quite familiarly and looked me in the eye. "I'm grateful to you for that." Gratitude wasn't exactly what I was looking for from her, but ... Without my encouragement, she went right for another diversion. "And clothes, it seems, are not necessary – am I right?"

That was true. She embarrassed me all over again. We had spent almost 24 hours a day in bed; I shivered with pleasure. Then I said, regretfully, "Too bad I have to go back to work tomorrow."

She bit into a roll. "I have to work on Monday myself," she said, completely unintentionally.

I felt like I'd been punched in the stomach. The whole time she'd been here, I'd never once thought about that. "You have to go back to work?"

She looked at me without thinking. "But of course. My vacation is over, too."

I just hadn't been prepared for that. Sure, she had her profession and I mine. And we'd both taken a vacation.

"Don't look so sad," she said comfortingly. "You'll still have time in the evenings. And I'm usually free then, too."

Just as I'd thought, love in the morning was her specialty. I pulled myself together. I'd known this all along. If I'd put it out of my mind, that was my own fault. I agreed reluctantly. "Yeah. We can get together in the evening."

She came over to me and looked at me lovingly. "But we've only just . . .," I said, although her face was already bringing my insides to a boil.

"Yes." She was already at my mouth. "But I have years to make up for."

I had to laugh. I still couldn't quite believe that. Her kiss became more urgent. I rose against her. "No," she said, "stay in your chair."

I sank back. She leaned over me. Her hand lay gently on my shoulder, and she kissed me with every ounce of tenderness she could muster. Her kisses were absolutely incredible. I didn't think that was a consequence of her job. It had to be natural talent. Such things just couldn't be learned.

When she pulled back for a moment, I said, "I love it when you kiss me like that. Sometimes, I never want it to stop. I've always been partial to kissing, but with you, I've become completely addicted to it."

This type of compliment could always make her uneasy. Now was no exception. "We could just kiss, if that's what you want," she said. She didn't seem terribly excited by the prospect, but she'd offered it immediately. I'd have to be more careful with what I said. If it sounded like an honest wish, she would offer to fulfill it instantly. The woman of my wildest dreams! Now I knew, that could also be fatal.

This time, I teased her about it a little. "Yes," I suggested. "That's a good idea."

She seemed disappointed, but as always, she put her own wishes aside. "Yes," she said.

I batted my eyelashes innocently at her. "May I choose the place for it?"

There was a slight delay before she figured it out. "You lying dog!" she grumbled, almost lovingly, as she bent back down over me.

The sweetness of her kisses was simply indescribable. When I could no longer stand the tension, I pushed her hands down over my body and between my legs. She let them hang there, motionless. "Do you want it now?" she asked sensuously.

"Yes," I moaned, at the very edge of sanity. She did nothing. "Please," I said urgently.

"Do you really want it?" she asked again. Something stirred in the back of my mind, but I could no longer think. She had something in mind. The presence of her tongue in my mouth robbed me of all conscious thought.

"Yes," I moaned again. "Please do it."

She pushed into me with two fingers. I yelped with surprise and tightened. Her fingers remained inside me, motionless. "You're very wet," she said. "This doesn't hurt." She began to move her fingers very carefully – very gently, and without rhythm. "Just the opposite – it feels good." She did everything to take away my fear. Her voice calmed me. And she was right.

At first, I didn't feel anything at all. Then, she stroked a spot just inside the entrance. That sent an intense feeling of warmth through my body. My arousal had disappeared from fright, but now, she stroked me gently back to the top again. When I began to move against her with more and more desire, she carefully pushed back. I tightened up again, but only for a moment. She repeated the motion until I'd gotten used to it again. Now I felt nothing but pure lust. I pushed against her, trying to take as much of her in as I possibly could. She matched my rhythm. I felt like she was completely inside me. She knew better than I did what I wanted. When I finally came around her fingers, she sighed. "I knew you could do it." I looked once more into her eyes, and then fell asleep.

When I awoke a short time later, I was in bed. She'd carried me over. I didn't remember anything about it. I had, of course, been aware of her strength and had given it a rather negative meaning at the beginning of our acquaintance. But when I thought about it now, it seemed completely improbable that this could be the same woman.

She came in and sat next to me on the bed. "I made coffee," she said. "Would you like some?"

"Would I like some what?" I teased.

She scooted herself a bit closer to the edge of the bed, farther from me. "No, no," she said, carefully fending me off. "I'm not on the menu."

She was like that sometimes. In contrast to her professional willingness, she was otherwise rather aloof. To allow oneself to be seduced by her was easy; to seduce her was another story – one that had caused me more than one headache already. First and foremost, she could never have the feeling that I wanted something from her. That often made her switch immediately to "pro" mode. If I gave her the feeling that it was her idea, and it was just "accidental" that she got something out of it, then everything was fine. I understood completely, but it did tend to make things rather tiresome. For that reason, I didn't start teasing her again, but rather asked, "Why did you go and do that?"

Careful, nervous attention crossed her face. "Did I hurt you?"

"No, of course not. You would've noticed that." I looked at her, and felt myself get almost dizzy with love for her. I smiled. "As gentle as you were."

She relaxed again. Mothers were called "overprotective" when they acted like this – could lovers be the same way? I leaned over toward her and kissed her very softly, so she wouldn't get the wrong idea. "You were wonderful," I reassured her. "And it was very good."

"For me, too." Now she smiled again. Then she answered my question. "I just think you shouldn't renounce anything you've never tried before. If you hadn't liked it, at least you'd know why." She was the pragmatic one, through and through.

"Will you bring me my coffee in bed, or do I have to try my wobbly legs?" I joked, in order to think about something other than making love to her.

She went for it. "Was it so bad?" she joked back.

"Much worse," I philosophized, with the most deadly serious face I could manage. "I've redefined the word 'orgasm.' They're going to have to rewrite the dictionary."

She laughed again, pleased, making me happy again for the moment. "Well, if that's how it is, I'll have to bring it to you." She stood up and went out in her usual graceful way.

I had to face the gloomy thought that this was our last day together. It occurred to me that I had no idea what she did on the weekend. Perhaps she'd have time then. But that really wasn't enough. I wanted her forever.

She came back in with the coffee. "Do you have the weekends free?" I asked casually.

She laughed unconcernedly. "Like a regular worker, you mean?"

I had to laugh at the picture myself. "Yeah, sort of."

She answered as though I'd asked her about a dentist's appointment. "Not generally," she said. "But most of the time, I'm not busy the whole day. Just in exceptional cases."

These "exceptional cases" didn't please me a bit, but what could I do? I tried to think about the positive aspects of the situation. "So maybe we'd have the weekend to ourselves sometimes?" It was the first time we'd ever discussed the future. I noticed some hesitation. She didn't want to set anything in stone.

"Sure," she said, unconvincingly. "Sometimes."

"Good," I said. I wasn't really thinking that, but perhaps I'd be able to convince her over time to keep the weekends free.

Over time? What was it that I had in mind? A steady relationship with a . . .? Even in my thoughts, I couldn't say the word. Could this ever turn out well? But what relationship ever comes with a guarantee? And for that matter — what had she said before? *Don't knock it if you haven't tried it.*

I looked at her and adored her. How should I continue from here? Any attempt to get closer to her would be met with avoidance or with the professional routine.

"Bring your coffee in here," I said, as harmlessly as possible. "I hate to drink mine alone."

She looked at me warily, but I must not have seemed too dangerous. Perhaps she assumed that I was still too weak. She guessed wrong about that!

She got her cup and sat next to me on the bed. I slid to one side to make room for her. "Come here," I said, "I want to lean against you, you big strong woman."

Now she was torn. On one hand, I'd expressed a wish. On the

other hand, she knew that if she did what I asked, she'd be within my reach. As she most often did, she fulfilled the wish. She sat closer to me.

That still didn't solve the whole problem. If I'd started to behave tenderly toward her, she would've gotten out immediately – either out of bed or out of her private persona. And I wanted her so. My fingers strained to touch her. Instead, I held my coffee cup with both hands, trying not to make her suspicious. "May I?" I asked before leaning against her. That always calmed her.

I finished my coffee slowly. Since she was sitting next to me, I had to reach across her to put the empty cup on the nightstand. Nothing could be more innocent! On my way back, I let my hand fall onto her thigh – completely coincidentally, of course. I stretched myself out a little closer and laid my head on her breast. She was wearing one of my long men's shirts. I would have liked most to undress her, but that would've been absolutely deadly. She would've turned to ice. I yawned. "Are you tired, too?"

That finally convinced her that I didn't want anything from her. My hand moved on her thigh as if I were seeking a comfortable position in which to fall asleep. In doing so, I brushed up against one of her erogenous zones – again, as if by coincidence. She became restless. I rearranged my head a bit on her breast. I accidentally brushed against her nipple. Her unrest grew. My hand still brushed sleepily against her thigh. I tried to breathe deeply, as though I were falling asleep.

She squirmed back and forth on the bed. Then she put down her coffee cup and laid an arm over me. Slowly, her hand began to stroke my breast. I rejoiced internally. At the same time, I gritted my teeth to avoid reacting to her touch too quickly.

After a little while, I acted as if I'd been woken up. "What are you doing?" I asked sluggishly.

That made her smile. "Don't you like it?" Now I had her!

I turned to face her more, and slid one hand absently under her shirt.

"Yes," I murmured, still a bit sleepily. "Keep going." I wanted to kiss her so badly, but I had to wait for her to come to me. It took a while, but then she lay down next to me and turned me onto my back. She kissed me. I noticed that she was already pretty turned on. As soon as I felt her mouth against mine, I lifted myself slowly and turned over with her, until she lay beneath me. Now I'd passed the critical point; I could continue. I loved her so much – we'd have to work on this problem!

I kissed her long and deep. She moaned in my mouth. I'd learned a few tricks from her! With both hands, I slowly pushed her shirt up. When I could see her breasts, I wondered anew at her beauty. I stroked her silky skin over and over. Her skin was simply incredible. I followed my fingers with my lips.

"Let me take this off." Her voice sounded forced.

I didn't want to be distracted. "It's Okay."

"Please." Her voice became more urgent. "Let me take it off."

Now I knew what was going on. She was reminded of how most women slept with her while she still had all her clothes on. A new point I'd have to watch out for in the future. I had to let her do it herself, so I sat back on my heels and said, "OK, go ahead."

She pulled the shirt off over her head and lay back down. Now I'd have to start closer to the beginning, because she'd been thinking about her job. Nothing I did could seem even a little bit like a client. I leaned back into her arms. My hand caressed her stomach gently, tracing little patterns over her skin. "Are you all right?"

She didn't answer right away. That in itself was an indication that I hadn't guessed wrong about the situation. Then she said, "It's been a long time since I've felt as good with someone else as I do with you."

This was the first time she'd ever told me anything like that. I'd only occasionally believed that I detected it. The fact that she said it out loud was a huge boost to my confidence. "That makes me very happy," I said, genuinely pleased. I propped myself up on one elbow and looked down at her. Tenderness overwhelmed me once more. "I hope that it always stays that way." I looked at her earnestly and lovingly. She just looked back up at me and said nothing.

I moved my hand slowly back in the direction of her breasts. I held her gaze tightly. "You are so beautiful," I said. "I still can't quite believe it. Every time I see you, it feels like a gift."

With this kind of compliment, ones that only dealt with her appearance, she was fine. She smiled, relaxed. "But I didn't choose that," she said simply.

I touched her breast and began to caress it. Her nipple hardened immediately, stretching the skin. I wanted her dreadfully, but I would still need to take my time. I smiled at her, leaned down, and kissed her gently, without expectation. I played my tongue across her lips, then traced it slowly down to her breasts. I took a nipple between my lips and teased it. Her nipples weren't as sensitive as mine, but after a short time, she began to react with restless motion and light moaning.

I laid my body onto hers and kissed her again, this time with increasing desire. She returned my kisses in kind.

My hand glided down between her thighs and spread them. She gasped when I brushed across the center. I couldn't wait much longer. I slid down over her body and opened her legs completely. She tossed back and forth across the bed impatiently. I found her entrance with my tongue. Her hips rose to meet me. I pushed inside. She cried out. "Darling!" That word was one she saved for moments of extreme passion – otherwise, I never heard it from her.

I circled my tongue around inside her. She moaned louder and louder and threw herself about wildly. I sought her clit with my tongue. I stroked it. Simultaneously, I reached inside her with one finger. She pushed her hips into me with such force I didn't think I could hold her. Suddenly, she stopped at the highest point in her thrusting and shuddered. I kept caressing her with my tongue until she collapsed. She was breathing heavily.

I made my way slowly back up her body caressing her once more all over. She pressed herself eagerly against my hand and sighed with contentment. When I'd made it back up to her level, I looked back over her whole body with an unbelievable feeling of tenderness.

"I love you," I said.

She looked at me, relaxed and satisfied. Her eyes spoke, but she didn't say it.

"I know," she said instead.

I asked myself whether I'd ever hear her say it.

—— 11 ——

She woke me with a kiss. "I'm going now," she said softly. Everything in me pulled itself together. I wasn't quite fully awake yet, but the day was already gone. I didn't want her to go, but I knew it had to be this way. I, too, would soon go back to work as usual. The dream was over for the time being.

She had a coffee cup in her hand. "One more cup of coffee in bed," she said. "To wake up." Was something flashing in her eyes? Had she noticed it herself? No, she was looking at me quite innocently.

I couldn't comprehend how she could be so awake this early in the morning. I had, after all, slept as much – or as little – as she had. But I felt like I'd been put through a wringer, and she looked like she'd just spent a refreshing weekend at the spa.

I sat up and took the mug from her. She was sitting at the foot of the bed, but there was nothing erotic about it. "I never would have thought I'd be so sorry to leave, after the way you dragged me over here."

"Oh, let it be already," I deflected. Did she have to start with these stories so god-awful early in the morning?

"No." She held her ground. "It was wonderful being here with you. I want you to know that."

She acted as though this were farewell forever! Or was that what she was trying to say? I felt a terrible fear course through my bones. I looked at her and tried to figure out what she was thinking. Her face was open and friendly. There was something else as well, but I couldn't quite make it out. Perhaps she wasn't completely awake either. I reached out my hand and laid it on hers. "Will you call me this evening?" I wanted to make absolutely sure that I wouldn't have to call her. That would be too much like work. I looked at my alarm clock. "I'll be home after about six."

"I can't before . . ."

I interrupted her. "Or whenever you have time." I didn't want to know how long she would be busy with other women. Apparently, she already had appointments from before her "vacation." She really had a strong grasp of her business. Probably the "regulars" again!

I would simply have to learn to deal with that. I had pursued her, and I couldn't make her responsible for my squeamishness. I smiled at her. "I'm looking forward to it," I said.

"Yes," she said hesitantly. Something was there!

"What is it?" I asked directly.

She shook her head. "Oh, nothing. I just don't want to leave yet."

"Then stay a while," I said. It was still early.

She stood up. "Unfortunately, that's not possible. I have . . . ," she broke off.

I understood her nonetheless. She had an appointment soon. Love in the morning. And the way it sounded, today could be one of those ten-client days. Straight through from morning 'til evening. Probably, I wouldn't even be able to touch her suggestively this evening. What a great start!

She leaned down and kissed me on the forehead. "Ugh!" I grunted disappointedly. "Not even a real goodbye kiss? When we're not going to see each other all day long? An eternity!"

She laughed. "You really know how to get me!" she said good-naturedly. So she had seen through it! But I couldn't tell for sure.

She leaned over me, propping herself up on the bed. I wrapped my arms around her neck. She kissed me softly, but it was clear that she was holding back. Nevertheless, I felt how her kiss started a fire inside me. Just a little bit more, and maybe she would stay! I increased my pull on her neck and sighed in her mouth. Carefully, she pulled away. "No." She was loving, but firm. "No more."

"Too bad." I'd never said anything truer.

She smiled understandingly. "Yes. But I really do have to go now."

I observed her beautiful lips and wondered when the next woman would kiss them. Was she already there waiting? Jealousy flooded me.

I tried to calm myself. This was neither the time nor the place for that. Then I felt ashamed. She had perhaps ten women to please today, all of whom would expect a full show, and I was putting the moves on her!

I reached an arm out. "Fine," I said, without any particular intonation. "Until this evening then."

She touched my hand briefly and left.

— **12** —

All day long, I didn't have much time to think about her. In my absence, so much had collected on my desk that I felt like I was chipping away at a mountain that never got any smaller. Toward the end of the afternoon, I finally saw the surface of the desk peeking through.

When I opened the last project folder, her face suddenly forced itself between the pages. Her face, as it looked when she lay there in complete relaxation. Her face, as she leaned down and kissed me. Her beautiful face, looking right at me. Longing overtook me like a torture device. I looked at the clock. I'd be home in an hour, just like I'd said, but I didn't know when she'd call. And I couldn't call her. Who knew what she was doing right then? I preferred not to imagine that. But of course, I couldn't prevent it. The images cascaded before me of their own volition. I saw her in bed with another woman. I saw her caressing and kissing the other woman. No, you're much too romantic! Remember what she told you! No! For God's sake, no!

I leapt up and threw the prospectus on the desk. Work was out of the question for the rest of the day. And I couldn't think about her without ... I would soon forget how to think altogether, given those choices.

At home, I waited restlessly for the phone to ring. I tried to distract myself. I put on a CD; after a short time, I didn't care for it anymore; I chose another, after five minutes, the same thing again. The third time, I came across the Vivaldi. I looked at the cover for several minutes. I didn't play it. I started to pace back and forth through the apartment, just like after our first night together. Suddenly, I jerked to a halt. She'd never actually said she was going to call me! And this morning, she'd been noticeably reserved. What if she wasn't going to call? What if she was never going to call? What if that was it? I didn't know her well enough to guess at the probability that she had really just taken a "vacation" with me – a vacation fling at home. And after that the usual: a phone number that you never used, and then threw away after a while.

I'd had the feeling this morning that she was making the farewell a little too dramatic for just one day.

The phone rang. I froze for a moment because it startled me so badly, then I dove for it.

I answered. The line was quiet, but I could tell that someone was there. Another prankster who harassed women, I bet! I took a breath to let loose my usual tirade against such callers.

"Hello," I heard her say.

My heart skipped a beat. I let the air rush back out of my lungs.

"Hello," I said. It sounded scratchy. I cleared my throat. "It's nice of you to call."

"Isn't that what you wanted?" she asked. Oh, no, the day had really worn her out! She sounded exhausted, she sounded uninterested, and she sounded professional.

"Yes," I confirmed, as if I hadn't noticed her tone of voice. "But it's nice of you anyhow." I didn't much want to continue this conversation over the telephone. I wanted to see her. "How are you?"

"Fine," she said. "A little tired." If that was a little tired, then I was the Queen of Sheba!

My longing for her grew. I didn't have the impression that she was particularly interested in having any more company that evening, myself included. The most direct route seemed like the best one in this case. "You don't sound tired, you sound completely exhausted," I said. "I'd like to do something for you."

At first, the line was quiet again. She would have to think about what I could possibly mean by that offer. "For me?" she said in the same, astounded tone with which one questions a winning lottery ticket. Complete disbelief.

"Yes," I said winningly. "and only for you. I promise, cross my heart and hope to die, that this is not a come-on in disguise."

She had to think about that a little while longer. Then her curiosity started to take over. "What did you have in mind?" she asked, if rather skeptically.

I didn't want to discuss it with her over the phone. Either she trusted me, or she didn't! "You can try it out if you want, but I can't do it over the phone!" Had that maybe sounded a bit too insinuating?

She thought about it again for a few seconds. Then she gave up. "Well, fine. Come over." A little sigh in her voice indicated that she felt this was the lesser evil. The lesser evil, compared to having to discuss it with me. After ten women, what difference could an eleventh make? That's exactly how it sounded.

But I was happy that I'd convinced her. After I hung up, I hummed a few bars of a little waltz and danced over to my closet. I could've danced all the way to her place.

She opened the door and looked just as exhausted as she'd sounded over the phone. Although everything in me wanted to take her in my arms and hold her tight, I just kissed her on the cheek in greeting. That seemed to take her somewhat by surprise, but she said nothing.

She was dressed in her silk robe again, though this time she wore a pair of silk pajamas underneath. It must feel wonderful to take those off of her! My fingertips might've been buried in an anthill, as much as they were tingling. No, tonight it was her turn – and only hers!

"Do you have a hot water bottle?" I asked as I followed her across the room. She stopped abruptly. I almost ran into her.

"A hot water bottle?" she repeated skeptically, turning to face me.

"Yes. Or a heating pad. Although – a hot water bottle would be better."

"A hot water bottle is better?" Now she was fully convinced that I had some unspeakably perverted activity in mind.

I brushed her cheek with the back of my hand. I didn't much want to stop that, either, but I controlled myself. I laughed. "To keep you warm, darling." That term of endearment still sounded very strange, but I could at least use it with her at carefully chosen times. Then perhaps she'd start to get used to it.

"But I'm not cold," she said with irritation. So I could imagine. She certainly had a hot day behind her.

"You might get cold while I'm massaging you." That was another tricky point that might cause her to bail out. "That's what I have in mind."

I watched the wariness in her face increase. I had to do something. "I told you over the phone and I'll tell you again: you can rest assured that I'm only going to give you a massage." I raised my right hand. "Indian brave's honor. How!"

She was beyond irritated. She'd probably never played Cowboys and Indians as a kid. I had.

"Do you know the scene in Victor/Victoria where Toddy says to Victoria that she can come to bed with him because it'll be much more comfortable than the sofa ...," I imitated Toddy's voice, "'and infinitely safer'? He's a fairy," I explained.

She obviously didn't know the scene. "But you're not a ..." she said, now apparently rather confused.

"No, that I'm not." I laughed at the idea. "But that's exactly what I mean." I couldn't help imitating Toddy's voice one more time – I loved the film! "Infinitely safer."

She didn't really seem convinced – at least not about my present mental state – but she said, "I have a heating pad." If it was made of silk too, it would be clear why she didn't own a hot water bottle: they didn't come in silk.

"Good." Cheerfully, I sailed past her confusion. "Can you get it?" Somewhat disoriented, she glanced around the apartment as if she'd never been there before, then she went into her bedroom, I would've followed her anywhere else, but this time I'd have to wait until I was invited in.

She did, in fact, return with a heating pad. It did not have a silk cover.

I looked around. "Well," I said uncertainly. "Where should I massage you?" There weren't all that many possibilities.

She seemed extremely conflicted. I was sure she had, up until this point, expected something entirely different. But now her doubts were returning. Apparently, she decided to jump in with both feet anyway. She turned toward her bedroom. "Here."

I followed her in. I was really curious. Her bedroom was rather luxurious, as I'd guessed, but neither overdone nor – as I should've known – sleazy. I smiled to myself when I noticed the silk sheets. "You love silk, don't you?"

"Yes. It's so comfortable against my skin."

For someone who'd gone without tenderness as long as she had, I supposed that was the next best thing. And completely risk-free. I thought of her skin, smooth as that silk, and felt the urge to touch her. But today, it was entirely up to her to set the pace.

Now came another difficult bit. For a good massage, she'd have to lie down on her stomach. I'd had good luck with a direct approach once already, so I tried it again. "I can, of course, massage several spots with you on your back, but for the truly relaxing ones, you'll have to lie on your stomach," I said. "Would that make you really uncomfortable? If it would, we can leave it be."

She stood across from me, about three steps away. I could tell that this was a situation she'd never encountered before – and one she'd never imagined she'd have to deal with. She didn't know how to behave, and she didn't know what to expect. On the one hand, I was sure she still believed this was some sort of seduction tactic. On the other hand, all these odd things kept coming up that just didn't fit with that scenario. The hot water bottle, for instance.

I could certainly imagine what she was going through. This morning, we had been a pair of lovers – or at least something very like that. This evening, after a day like today, anything including the word "love" probably didn't sound nearly as appetizing as it might. So where could I fit in?

And now this. We both knew what kind of risk she took by placing herself in a position that, for most people, entailed nothing more than complete relaxation. For her, it was obviously associated with a traumatic experience. I could still recall its consequences quite vividly.

I made a suggestion. "How about if we start on your back? You can turn over onto your stomach later if you like. And if not, then that's fine, too." Despite all its luxury, her bedroom had suddenly taken on the atmosphere of a doctor's office. Nothing said here could be remotely suggestive. In any other case, that would've been just the opposite of what I wanted. Today, it was just right.

She looked at me. She untied her belt slowly and removed her robe.

Well, perhaps the bit about the doctor's office had been somewhat rash! I pretended to look for an outlet to plug in the heating pad. By doing so, I could stick my head under the bed until it cooled off a bit.

When I stood up again, she'd undressed completely and lay under the blanket. I handed her the heating pad. "I plugged it in. It should start getting warm any minute. It'd be best if you put it under your shoulders. They usually tense up first."

She examined the pad – she'd probably never used it – and laid it between herself and the pillow. She held the blanket firmly over her breasts. I almost had to laugh!

And so I began. She followed me with her eyes as I crossed the room. I got some massage oil out of my jacket pocket, took the jacket off, and rolled up my sleeves. The massage oil made quite an impression on her. She was more than surprised when I pulled it out of my pocket. I could tell from her eyes that she thought this increased the probability that I was actually going to give her a massage. I grinned. "A good housewife always has something like this around," I kidded.

I sat at the foot of the bed and looked at her expertly. "I think I'll start with your shoulders, what do you think?" Given that her shoulders were the only part of her body currently exposed, she wouldn't have to give up any of the blanket for me to do that.

I opened the bottle and rubbed a small amount of oil into my hands. Now was the time for me to practice self-control! I laid my hands carefully on her shoulders. If she didn't jump … I did – or was it both of us at the same time? The silky softness of her skin didn't exactly catch me unprepared, but I felt butterflies anyhow. All evening, I'd wanted to touch her – and now she lay here, I was touching her, and this was it. But I had made a promise to her – and in any case, I wanted her to get what she needed for once.

I began to massage her muscles gently with my thumbs. Tense was an understatement – she was hard as a rock! She must've had quite a day. When I increased the pressure a little, she let out a small yelp. I softened my touch again. "I'm sorry," I said, "but you're so tense. It's going to take a while before it gets much better."

"You're actually massaging me." She was nothing short of amazed.

I looked at my hands with a bit of uncertainty. "Uh, yes. I think that's what this is called."

"But you're really doing it." She still couldn't believe it.

"I think that's what you need most right now. Why shouldn't I do it?"

How could I make her understand that she had an obvious and in-herent right to this? Not to the massage, but simply to have some-one who cared about her. That notion seemed completely strange to her. I busied myself with practical matters. "If you had a bathtub, I'd have put you in there first to soften your muscles. It takes long-er this way." I didn't want her to think about anything other than relaxing.

She closed her eyes. "It can't possibly take long enough," she murmured savoringly.

I rubbed her shoulders until they finally loosened up. Then I pulled the blanket back a little and massaged her arms. The next time I pulled the blanket down, her breasts were uncovered. I swallowed as discreetly as possible. How could I be so naive to think that I could control all feeling – with this body? Her breasts rose and sank with her breath. My hands began to move toward them all on their own. Just before I touched her, I stopped myself. Unfortunately, there was nothing to massage there. I had no excuse whatsoever. Sighing to myself, I pulled the blanket down a little more. I watched her very carefully throughout this. I didn't want her to tense up again.

She blinked a little. "Are you cold?" I asked.

It took her a good minute to react at all. "No," she answered then. Her voice sounded much more relaxed than before. "It's wonderful."

"You should get a massage more often." I began to knead her hips. I almost followed that with "in your line of work." I held my tongue at the last second.

"Maybe I will," she replied casually.

I wandered over to her thighs and massaged them as well. I tried with all my might to look only at her thighs, and only where I was massaging her. I started to sweat. Thank God, that wasn't too ob-vious or unusual for this activity. I could always say it was from the effort.

"So," I said after a moment, "now, unfortunately, you have to make a decision. Do you want to turn over?" I said it consciously, doctor's office style.

She tensed a little, but that was to be expected. She opened her eyes halfway. It appeared that her eyelids were too heavy for her to open them all the way. Heavens, those were bedroom eyes in the truest sense of the word! I looked in a different direction.

"I'll try," she said after a slight hesitation.

I was touched by her trust. After all, she didn't exactly have the best memories about the last time, and that had been with me. I let her do it as slowly as she wanted. She did it very slowly.

When she finally lay on her stomach, I said quite cheerfully, as I observed her beautiful curves, "I'll start with your shoulders again." She should have the chance to prepare herself for my touch.

I took some more massage oil from the bottle and rubbed it between my hands. Again, I said, "Here we go." Nonetheless, she jerked when I touched her. My God, how must it have felt for her the last time? I still felt ashamed when I thought about it. Even if I hadn't known any better.

Despite the massage from the front, her shoulders were still rather hard. Her whole body must've been one tightly strung bow before I got there. I worked my way slowly from her shoulders across her back and down to her bottom. I took my time about it. It did her good, and it gave me a chance to enjoy at least a little bit of her warmth and her soft skin. Finally, I massaged the backs of her legs briefly.

"So," I said in conclusion. I couldn't help myself. Before I could think about what I was doing, I'd slapped her very lightly on the butt.

"Oof!" She didn't seem too averse to this sort of affection. In any case, she was relaxed enough.

I continued, "And now for the nicest part."

She tensed again slightly. This time, though, that was my intention. I was sure she was thinking this had all been a seduction scene, albeit a very long and comfortable one. Her back loosened again. She'd allow it, if that's what I wanted.

"For this, you need to turn back over onto your back," I said, still secretively. She did it. She looked at me expectantly. Her face showed exactly what I'd expected.

I took the blanket and covered her up. "So you don't freeze," I said, grinning at the astounded look on face. "I only need your feet."

I slid back to the other end of the bed and pulled the blanket up just enough to see her feet. Of course, I would've liked to see more of her, but I was sure I'd have a chance to do so another time. I took a foot in my hands and massaged it carefully. She moaned lustfully. One would've thought I was doing something entirely different with her. "That's a lovely feeling!" she said wonderingly.

"Yes," I confirmed with satisfaction. "And now relax. You can go to sleep."

"But I don't want to." Her protest was rather weak.

I grinned. Her will wasn't going to hold up much longer on that one!

I massaged the other foot. After a short while, I heard her breathing deeply. She was asleep. I ended the massage and stood up. I walked over to the head of the bed and looked down at her. She slept like a baby, totally relaxed. Not even after the best night of lovemaking had she ever looked like that. I loved her even more. How could I stand it? Today was only the first day she'd gone back to "work".

I took her pajama top and laid it over her. She murmured lightly at the disruption in her sleep. I stroked her face. "Sleep," I whispered lightly. "Sleep, my darling." I kissed her on the forehead and straightened.

I would've liked to stay the night, but I didn't want to make that decision while she was asleep. Perhaps she would want to wake up alone after such a long day. I put on my jacket, glanced back one more time at her face, and smiled. I locked the door behind me as quietly as I could and left.

—— 13 ——

At eight o'clock the next morning, just as I was about to leave for work, the phone rang. Unusual this time of day. Most days, I'd already be at work by now.

I picked it up.

"Good morning!" she said, obviously in a good mood. Apparently, the massage had done her good.

"G'morning," I mumbled. We truly didn't have much in common first thing in the morning!

"Oh!" she joked playfully. "Aren't you awake yet?" She really was in a good mood.

"At this hour?"

She laughed. "Yes, I remember. Would you like to come over for a cup of coffee before you go to work?"

I stopped short. "It's getting kind of late already," I objected.

"Yes, I know," she admitted. "But can't you squeeze it in somehow? Just for a little bit."

She sounded urgent. What did she want? "Fine," I consented, somewhat disgruntled. "But only for half an hour." If I were all the way awake, I'd be overjoyed to see her, but now . . .

"I don't need any more," she said, pleased. "I'll turn the coffee-maker on now!" With audible satisfaction, she hung up.

I stood with the receiver in my hand and asked myself what she wanted with me, for just half an hour.

The five-minute walk from my place to hers didn't help to wake me up, either. The fresh morning air tickled my nose and the sun shone brightly, but it was no use. I was a typical victim of "night-lag." What other people felt after a long flight across time zones and called jet-lag, I felt every morning for at least two hours after getting out of bed, or at least until after my second cup of coffee.

I rang the doorbell. She opened the door. She was dressed. I'd expected to find her in her robe, but instead she wore jeans and a blue shirt that became her so well that even I, in my morning haze, noticed it. She pulled me into the apartment without a word, shut the door, took me into her arms, and kissed me. I got dizzy. All this so early in the morning before I'd had my coffee!

She stopped kissing me. She loosened her grip on me slightly and looked me in the eyes. "I just wanted to thank you," she smiled roguishly.

"For what?" I'd just gotten out of bed!

"For yesterday," she said sweetly.

"Oh, that," I dismissed – I still wasn't quite awake. "Couldn't you have waited until this evening?"

"You really are not a morning person!" she laughed. She took my hand. "Come on," she ordered, leading me into the kitchen. "The coffee is ready."

I clambered up onto the stool at her breakfast bar. She busied herself with the coffeemaker and hummed a little folk tune. Then she set a cup in front of me. She said nothing and watched me. I drank the coffee and slowly began to wake up.

"Why didn't you stay here?" she asked softly.

I looked up from my coffee cup. "I didn't want to disturb you when you woke up. You might've wanted to be alone."

"I might've thought that myself at one time," she admitted, smiling.

I smiled back. "Your coffee is good. Could I have another?"

She took my cup and set it back under the machine. The beans crackled, as they were ground. Then the coffee ran down into the cup. I watched, fascinated.

"If I didn't have a coffeemaker, would you still come see me?" she teased lovingly.

I jerked to attention and looked at her. I'd actually forgotten about her for a moment.

"Excuse me," I requested a bit remorsefully, "but no one can get through to me in the morning, you know that."

"I know." She was much too contented to fault me for such a small thing. She put the coffee cup back in front of me and looked deep into my eyes. "You don't need to be excused for anything." She looked at me piercingly once more. "Absolutely nothing."

She could've woken the dead with that look. At any rate, she woke me up with it. I started to tingle. I slid off the barstool. "I have to go to work now," I said, already halfway to the door. I didn't want her to kiss me again. If she did, I'd never get out of there today.

She could tell what I was thinking and laughed knowingly, but she stayed on the other side of the counter. "Have a nice day at the office!" she called after me.

—— 14 ——

That I did not. At noon, she called me. "Have you eaten yet?"
"No," I said, surprised. "Not yet."

"Shall we eat together?"

What was she planning? "You mean go out to eat?" I asked with astonishment. Our last attempt at that was still quite fresh in my mind.

"No. I meant at my place." What was with all this?

"You're going to cook?" Now I was really confused.

"No, not really." Her voice had suddenly changed. It sounded almost desperate. "Actually, I hadn't thought about food at all." She paused, and I asked myself what she was up to with all this sneaking around. Was she just trying to make me uncertain? "I want to sleep with you," she whispered suddenly, out of nowhere – seductively, temptingly, erotically.

The telephone receiver almost melted in my hand at her sensuous intensity. If I hadn't been sitting down, I would've fallen over. When I'd gathered myself halfway together again, I whispered back. "Are you crazy? I'm not alone here!"

"Really? If I'd known that, I would've called earlier." Her gentle laughter followed.

The situation seemed to amuse her greatly. It amused me less. She was driving me crazy with her voice. It felt like she was reaching through the telephone and stroking every one of my erogenous zones.

"What's this supposed to be?" I asked, horribly tortured. "Phone sex?" Too late! I hoped she wouldn't take that the wrong way. She wasn't insulted at all. Her voice sounded like a feather caressing me. "Normally, I don't offer that," she said, almost giggling. "But with you, I could get used to it."

"Stop it!" I whispered from the very edge of sanity.

"Come over." She didn't let up. Her voice was arousal itself.

"I can't!" I could've screamed. "I have a lunch meeting." She'd have to understand that!

"Then come afterwards," she tempted promisingly.

"I have two appointments afterwards. I can't cancel them." Didn't she have any clients today? Then again, the morning was over. How could I think such a thing? She really drove me to the end of my wits! "I can't be done before four."

"Too bad." Her disappointment was clearly audible. Then she chuckled. "I could always come to your office."

"No!" This time, I really did scream. Everyone looked over at me. With great effort, I calmed my voice. "No," I whispered nervously, "don't you dare!"

She laughed boisterously. Playing with me like that probably helped her get over her disappointment. "All right," she agreed. "I won't." Her voice took on a motherly strictness. "But at four o'clock, you'd better be home!"

"My place or yours?" I asked, still completely helpless.

"Pick me up at my place," she said without hesitation.

I hung up. My colleagues stared at me with a combination of concern and extreme curiosity. "Just a logistical problem," I called across the room, somewhat irritated. And that's what it was, too, after a fashion!

—— 15 ——

She must've already been standing at the door when I arrived. She opened it immediately, came out, and locked the door from the outside.

"Let's go," she said. She didn't kiss me, she didn't touch me, she didn't even say "hello". Had something gone wrong again already? I didn't know how long I would be able to stand this emotional roller coaster. I could never be sure what to expect with her.

On the street, she walked next to me, but without looking in my direction. She took those long strides of hers that I always had to jog to keep up with. In the meantime, though, I was ready for the Olympics!

"What happened?" I asked, reaching for her hand.

She dodged me. "Don't touch me!" she warned forcefully.

"What's up with you?" It couldn't possibly have anything to do with me. What had changed since our telephone conversation?

She looked straight ahead once more and spoke through gritted teeth. "If I touch you now, I'm going to have to take you right here in the street. Is that what you want?"

So that was it! I grinned, gloating just a little. She'd gotten me so worked up over the telephone; that the whole afternoon had felt like I was sitting on hot coals. But it obviously hadn't gone any better for her. I looked at her, racing along beside me. More likely worse.

We arrived at my building. She dashed up the four flights of stairs as though she were being chased by invisible ghosts. I'd never seen her like this before! If a little massage could lead to this, I'd have to be more careful in the future. Then again – why? What did I have to lose? Just the opposite.

She waited impatiently for me at the top of the stairs. While I was turning the key in the lock, she grabbed my backside and shoved me up against the wall. I'd been through that once with her before, but this time it was something completely different. She pushed against me, and her hands pulled my groin against hers. I felt the heat between her legs. My goodness, she must be on fire! What a coincidence – I felt exactly the same!

"Please!" I begged her. "Let's at least go inside the apartment. We've made it all the way up here, haven't we?"

She allowed me a little bit of room. I turned the key, and the door swung open. We almost fell inside. I grabbed at the key, pulled it out, and slammed the door shut behind us. She was already at my mouth, on my breasts, everywhere. We sank to the floor. She pulled my shirt out of my pants and unzipped them. She slid one hand inside, right between my legs.

"You're so wet!" It sounded as if she were surprised by this.

"Ha, you're funny! After your phone call this afternoon, and now this!" Sometimes I wondered where she got her naiveté, given her experience.

She grinned. "Did that turn you on?"

I acted indifferent. "No, not at all. Women call me at my office every day and drive me to the brink of orgasm."

She pulled me on top of her. "Then perhaps I'd better come see you in person the next time."

"Behave yourself!" I replied threateningly.

Her mouth was already on mine, stifling any further protest. The tightness between my legs almost drove me crazy. Her hand was being pressed into the middle by the fabric of my pants. I began to rub against it. She moved her hand with me, as much as she could. She'd barely begun to do that when I came the first time. She held me off the floor.

"My heavens!" she remarked. "and I thought I was turned on!"

I gasped, "I hope you are." I propped myself up next to her. "Since it's your turn next."

"Ahem," she said, "understood. But could we maybe go to bed? I've got bruises all over already."

I rolled over and stood up. She rose with her usual grace. While she turned, smiling, to walk toward the bedroom, she began automatically to unbutton her cuffs.

"Wait!" I said. She stopped. I walked past her, in order to look her in the face. She looked at me questioningly. "I'd like ... please ... May I undress you?"

Her reaction was almost invisible, but it was there. She put up a wall.

"It's ok," I said. "It was just a question. I thought ..." I thought you trusted me, I wanted to say, but that would've caused her more than anything to grant my wish. And as well as she could act, I might never even have noticed that she was doing it against her own will. I took a step toward her and took her in my arms. "Forgive me; I always want too much at once from you."

She laid her arms around me as well. "It's odd," she mused, "there was a time when I never would've allowed it, but now . . . I think I actually want it." It sounded as though she were genuinely surprised at herself.

I looked up at her. "Are you sure?"

"No," she said. She smiled enchantingly. "But we can certainly try it." We went into the bedroom together, and she lowered herself onto the foot of the bed.

I leaned over her and kissed her. While I was doing that, I slowly pulled her shirt out of her pants. When that was done, I crouched in front of her. I put my hands on her waist and looked at her. Was there any sign of discomfort, of defensiveness? I held her gaze and let my hands wander around to the front. She was still watching me calmly. I undid the button and waited. Then I bent over her and kissed her again.

In contrast to the incredible arousal she'd demonstrated earlier, she was now very reserved. I ran my hands up beneath her shirt until I felt the velvety roundness of her breasts. It overwhelmed me. "I love you so much," I whispered, my lips nibbling devotedly at her ear.

This time, she reacted. She wrapped her arms around me and pulled me close to her. I leaned against her, and she sank slowly back onto the bed. I began to unbutton her shirt. She still showed no sign of excitement. I pushed her shirt back over her shoulders. "I can stop any time you want," I offered soothingly. I sought her eyes. They were closed.

"No," she said weakly. She grasped my head and pulled my mouth down to her breasts. "Please, make love to me!" Her voice was even hoarser than before.

I kissed her breasts and moved my lips downward. She shivered. I didn't know if that was from arousal or fear. I hoped it was arousal. I heard her breathing heavily above me. I unzipped her pants and slid one hand inside. She moaned. I looked up, but couldn't read her expression.

Slowly, I pulled her pants down over her hips and laid a hand between her legs. Immediately, she began to push against me lustfully. "Yes." I found the center and began to massage it gently. Her hips rose, thrusting desperately into the air. My mouth wandered back to her breasts. I entered her with one finger and began to stroke her inside. She moaned, loud and gasping. I pushed myself up a little higher and looked into her face. She tossed her head back and forth with excitement. With her eyes still closed, she whispered, "please, I've been waiting for you all day . . ."

I glided quickly down between her thighs and took her in with my tongue. She went stiff immediately. She screamed. I'd never heard such a yell from her. She collapsed.

I moved back up next to her and took her into my arms. She was breathing as though she'd climbed more than just one mountain. I suddenly had the feeling that this was the first time she'd ever truly given herself over to me. Today, she'd decided to trust me completely.

I brushed her hair out of her face. "My darling," I said.

She twitched, then lay quiet. She still held her eyes closed tightly. She didn't answer. I thought she'd fallen asleep.

I laid her on the bed and started to stand up.

"Don't go away," she said softly.

"I thought you were asleep."

"No. I'm just . . ." She opened her eyes and looked at me. "I never want to go through another day like today," she said, shuddering. "It was awful."

It sounded like she'd really been suffering. I laughed. "It's your own fault. If you make phone calls like that . . ."

"I don't understand it myself. You're not going to believe this, but I've really never done that before."

"Never? But when you're newly —" Dammit, there it was again! People newly in love did things like that. But was she newly in love? I was, I knew that, but was she? For her, love might still be a chore. I'd better not say it. "When people haven't known each other long, they feel a need to do things like that," I stated.

"Oh yeah?" As if this was a completely new concept for her. It couldn't possibly be that she'd never experienced anything like it before!

"Oh, yeah," I attested, laughing. I stood up.

She reached out a hand toward me. "Please stay."

"Nothing would make me happier," I swore, "but I still have to pack."

"Pack?" The surprise in her voice was incredible. "You're going away?"

"Only for a week." It now seemed unbelievably long to me, too. "Business trip."

"A week," she repeated gloomily.

I tried to cheer her up. "We can talk on the phone every day," I suggested. I tried to put a hint of cheerful temptation into my voice.

"Your voice on the phone is almost as good as . . ."

"Almost." She didn't seem convinced in the slightest.

"Oh, come on," I comforted her – and myself. "It will pass." At least she could imagine still being with me a week from now. That, in itself, was something. "Let's think about what we'll do when I get back instead."

For a moment, she still looked depressed, but then she began to smile a bit mischievously. "Is there any doubt?"

"Knock it off," I said. "You're just trying to coax me back into bed." I was already starting to feel warm again. Seeing her in bed was temptation enough. She saw my expression. She stretched. Normally, I wouldn't have been able to stand seeing her beautiful, long limbs laid out like that before me. I had to call on every bit of self-control. "Be sensible," I implored her desperately, "I don't just have to pack; I still have to go through some files. Otherwise, I'll get up for my presentation tomorrow and just stand there like an idiot. Would you want that?" I appealed to her sense of pity. That had always worked for me in the past.

It worked this time also. She sighed in surrender. "You're heartless." Her winks indicated that this was a complete lie. Then, she rolled up into a ball and covered herself with the blanket. "I want nothing more to do with you." She turned over onto her other side.

I laughed at her theatrics. They were really her greatest gift. Well, maybe her second greatest. "We'll make up for it when I come back. For certain." I turned toward the closet to get out a suitcase.

"That's what they all say," she murmured with resignation, but loud enough that I could understand her.

"Yeah, I know," I said laughing. "Life is hard."

"Pff," she replied contemptuously.

I laughed as I pulled down a suitcase and began to pack.

—— **16** ——

I had never realized how long a week could be. And this despite the fact that she'd "talked me into" one more time on the morning I left. Resisting her more than once required superhuman strength, and I did not have that.

Now, on the last day, I was already thinking about her with unbelievable desire. The phone calls had only served to amplify that feeling, as I might well have expected. As soon as .I heard her voice, I was in flames. And she did her best not to extinguish those flames.

She called.

"I'm just about to walk out the door," I said in answer to her question.

"How long is the ride?" The need in her voice was unmistakable.

"If the train is on schedule, about four hours. So I'll be there around eight."

During the ride, I thought almost exclusively about her. I began to imagine how she would greet me, how she would look, what she would be wearing. But there was really no question about that. She'd be wearing her robe, because she knew I liked it so much. And I would take it off her . . .

I ran my things home quickly. Then I whistled all the way to her place. In the elevator, I closed my eyes and pictured her face. Her lips came nearer . . . The elevator stopped.

When I was almost to her door, it opened. Aha, she'd heard me coming! I almost collided with someone. A large woman in leather came out of her apartment. A large woman in leather. She had to stop as well. At first, she looked at me with surprise, but then she grinned lewdly. "She's in good form today," she said. "I'd take advantage of it." Then she laughed maliciously and walked past me.

I was stunned. It was as if a bomb had exploded next to me and I hadn't yet noticed that I was dead. The other woman had left the door open. I entered, still numb, and shut the door behind me.

She stood in front of the bed with her back to me. When she heard the door close, she said angrily: "For the last time, no! Go away!"

"But I just got here." I was still so stunned that I answered her outbreak automatically, as though she'd spoken to me.

She spun around. "You!" she said, horrified. She looked hot under the collar. Obviously, she'd been buttoning her vest. The two top buttons were still undone, pushing her breasts up over the top in an obscene manner.

This was not the woman I'd expected. She'd known that I was coming, and she'd still "worked" up to the very last minute. Her whole spiel on the telephone and before had only been an act. She just wanted to keep me ready as long as possible. A stupid, infatuated fool who'd do anything for her. An attractive diversion from her routine!

"Yes, me," I said, still dazed, but beginning to feel the anger growing in me. "We had a date. But you've apparently forgotten that."

She stood there, speechless. Of course she was horrified. I'd obviously caught her at the game she was playing with me.

I took a step back. "There's no sense in me staying." I started to turn around.

"Wait," she replied dully. "This is all a misunderstanding."

"A misunderstanding? I believe we had one of those before, or do I not recall correctly?" I laughed aloud, full of scorn. "I may be dumb, but not so dumb that the same trick works twice with me."

I turned around. I almost had the doorknob in my hand when she said, "This isn't a trick." She sounded like she'd been completely destroyed. But I was already quite familiar with her abilities as an actress. I wasn't about to fall for that again. Now she wanted me wrapped back around her little finger, and if I let her, she'd be able to make me believe anything she wanted. No, I won't do that! I turned the knob.

At the same time, I felt her hand on my shoulder. "Please, don't go," she pleaded.

Yes, she was really good at this! The right tone of voice for every situation. "Why should I stay?" I asked bitterly.

"I want to explain . . ."

"We've had enough explanations already, don't you think?" My whole body rejected her. I shook her hand from my shoulder and turned back around. She'd put on a robe, a kind of kimono in black. It looked particularly sleazy to me.

"It's not because you slept with another woman. I know that's your . . . job." I could imagine better than ever that she really did her job with zeal. "But you knew I was coming. We just spoke," I looked at my watch, "not five hours ago on the phone. And you told me some lie along the lines of 'I'll be waiting for you.' Was it taking too long for you?" I was so wrapped up in my anger, I could barely stop. Still, I was curious how she intended to straighten this out.

"I didn't lie to you," she contradicted dejectedly. "I waited for you all afternoon." She tried to look me in the eye. I dodged her. "Alone," she continued earnestly.

"How thoughtful of you!" I replied sharply.

She recoiled, hurt. But she still didn't want to give up. "She," she nodded toward the door, "came here an hour ago, unannounced. She was here once before, but I didn't like her. I had told her that I wouldn't make any more appointments with her."

I was astonished. That happened too?

"She wouldn't leave. She tried to . . ., she tried to take it by force." She turned away and took a few steps. Then she turned back to face me.

"Yes, I'm strong enough. She didn't succeed. But she didn't go away easily, either. What was I supposed to do? Call the police?"

Now I understood. This was all supposed to be an excuse for the fact that she'd misgauged the time. "So you did do what she wanted?"

"Not everything," she qualified.

"Sure." I was completely cold now. "Why should you pass it up? Such an opportunity? It's not exactly pocket change now, is it?"

Her eyes blazed. Was she furious now? Was she going to hit me, after she'd so clearly resorted to violence with the last woman?

"It's still my profession," she stated extremely calmly.

"Oh, yes," I replied caustically. "I'd forgotten about that." A thought came to my mind, and I spoke it aloud. "And I'm sure she tipped well for the good service, am I right?"

She trembled, unblinking. "She paid more than the usual price," she confirmed. "That is true."

"Well, then," I jeered, "then at least it was worth the trouble."

She didn't answer. Her expression was unreadable. I couldn't have guessed what she was thinking, but I didn't care, either. Now that everything was over.

I left her standing there.

—— **17** ——

Since meeting her, I'd thought about nothing else. At least, as little as possible. I noticed this now. I worked late into the night. My colleagues were beginning to joke that I should bring a bed to the office, since I never left anyhow. It was fine with me. I repressed the slightest hint of regret.

If ever a thought of her entered my mind, I hunted it promptly to extinction. I reassured myself again and again – when it came to that – by reminding myself that a relationship with a prostitute (I could say the word now) was doomed to fail from the very beginning. Sure, I was still in love with her now, but how would things have looked in a year or two? She'd never even hinted that she might give up her trade and do something else with her life. And I'd only been denying that I was jealous of every one of her clients. I wanted her for myself alone.

So? That's normal, isn't it? A relationship with a woman who definitively did not live in the "normal" world, whatever that meant, who sold her body like a commodity was a contradiction in itself. From the very beginning, we'd had completely different views of the world.

Did we? So what had we laughed about together? Oh, that was just banal stuff! Things that anyone would laugh at.

I became more hermit-like every day. I was rarely home, and when I was home, I never answered the telephone. I'd long since taken it off the hook. I went shopping in another town, or at least another part of town. As close to each other as we lived, the danger of meeting her accidentally was much too great if I did such things in my own neighborhood. Back when I was looking for her, it of course hadn't worked out. But now when we'd rather avoid each other – I would, anyhow – I was certain we would end up running into each other.

After a couple of days, an old girlfriend of mine called me at work. When I answered, she said, "Well, at least you can be reached here! You don't seem to have a telephone at home anymore. Or don't you still live there?"

"Oh, hello Karin," I greeted her weakly.

"And you don't seem to be doing terribly well, either." She was right about that. "Are you in love?" she asked curiously. She knew me well.

"No," I denied disapprovingly.

"Mm-hmm." She'd known me much too long to be satisfied with that.

"Did she leave you?"

I laughed scornfully. "Leave me? I left her."

"But you're not happy about it." That wasn't a question. She was simply stating a fact.

"No," I contradicted her defiantly. "No, I'm very happy about it."

"Mm," Karin continued. "Then it's worse than I thought."

"Nothing is wrong." My stubbornness grew. "I'm doing very well!"

"Yes, I can see that," said Karin, without any particular inflection. Changing the subject entirely, she continued, "Do you still have some vacation time left?"

"All kinds of comp time," I reported, surprised. "Why?"

"The reason I'm calling is that I want to go away for a couple of days, and I'm looking for another woman to go with me. And I thought about you right away."

"But Corinna . . ."

"Corinna doesn't have time. She's right in the middle of final exams. And really, I'm just disturbing her studies. That's why I wanted to go away – so she can work in peace."

That sounded entirely logical.

"Yes, but . . ." She'd always caught me off guard with ideas like this. Now, the effect of the surprise was even greater than usual.

"Corinna doesn't mind if you come along. She knows there's nothing more going on between us." She didn't seem at all like she was trying to convince me of something. She just listed one fact after another.

I'd always been amazed by her powers of logic. This was all moving too fast for me. "Still . . ."

"No excuses! We're going up into the mountains. Do you still remember the cabin?"

I remembered it well. The cabin had been our first love nest together. We'd spent our best times together there. I felt a tear in my eye when I thought about it.

"Yes." I swallowed.

She ignored my dismay. "How soon can you get out of here?"

I glanced across my desk. "Actually . . ., actually, I have an awful lot to do. I'm a little behind."

She laughed. "I understand," she thought aloud, "you've always been that way."

I was insulted. "What's that supposed to mean?"

"Oh, come on." She brushed that off. "When can you go? Tomorrow, the day after tomorrow?" Words like "next week" or "next month" didn't seem to be part of her vocabulary.

I surrendered. When she wanted something, she got it. In the end, I knew her well enough. "In two days," I supposed, "I could have most of my work either finished or delegated."

"Very well then," she confirmed, as if she'd already known it. "So Wednesday then. I'd pick you up at 8 a.m." She already had the whole thing planned.

"At eight?" I echoed.

"I know you're not awake yet then. But it takes two hours to get there. I'll drive. And then we still have to hike up another half hour." It sounded like a firm itinerary. Changes not accepted.

The cabin was really quite remote. There wasn't a paved street up there, or even a passable dirt road. "Fine." I admitted defeat. "If you drive."

She laughed. "Didn't I always?" She waited a moment to see if I had anything else to say. "Well, then, until Wednesday. And be punctual. Otherwise I'll toss you out of bed myself!" She was laughing when she hung up.

All that threw me for something of a loop. I'd gotten so used to my solitary melancholy; it seemed like someone had suddenly shot me out of a catapult.

—— **18** ——

On Wednesday, we almost left on time. Karin really did make enough of a racket to drag me out of bed at eight in the morning. She even forbade me my morning coffee – despite my forceful protests – and we hit the road as soon as I was decently dressed. I grumbled about the lack of coffee for a while, and then fell asleep in the car. When I woke up, we were already heading through the pass. She noticed that I was awake.

"We're almost there, you see? You really love to sleep, don't you!"

"Yeah, yeah," I mumbled again. She made me nervous with all that energy. It reminded me of . . . *Stop it! That was no longer an issue!*

She parked the car at the trailhead, and we loaded up the backpacks.

"I thought we were only going to stay a couple of days," I protested when I felt the weight of the pack she gave me.

"You can't have forgotten that we have to carry up everything we need for the whole time," she explained cheerily, handing me yet another bag, "and back down again, too. There's no supermarket and no garbage service here."

"That always did annoy me," I grumbled crabbily

She looked at me coquettishly "I don't remember you ever complaining about it back then."

I dismissed that. "That was something entirely different."

She was not to be deprived of her good mood. "The longer we stand around down her, the longer it'll be before you get your coffee. As a matter of fact, you're carrying it in your backpack." I sighed. "That's why it's so heavy."

"Now, then!" Happy as the leader of a Girl Scout troop, she marched on. I tramped along behind her.

Up top, we had to prepare the cabin for use first; it was apparent that no one had used it in some time. That meant starting everything up – heater, boiler, gas. By the time I got my coffee, another hour had passed.

When we finally sat down, she cornered me. "Now then, tell me all about it." She was totally serious.

"There's nothing to tell," I deflected brusquely.

"Of course there is," she persisted calmly. "Otherwise, you wouldn't be so guarded."

I shrugged my shoulders. "It was just an affair. A rather short one at that. It's not that important."

"So unimportant that you retreat to a hermit's existence? Or were you planning to enter a convent all along?" She looked at me. She knew? She knew me too well to believe anything I was likely to make up. She gave me a foothold. "Not too long ago, you fell in love with a woman."

"A woman!" I snorted contemptuously. "She's a . . ." How could I explain it to her?

Karin looked rather irritated. "Well, of course she's a woman, and it doesn't matter much what else she is, now does it?"

"Yes." I just couldn't hold my own against her logic. "Yes, she's undoubtedly a woman. And what a woman!" I made another contemptuous gesture.

"So what did she do to you that's making you so mad at yourself?"

At first, I didn't quite hear what she'd said, but then it sank in.

"Mad at myself? At the very most, mad at her!" *What did I have to do with it? I hadn't done anything wrong, had I?*

"No, I don't believe that. I know how you act when you're mad at someone else. That doesn't make you flip out like this. You only do that when you think you've made a terrible mistake." She'd made her diagnosis of me.

Reluctantly, I had to admit she was right. "What else is it but a terrible mistake to fall in love with a woman who . . .," I couldn't say it out loud. I might be able to think it, but I couldn't say it.

"You're jealous," Karin stated without another word from me. "Did she cheat on you with another woman?"

"With one?" I laughed bitterly.

Karin looked at me with interest. "It sounds like she's some sort of nymphomaniac."

"She's no nymphomaniac." Even I didn't think that. "She's a prostitute." Now it was out!

"Oh." She was surprised, but not particularly shocked. "That's a new one."

"Is that all you have to say about it?" I poured out my despair for her to see, and she just found it "new"?

Karin looked at me empathetically. "But you said she cheated on you with other women. Doesn't she sleep with men, too?" She hesitated. This truly was all rather new to her as well! "I mean . . . professionally?"

Although I thought I'd gotten used to it, the word took on a new feeling of obscenity in this context.

"No," I replied dismissively. "As far as I know, no."

Karin put one and one together in her head. "That means she's a prostitute for women?"

"Yes." In that time, I'd gotten used to the topic again. "That's what she is: a prostitute for women."

Karin let out a whistle. "I've heard that there is such a thing, but somehow I could never quite believe it. That there's enough demand for such a thing . . ." She discussed it like an economics exercise. A simple matter of supply and demand.

"Oh, yeah," I assured her bitterly. "The demand is greater than you think."

"Excuse me, please." Karin looked at me sympathetically again. "I'm handling it like an abstract problem, but of course for you it's very concrete."

"No it isn't," I denied stubbornly. "Not anymore."

She smiled understandingly. "So you're getting all upset about nothing, right?"

I flared. "Oh, if you only knew . . ., that's not nearly all!"

"Okay," she said, leaning back comfortably in her chair. "So tell me everything then."

At first, I didn't want to. There was just so much that I didn't understand myself. But then I slowly began to thaw under her understanding gaze. And I told her everything.

She listened quietly and let me talk. She didn't ask anything – she didn't want to question my view of things just yet. When I finished, she said, "Boy, you've been carrying a lot around with you!"

Although that didn't exactly help me at the moment, it calmed me straight off and made my anger with myself easier for me to understand.

She went over to the stove and got us each a fresh cup of coffee. During this, she said nothing. She was thinking. After she sat down again, she said, "You're still in love with her." She raised her hand to stop my protest before I could start. "And if I'm judging correctly – the way I know you – I'd even say that you really love her."

Now I couldn't say anything, because I was completely confused. How could she say that with such certainty? Something that was so wrong?

She smiled at me understandingly. "I remember your jealous streak well. It makes you completely irrational. After everything you told me, I don't believe her to be the woman you describe. Of course, I don't know her, and my experience with prostitutes is rather limited," she laughed a little, "but in the end, I have no reason to defend her. Whether she will speak to you again after that confrontation, I'd have to bet not." Her conclusions were as logical as they were plausible. I had nothing with which to refute them.

"I don't think so either. But a relationship like that never had a future anyway." That was, for me, irrevocably certain.

"That may be." Karin thought about it for a moment before continuing. "It's even probable. But that's still no reason to behave like a bull in a china shop." She looked at me with mild reprehension. "To put it mildly."

I was ashamed. All this churned inside me. The memories came rushing back. Above all, the good memories. But I just wasn't ready to allow that. I shut them off.

My days with Karin were full of deep internal recovery. She knew me. She knew how I reacted to a relationship, and she'd fought her own battles with my jealousy when we were together.

I felt that she'd allowed me to bathe in her concern and sympathy. As my body began to relax, I realized how I'd been mistreating it. The sleep deprivation made itself noticeable, such that I sometimes slept through half the day as well as the night. The isolation of the cabin did me good as well. There was no telephone, no radio, no connection with the outside world beyond what we carried up on our backs and saw there with our own eyes.

The last evening, we opened the last bottle of wine that we'd tiresomely hauled up there. Karin had planned everything so well; we'd be carrying nearly empty backpacks down the hill in the morning.

I still hadn't come to a decision. I said, "I know I won't be able stand it for any length of time to wonder constantly what she's doing. And I can't ignore it either."

Karin shook her head with annoyance at my obstinacy. "But that's not what a relationship is made of. With whom and how many one sleeps." She looked at me penetratingly. "Certainly not in this case, where it really doesn't mean anything."

"I know," I said. "You said that back then. But I can't change it. I'm jealous. I can't differentiate love from sex." I laid my head in my hands and looked up at her. "So of course it had to happen to me, meeting a woman whose profession that is."

Karin laughed. "Serves you right. When I think about how much you drove me crazy back in those days . . ., I couldn't even look at another woman!"

"You didn't have to do it when I was standing right next to you, did you?" Why did I always have to repeat such self-explanatory things!

"When else could I have done it? We were almost always together." Karin looked at me good-naturedly. "I'm sure she doesn't look at other women on the street – for her job, does she?"

"No," I said distastefully. "She doesn't like to go out at all."

"I can understand that." Karin nodded. Then she laughed as a thought suddenly struck her. "That makes for a lovely little 'in-house' relationship, doesn't it? That must really be your ideal!"

I didn't want to be convinced so easily. "Yes, but . . ."

"No 'yes, but . . .'" Karin let out a heartfelt groan. "She sleeps with other women. She's going to keep doing that. That's how she earns her living." I shuddered. Karin saw this and continued sympathetically, "But the most important thing is that you talk to each other, laugh with one another, sit in front of the television together and nibble on peanuts – those are the things that hold people together, just doing the most mundane things together. Talking about what you want to cook for dinner, going shopping together, spending a lazy weekend together, doing nothing but enjoying each other's company."

Karin looked at me probingly again. "That, for me, is the difference between an affair and a relationship. Of course, they have a basis in common. There has to be sexual attraction involved, but how much of a relationship is sex? Maybe five percent – ninety-five percent has to be filled with other things."

I protested with an energetic growl.

Karin laughed congenially. "Yes, I know, at the beginning it's more – a lot more. I still remember our first weeks very well." She grinned. Then she sobered again. "It's not the nights that you have to get through, it's the days."

She leaned over and brushed the hair out of my eyes. "Would you like to sleep with me tonight?" she said amicably.

I looked at her in astonishment. I hadn't had the impression before now that she was interested in that. I hesitated. She'd done so much for me in the last few days, but I couldn't quite imagine thanking her in that way. But I didn't want to hurt her. I looked up at her. "I don't think that would be such a good idea," I said, hoping she wouldn't take it the wrong way.

She understood it completely. "Oh, that wasn't a sexual offer," she corrected with a degree of self-confidence that I'd never achieve in these matters. "I just thought a little snuggling couldn't hurt."

I knew that was unusual for her. "So are you monogamous now?" I asked in disbelief.

Karin laughed out loud. "You can't imagine that, can you?" She settled down again. "And you're right I'm not monogamous." When she saw my reaction, she continued, "but that definitely doesn't mean that I constantly think about sex and chase after every woman I see – particularly an ex-girlfriend, with whom the relationship ended because of her jealousy over my non-monogamy."

I had to swallow. "Still ...," I said, although a little cuddling with her sounded like a very good idea.

"Still," she repeated earnestly, "you're faithful to her."

My head shot up. I hadn't thought about that at all!

Karin said seriously, but with a smile in her eyes, "You say that you hate her. You never want to see her again. But you could never betray her." She came over to me and kissed me on the cheek. "You love her," she concluded gently.

I sat there, unable to move. She walked as far as the door, then turned around. "My offer still stands," she said, smiling. "And I swear by everything I hold sacred, I won't take anything away from her."

—— 19 ——

The next day, I returned to my apartment in a rather different mood than the one I had left it in. Nevertheless, I was still uncertain. It would surely take a couple of days before I could really absorb everything Karin had said to me up at the cabin. And then – what would I do then? I really didn't know. One thing was clear: I couldn't live with the situation as it stood. I would probably have to move to a different town. That was the easiest way.

Calmed somewhat, I went into the kitchen to put on some water for coffee. I already had the kettle in my hand when the phone rang. I'd made such a habit of not answering that I didn't react initially. It didn't stop. It made me nervous – for a number of reasons.

Then it occurred to me that Karin had promised to call when she got home. I could already hear her admonishments if I didn't pick up, so I answered.

On the line, someone was breathing heavily. This time, I didn't even assume that it was a prank caller.

"What do you want?" I asked, more brusquely than I'd actually intended.

The breathing got louder. It sounded very labored. Suddenly, it got very quiet. Then, an unrecognizable noise came through the receiver. It went still again for a moment. From phone sex to phone harassment? Perhaps she should've spent the weekend at the cabin with Karin!

"Say something," I said rather threateningly, "or else I'll hang up." I heard that strange noise again for a moment and then – suddenly – her voice. "Please . . .," she said very softly.

Was that really her voice? It sounded like it was coming from a basement or through a wad of cotton or both.

"Yes?" I asked expectantly, anticipating the way she sounded the first time I called her.

"Please," came from the receiver again, very quietly. "Can you come over?"

So soon? And Karin had thought she'd never even speak to me! Her breathing was still heavy. What was she doing over there?

I couldn't. Not that evening. I had to think about what had been going through my head for the past few days first.

"I just got home, not fifteen minutes ago," I said. "I didn't particularly want to go out again tonight."

Again came this unrecognizable noise – this time louder. No, it wasn't unrecognizable at all – it sounded like moaning!

"Please, help me!" What was going on? Could her desire for me be that strong?

"What's the matter?" I asked, irritated.

"Please, come," she whispered again, very weakly. Something was wrong there! The line was quiet. I didn't hear any more breathing, but she hadn't hung up either.

I waited a while and then I hung up. What should I do now? Her voice had sounded very odd. Really desperate. On the other hand, I knew all about her talents in that area. What could I expect if I went to see her?

I walked slowly back to the kitchen. My disquiet grew. I couldn't just stay here. I had to know what was going on. And if she just wanted revenge – if she'd come up with some sort of payback for me – I'd notice soon enough.

I grabbed my jacket and walked hesitantly over there. I pushed the intercom button for her apartment. She buzzed me in immediately. I took the elevator up. At her door, I hesitated. Then I laid my thumb on her doorbell. The door opened slowly. She was nowhere to be seen. I went in and looked around carefully. I turned around to close the door. Then I saw her.

She stood behind the door in a crumpled heap, barely supporting herself against the wall. She was wearing her black kimono, but she hadn't tied the belt. Underneath, she was naked. She hung her head. Then she looked up.

"My God!" I cried in horror. Her face was covered with blood; I couldn't even see her eyes. I leapt toward her and tried to support her. She moaned with terrible pain. "My God," I heard myself say again. I took her arms, trying to ignore her cries of pain.

"Come," I said gently, "we've got to get you into bed." She groaned at every step. I opened the bedroom door and laid her down as carefully as possible. She was moaning awfully.

I looked at her and felt completely helpless. I sat down next to her on the bed. Even that slight motion elicited another whimpering sound from her. I wanted to comfort her, but what could I do if everything hurt her?

"What happened?" I asked.

She tried to answer, but her lips were split open and grossly swollen. I motioned for her not to try.

"Leave it – that's not important now. I'll call an ambulance." I reached for the telephone on the nightstand.

"No!" she groaned firmly.

I didn't understand her. "But you absolutely have to go to the hospital. You need to see a doctor!"

She tried to speak again. "No hospital," she whispered laboriously. "No police."

I hadn't even thought about that. I'd certainly have to call the police as well. Why didn't she want that? She'd obviously been assaulted.

"But be practical – I can't help you! You're seriously injured. Let me call an ambulance, please."

She shook her head laboriously, her face twisted in pain.

I was helpless. My medical knowledge did not extend beyond that little bit of massage, and that definitely wouldn't help her now.

She lay there and moaned again. I had to do something. I called Karin.

"I just tried calling you three times," she greeted me cheerfully.

"Were you sleeping again already?"

"No," I answered softly.

She noticed it immediately. "What's up?"

"I need a doctor," I said.

She was startled. "What did you do to yourself?" she asked. "We just got back."

"Not for me."

Strangely, that seemed to explain everything for her. "You're with her," she said – a statement, not a question.

"Yes," I confirmed.

"Give me the address," she said. She didn't ask why. She didn't refer me to the hospital. If I hadn't figured out how helpful her natural, calm attentiveness could be over the past few days, I would've seen it now. She was something special. I gave her the address.

She said, "I'll try to contact a doctor I know. I hope she's home."

"I hope so, too!" I said urgently, "And please, hurry!"

Karin said nothing more, and hung up. I knew she would do what she could. Now I could only wait.

It seemed like an eternity. I tried to clean up some of the blood with a washcloth. She moaned so horribly that I gave up. The doorbell rang. I looked at the clock. Forty-five minutes had passed. I opened the door.

A grey-haired woman in her mid-fifties stormed in. I assumed she was the doctor. She didn't introduce herself. "Where is she?" she asked curtly.

I pointed toward the bedroom. She stormed right past me. I followed her in. She stood by the bed, rolling up the sleeves of her white blouse. She took a stethoscope from her bag.

She looked down at the bed. "Those damned guys!" she said angrily.

I looked at her. I said nothing, but I was pretty sure that this hadn't been caused by a "damned guy."

The doctor examined her quickly and professionally. She moaned. The doctor said soothingly, "It's all right, kiddo. It's almost over."

When she was done, she stood to face me. "I think she got lucky. No internal injuries as far as I can tell. But she should be x-rayed anyway."

A weak sound of protest came from the bed. The doctor turned around.

"I know, kiddo. I already saw the bed."

To me, she continued, "I don't think she's in any immediate mortal danger. As soon as she can walk again, bring her to a hospital and have her x-rayed. At that point, they won't ask any questions."

She looked at me. "Promise me you will!"

It was an order. I nodded.

She asked. "Is she your girlfriend?" I was taken completely by surprise. At any other time, I wouldn't have answered, nor would I even have known what the answer was. Now, I nodded, just like before.

The doctor sighed. "You girls should look out for each other better, in your line of work!"

She thought I was a . . .! Despite the gravity of the situation, I had to smile. "I'll look after her," I promised. "As soon as she can walk, she'll be x-rayed."

The doctor looked me right in the eye. Then she said, "Good. I believe you mean it." She took out a prescription pad and wrote something on it. "Get this now at the all-night pharmacy. Give her one pill every hour for the next twelve hours."

I nodded obediently. She wouldn't have accepted no for an answer, anyhow.

She turned and headed for the door. I reached out an arm. "Yes, but . . ."

She stood in the doorway. "It's taken care of," she said. Then she was gone. I still stood there, completely flabbergasted.

A soft moan from the bed brought me back to my senses. I went over. I looked down at her. She looked at me through a slit of an eye. The other was swollen completely shut.

"I'm going to run over to the pharmacy," I announced. "To get your medicine."

"No," she protested weakly. I could barely understand her.

I kneeled by the bed. "I'll be right back. But I have to go. I'll lock the door from the outside. Where are your keys?"

If I interpreted her gesture correctly, she was indicating a purse. I opened it and found the key. I took it out. "I'll be right back," I reassured her soothingly. I stroked the air next to her face, so as to avoid touching her and causing her fresh pain. Then I left hurriedly.

The night was a sea of horrors for her, despite the tablets that I patiently gave her every hour. She could barely swallow.

I just sat with her and watched her. After I gave her a pill, she usually slept a little, but even in her sleep, she still cried out in terror. Once she yelled aloud, "No!" She woke from that, and although the hour wasn't quite up yet, I gave her another tablet.

So it went until morning. Then she fell into a restless sleep from which she would not be roused. I sat in an armchair with a blanket and fell asleep quickly. Her moans woke me. When I came to my senses, I saw that she was trying to get up.

I leapt up. "Are you crazy? Lie down!"

She sank back, groaning. "I have to go," she whispered through her swollen lips. She almost looked worse than the night before. Now I could see her upper body, from which the kimono had fallen. Her skin was covered with bruises and welts – or, more precisely, I could see a patch or two of skin between the bruises.

"Nonsense," I replied sternly. "You stay in bed and tell me what it is that you want. I'll get it for you."

"I don't want anything," she sighed with labored resignation.

"Fine," I said. I went over to the bed and kneeled next to her. "Are you in much pain?" Dumb question – that was obvious!

"I'm ok," she claimed. Then next moment, she winced again.

"Do you want another pill?" I asked, concerned.

She whispered. I leaned over her, so that her mouth was right next to my ear.

"I ... want ... to ... get ... away ... from ... here." It took a terrible effort.

I could understand that! "Should I bring you to my house?" I dreaded the four flights of stairs already, but if that's what she wanted ...

She shook her head only just visibly, but had to groan from the pain anyway. "Paris," she breathed, barely audibly.

"To Paris?" How did she intend to do that? And then, did she want to lie in a hotel for days in this condition, unable to stand? She'd be better off doing that here. I said: "When you're feeling better, we'll go to Paris."

Her hands curled convulsively into fists. "Now!" she insisted with all the strength she could possibly muster.

I spoke soothingly to her. "That's not possible. You can't take it. You'll have to wait a couple of days."

"Please ...," she whispered, completely exhausted.

What was I supposed to say to that? I sighed. "All right, fine. I'll take you to Paris. I don't know how, but I promise I'll do it."

The tension in her body let up. I stood up. "I'll reserve a room. Do you prefer a particular hotel?"

She tried to say something again. At first, I couldn't understand her, but then I heard, "no hotel."

"No hotel? Do you intend to sleep under a bridge in that condition?" I was beginning to doubt that only her body had been affected by the injuries.

"Apartment," she said weakly. She raised her hand and pointed toward her purse again. I was confused. An apartment in her purse? I picked up the purse and laid it next to her on the bed. She said: "Open." I did. Then she said: "Addresses." I assumed she wanted an address book, and looked for one. I found a small pocket calendar — not the voluminous leather-bound book in which she wrote her appointments. She was breathing very heavily. With a last effort, she gasped: "First page."

I opened the calendar. On the first page stood her name and an address in Paris. I looked at her questioningly. "Do you want to go there? Do you always stay there when you're in Paris?"

She nodded, eyes closed. At least I interpreted it as a nod.

"Should I call? Who lives there?"

She whispered incomprehensibly. I leaned over her again. "My . . .," I understood. Who? Her friend, mother, cousin? It occurred to me that I'd never realized she must have a family, too. She took a deep breath, to the extent that she was able. "My . . . apartment," she said.

"That's your apartment?" Her reaction was weak, but I assumed that she was trying to confirm. What else this all meant, I didn't want to think about just then. I had the address; I knew what she wanted. Now there was just the transportation problem.

I thought aloud about it. "You can't walk. I can't imagine getting you on a train or an airplane." I paced around the room. "That leaves my car." I looked at her, trying to imagine how someone in her condition could tolerate a half-day-long car ride. "I don't know how you'll get through it."

She murmured something again. "I'll . . . manage . . . it." She had to have it. And her will could move mountains, or so I hoped. Or at least move her body to Paris.

"Well, then," I gave up, resigned. If it wasn't going to work, I'd see that, and then she'd just have to get used to the idea of staying here until she was better. "I'm going home to pack a couple of things. Then I'll come back with my car. It won't take long." She'd tried to open her swollen eyes in an instinctive expression of fear, but the pain prevented her from doing so. She moaned terribly.

"I'll be right back. I'll lock the door from the outside again. That worked well last night. Don't be afraid!" I took the key and left.

At home, I threw a few things together, got out money and travelers' checks, and hurried as much as possible. I took every soft thing I could find: blankets, pillows, and – what I didn't dare forget – a hot water bottle. Finally, I had everything in the car. I drove, illegally, into the pedestrian zone and parked the car right in front of her door. When I got up to the apartment, she was trying to get up by herself again. She'd managed something between lying down and sitting up. I helped her sit up the rest of the way.

"I'm afraid it's time to get going," I warned her. "We have to get you dressed." I went over to her closet. Apparently, she drew a sharp distinction between work and her private life here also. There wasn't a single thing in leather.

I looked for a few soft, comfortable things, finding nothing but silk underclothes but taking them anyhow. In her closet, I found a suitcase. I put everything in there except what I wanted to dress her in, a jogging suit. Good thing she at least had one of those. But I'd already determined that she was athletic.

I came back to the bed. "Do you think you can help me?" She nodded weakly. I gave her the top. She couldn't lift her arms alone and let them fall back down, disappointed. "It's all right," I calmed her. "I'll do it." Afterwards, I was about to take her suitcase down to my car. "I'll come back and get you."

"No," she protested. She didn't want to be alone another minute.

I slung the bag over one shoulder and wrapped her arm around the other. She moaned. I ignored it, put my arm around her waist, and pulled her up. She moaned louder, but propped herself up against me as best she could. Where would this end? We hadn't even made it out of the bedroom yet!

"Don't you think maybe we should reconsider this?" I asked cautiously.

Her reaction was violent. She gathered up every ounce of strength in her body and took a step. I supported her. We got down to the car with great effort. I packed her in blankets and pillows in the back seat and hoped that that would be enough. She collapsed with exhaustion as I sat down in the driver's seat. Perhaps she'd fallen asleep. I had given her another pill back in the apartment. Awake, she'd never be able to stand so much pain.

As I pulled out into the street, she cried out. I looked in the rearview mirror. "Can you really do this?"

She gritted her teeth. "Yes", she growled. I'd better not ask her that anymore!

The first few miles, before we got to the freeway, were extremely awful. I wanted to turn around, or at least get some earplugs. She moaned continuously. Then, when we got on the freeway, I suddenly heard nothing more from her. She'd lost consciousness. That was best. I hoped she'd stay that way as long as possible.

During the drive, I stopped twice without her waking up. I watched her carefully. Her swollen face was twisted up in pain. Unconsciousness might protect her mind from thinking about her injuries, but it didn't shield her body from them. She continued to moan now and then, but thank God, she didn't wake up.

After the last stop, the industrial areas surrounding Paris suddenly appeared before me. As always, I was surprised by the sudden transformation. First, there was barely a house to be seen, just a few farming villages, but then all of a sudden there were wide streets and sprawling industrial complexes right and left.

This artificial landscape never seemed to end. One after another, the garishly-lit, phantasmagoric buildings slid past my windows. Tall buildings whose tops I couldn't even see from inside the car stood between flat, isolated, defenseless-looking warehouses. Flat, pointed, flat, pointed – it resembled a desolate futuristic painting, which, with its unusual lighting, looked almost filigreed.

The aesthetics of these constructions took me prisoner. My surroundings seemed to flash by me like images on a giant movie screen.

I didn't know how long it had been before the scenery changed. The poor suburbs of Paris and their own aesthetics couldn't compete with the industrial region. What perversion! Here lived the people who worked in that science fiction world.

I had to turn my attention to the traffic. Even at night, Paris always seemed to be at rush hour. I had to drive through the city. I'd have to take part in the incomparable experience of the Arc de Triomphe traffic circle! Now, at night, I felt up to it, but I'd never in a million years attempt it during the day.

I drove on, looking for the road that would lead us to her apartment.

It wasn't far now. She moaned.

I looked in the rearview mirror. "Are you awake?"

In answer, I got a horrible sound from her. Then a sort of rasping. It sounded like metal rubbing against metal. "Where ...?" she asked, barely understandable.

"We're in Paris," I replied in a friendly voice. "Your apartment must be right around here someplace." I was curious what the apartment would be like. Above all, I hoped it had an elevator.

I found the building and parked in the street. What was I doing in Paris, anyhow? I gave us both a moment to recover, then got out. I opened the back door. "Can you get out?" I asked carefully.

She moved around a little. "I'll try," she said softly.

I got her purse out of the car and looked for the key. It was hidden deep in an inside pocket. There was a beautiful silver key chain attached to it. I held it in my hand for a moment, admiring it. She let out a loud noise. I turned to her quickly. Her face was scrunched up in pain yet again. I went to her and wrapped her arm over my shoulder and mine around her waist. I brought her to the door and opened it. Slowly, I helped her inside. The door swung shut by itself.

We stood in a foyer of enormous dimensions. Left and right stood wide spiral staircases to the next floor. "Oh, my!" I was overwhelmed and deeply impressed. She trembled on my arm. That pulled me back down out of the clouds and to the business at hand. I didn't see an elevator anywhere. The whole thing seemed to be original eighteenth-century construction.

"What floor is your apartment on?" I asked her apprehensively.

"First." It sounded very weak. She just barely raised her hand and pointed to the right. "Elevator."

I was somewhat relieved. The first floor hadn't sounded so bad, but probably that which I saw at the top of the stairs was the first floor. And way up there – those stairs must be half a mile long! I preferred the elevator.

I led her slowly over to the right, although I couldn't detect any technological devices. When we reached the corner of the entry hall, I finally saw the elevator doors. They were completely hidden behind a marble column and very elaborately decorated. We got on the elevator. I closed the gate from inside and pushed the button for "1." As I'd suspected, it was actually the second floor. In between there was yet another story. We rode up.

On the floor designated here as the first, there were two doors. She started right away for the left one. I brought her to the door and opened it with the second key on the ring. Inside the apartment, she showed me wordlessly the way to the bedroom – if you could call this French boudoir that!

I laid her on the bed, a French dream of velvet and silk, and took her shoes off. I didn't want to attempt to undress her just yet. I pulled the blanket up over her and looked down at her. She could barely stay awake. I bent down over her and kissed her gently on the nose. That seemed to be the least damaged part of her. "Sleep," I said, "you're in Paris now."

She closed her eyes.

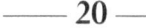

—— **20** ——

I had to drive around the neighborhood for half an hour before I found a parking place, and even then, it wasn't particularly close. I wasn't sure I'd ever find it again. In my exhausted state, the street signs shimmered before my eyes. Sighing, I parked the car and, after some searching, actually did find my way back to the apartment.

First, I looked to see if she was still sleeping. She was exhausted half to death but still restless. At the moment, there was nothing I could do about that.

I was too tired to take a good look around the apartment. I just had the impression that it was very large.

In the room next to her bedroom, I saw a chaise lounge that would suffice for a place to sleep. I could hear her from there if I left the door ajar. Despite the size of her bed, I didn't want to sleep next to her. I was afraid I'd touch her in my sleep and cause her more pain.

The next morning, I woke up and first had to figure out where I was. In my usual morning haze, I went through a mental list of possibilities. It wasn't my apartment, nor was it hers. Then I heard a soft moaning sound from the next room. Paris! Finally, I was awake.

I got up and looked after her. She tossed and turned restlessly, but she was still asleep. I didn't think it would be an improvement to wake her. I sat carefully on the bed and watched her.

It looked to me like her face was even more black and blue than it had been the day before. It was gruesome, especially compared to her usual beauty. But I reassured myself with what the doctor had said. And all of her external injuries would, in time, heal. How it would go with the internal injuries – the non-physical ones – I couldn't predict.

I guessed that she would probably sleep a while longer. There wasn't anything better for her to do. I got up from the bed and looked around. Right off the bedroom, there was a bathroom. I went in. Here she had a bathtub – and what a bathtub! It was a huge, freestanding one with lion-claw feet. The whole bathroom was one big orgy of luxury. Well no, perhaps "orgy" was something of an overstatement. It simply contained everything one could need to make oneself feel well, and all of that in first-class style. I could imagine how much she enjoyed her getaways here.

I left the bathroom and took another look at her on the bed. Her sleep was still a little restless, but she was breathing evenly. I stepped into the hallway outside her room. To the left would likely be the everyday rooms; to the right, I saw a door into another room and a few pieces of antique furniture, probably Louis XV. I chose to go left. I guessed I'd find the kitchen down that way, and what I needed most at the moment was a cup of coffee.

I was right. The kitchen was at the end of the hall. It was the sort of kitchen one would expect to find in a place like this, large, old, and perfectly appointed. I asked myself why she needed it, since she never cooked.

I looked for the coffeemaker. There were two. One was the fancy American style I'd seen before in her kitchen in Germany. The other was a traditional, French hand-cranked model. I chose the latter. It felt right for the first day in Paris. I found coffee, as well, but no milk, not even powdered, so I'd have to wait for café au lait. When the coffee was ready, I took my cup and went back into the bedroom. She still wasn't awake yet. Better that way. So I set off on a self-guided tour of the apartment.

Behind the kitchen, I had already discovered another small room. Probably the household staff had slept there once. What times those were! Down the hall from the kitchen, there was also a dining room and another room that had probably served the same purpose as the first.

When I left her bedroom this time, I wandered off to the right. The first door on the right opened into another bedroom that didn't appear to be in use. To the left, there was a sort of library. At least that's what I gathered from the old bookshelves lining the walls. Now, the room was obviously used for something else. A large desk stood next to the window, with a partially inclined surface. I went over to it. On the level portion of the desktop lay a couple of collages. On the inclined surface was a filigreed pencil drawing. She drew! I was so surprised I had to sit down for a moment.

I felt the tears welling in my eyes. I still wasn't quite ready to admit that Karin had been right, but deep inside, I knew that I loved her like I'd never loved another woman in my life.

I sat there, shaken and ashamed. If she hadn't been in such bad shape, I would've driven home right then. But I had to wait until she was at least a little better. At that point, she probably wouldn't want anything more to do with me anyhow. Surely, in her desperation, she simply hadn't known whom else to call but me. When she was no longer dependent on my help, she would certainly remember what had happened at our last encounter. But by then, I'd already be gone.

I stood up and wiped away my tears. On the other side of the room, there was another door. Through it, I came into a small, unpretentious salon. It was clear that she spent much of her time here. There was a comfortable armchair in front of a small fireplace, and next to that an end table on which lay – I could hardly believe it – a pair of reading glasses! By now, the tears were rolling down my cheeks. I looked to see what she was reading. Baudelaire, *Fleurs du mal, The Flowers of Evil,* in French! Was that the right sort of material? For her recovery, I'd have to find her something lighter.

At the opposite end of the room, there was yet another door. Behind it, I found the large parlor that I'd already glimpsed from the hallway, the one with the Louis XV furniture. It seemed to serve a more ornamental purpose and was not as cozy as the small salon next door. A large, intricately tiled hearth commanded one corner.

On the parquetry floor, there were a few scattered throw rugs that had clearly not been bought at a clearance sale. The furniture was very elegant and – as I'd feared – genuine.

This ended my tour. I looked down at the street through one of the high windows. The typical Parisian bustle made me smile. Several people were crossing the street with baguettes under their arms; a motor scooter grazed a passer-by, who scolded after it temperamentally. Two women met and conversed with a degree of physicality and animation unheard of on German streets. This was what I loved most about France.

Above all, this made me realize something. I'd need to go grocery shopping, for her and for myself. That was something new. It would be fun.

I went back into the kitchen, got a second cup of coffee, and rummaged through the cupboards. Apparently, she really never cooked, not even here. Other than the coffee and several varieties of tea, I found a few frozen entrees – for emergencies, I assumed – and that was it.

I mulled over the situation. It would be a couple of days yet, surely, before she could go out. But she needed something fortifying to help with her recovery. And I, myself, wouldn't want to do without baguettes or café au lait. Everything was set.

I made a little list and went back into the room where I had slept. I got dressed. Before I left, I looked in on her once more. She was still asleep. That was good.

I really enjoyed my shopping trip; just the chance to speak French was something special, though mine was rather rusty from years of disuse. And then there were the people, who simply laughed and scolded and yelled, and then in the next moment fell into each other's arms again. It was simply lovely.

My final purchases bore little resemblance to my original list, but that didn't matter. The pure pleasure was worth it.

I walked back to the apartment whistling. People I met wished me a cheerful "Bonjour!" and I answered just as cheerfully. Back in the apartment, I put away my purchases in the kitchen, whistling softly so as not to wake her. I set a pot of milk on to warm – for the first café au lait of the day – and went to her bedroom. When I came in, she looked at me. I stopped whistling immediately. She, of course, wouldn't know what I'd been doing and might find it inappropriate.

I went over to her in the bed. "Did I wake you?" I asked with concern.

"No," she replied, still quietly, but it was obvious that she was doing better, "I was already awake." Her speech was somewhat slurred. Her lips were still swollen.

I wanted to scoop her up in my arms to show my joy at her improvement. But that wasn't yet possible. "I went shopping," I explained. "Would you like something to eat?"

"No," she said again. "I was wondering where you were."

Oh, boy, that didn't sound good! Despite her soft voice, I could hear the ice crunching. *What did she mean, where I was? Did she think I'd left her alone? That I'd gone home?* She was too ill to discuss it now. "I'm making myself a café au lait right now," I told her, as though I hadn't noticed her tone. "Do you think you can drink something?"

She hesitated. I elaborated on my offer. "I also have oranges. I could squeeze you some juice. That'd probably be better for you anyway. Besides, you have a remarkably nice juicer." I grinned encouragingly

"Do I?" she asked gloomily

She was lucky that she was so sick! In any other case, I would've told her exactly what she could do with her juicer. But now I just confirmed, "Yes, you do. So orange juice it is – don't help, don't hurt!"

"Pardon me?" If I hadn't known for certain that we'd seen each other before – and more – I would've had serious doubts about that now.

"Even if it doesn't help, it won't hurt you, either," I repeated with my best grade-school diction.

She just looked at me.

I sighed to myself. Then I put on a friendly smile. "So I'll go to the kitchen now and squeeze you some orange juice. Besides, my milk is probably about to boil over by now." I turned around and left.

In the kitchen, I asked myself what her behavior was supposed to mean. She had been assaulted horribly. In her desperation, she'd called me. I had brought her here. Was she sorry to be forced to spend time with me like this? Did she want, now that she was here – obviously her most secluded and private retreat – to get rid of me? That she could have! But only when she was well enough that I could leave her alone with a clear conscience. She'd have to put up with me that long!

I made the orange juice, poured it into a glass, and took a straw from the package I'd bought. I put everything on a breakfast tray – she had one of those, of all things – and brought it to her.

She must really have been doing better; she had sat herself up without my help. I set the tray across her lap and took my café au lait bowl from it. Then I sat down – in spite of her bad mood – across from her on the bed. I indicated the straw. "I thought that would be more comfortable for you."

She took the glass carefully. "Yes." She drank a sip. "Thank you for thinking of it." She didn't look at me. Her voice did not indicate to me whether she meant that earnestly or was only being polite.

"Your apartment is absolutely enchanting," I gushed. *Like you,* I wanted to continue, even if she didn't want to hear that. But I left it unsaid. Perhaps it was still too soon for that.

"Do you think so?" she replied, reserved as expected.

I went on, ignoring her mood. "I looked around a bit while you were sleeping. I hope that was permissible."

She looked at me through narrow eye slits. Although I knew she couldn't open her eyes much wider if she wanted to, it looked intentional. It fit her tone. "I've never had to decide that before," she said.

With all the experience I'd had with her up to that point, I knew that it was most unforgivable to her when someone invaded her private sphere. I couldn't help that. I'd neither read her love letters – had she ever written or received any? Nor had I rummaged through her closets – except for the kitchen, but that didn't count.

"I hope not." I acted unimpressed. She should know that I wouldn't give in to her defensiveness.

She noticed. "I'm thankful to you for everything you've done for me," she said again, without indicating whether she was being genuine or not.

"How are you doing?" I asked. She certainly couldn't imagine an ulterior motive behind that question.

"Better." She didn't seem too excited to give out more information.

I reacted with mild irritation this time. "That's nice," I commented artificially. I was slowly beginning to get sick of this. What was her problem?

"Take your sweatshirt off," I demanded coolly. A small shock would do her good.

It worked.

"What?" Startled, she looked up.

I let her squirm just a little. Then I explained what I had in mind. "I bought a salve for your bruises. I'm going to rub some on you. Also, I found a medicinal bath. You're going to soak in that this afternoon. And you have to take that sweatsuit off anyway. You've had it on since yesterday." So, let her try to contradict that!

She didn't try to. She just stared at me through her swollen eyelids like a woman from Mars.

I set my coffee bowl on her breakfast tray and stood up. "Where do you keep your pajamas?" I asked. *If I'd gone through her closets, I would've known that already, wouldn't I?*

She pointed at the middle drawer of an antique bureau. I opened it and saw at least a dozen pairs of silk pajamas. I turned around. "Don't you have anything else besides silk?"

She swallowed. I'd really ruffled her. "No," she explained, much more cooperative than before, "it's . . ."

"I know," I smiled warmly. "It's so comfortable against the skin." I took out a pair and laid them on the bed. I went to the kitchen and got the salve. When I came back, she hadn't budged. She must still have been completely perplexed.

I took the breakfast tray and set it aside. I looked at her. I felt sorry for her already. Everything I was about to do to her was going to hurt, but it was necessary. "I'll help you." I reached around her waist and pulled the sweatshirt up. She moaned. Slowly, I raised her arms over her head and pulled the shirt over them. Her moaning got louder.

Finally, it was done. Her arms fell back to her sides and she yelped again in pain. "Now your pants." I pulled back the blanket. "You'd better lie down."

She got herself slowly and painfully into a lying position. It was easier to get her pants off. She didn't have to do much for that.

I could barely look at her. Everything was green and blue. I asked myself who could have done this. I'd certainly never ask her.

I took the salve. "If it hurts, yell," I said. "I'll be as careful as I can." I knew I couldn't protect her from the pain. Still, I suspected she could tolerate more pain than I wanted to give her credit for.

I began to apply the salve. She jerked at every touch. After a while, she began to moan softly. Before I made her turn over, I granted her a small break.

I looked at her. "Yell if you need to," I offered painfully. "Nobody's going to hear you." I wished I could have done it for her.

She looked at me dejectedly. "I can't," she said. We eventually got through the procedure. I put the pajamas on her, after which she collapsed back into sleep.

It became more and more evident to me that I was developing a sense of vengeance against whoever had done this to her. While I was treating her, I had discovered deep gouges in her wrists. Someone must have handcuffed her. No wonder she looked like that. She had been completely unable to defend herself.

It was still a mystery to me what exactly had happened. She had assured me that she wasn't into this kind of violence. So how did she get herself into a situation where she could be handcuffed?

Or had she done it willingly after all? I just couldn't imagine that. But until recently, there was a lot I couldn't have imagined. A number of those things involved my relationship with her, of course. That she was a prostitute and that I loved her, for instance.

I wasn't happy about that, and certainly not about her profession. However, I was more prepared to accept it now. Perhaps not in the context of a relationship, but at least as her lifestyle.

What that meant for me was already clear. I would always love her, but we wouldn't be together. If I was lucky, she might accept me as a platonic girlfriend.

I smiled through my grief. Platonic – with her erotic charisma! I could forget that already.

I suddenly noticed that I was getting hungry. I went to the kitchen and gathered together a few things I'd bought for breakfast earlier. I wouldn't have to deal with her for a while, after all. I took a baguette and some cheese into the small salon.

I knew why this was her favorite spot. I could feel the inner warmth that the room gave off. Again, she had sought the warmth from things that she didn't get from people.

Couldn't I change that? It had to be possible to give her back a little of what she gave out so freely, whether she realized it or not. The joy of beauty, love.

I would've loved to sit in the overstuffed chair, but I didn't want to take her seat. So I sat in the armchair across from it and imagined her sitting in her chair and reading her book.

It must be wonderful to spend the evenings with her, sitting there peacefully and reading, looking up to see her beautiful face. Would I ever experience that?

I let myself sink back into the chair and gave myself over to my daydreams. I must've nodded off, because I was suddenly awakened by her screams. It was such a blood-curdling sound that I dashed immediately to her room. She wasn't awake. She screamed in pain, but not the pain her body felt. It was a nightmare. I ran to her and shook her. Even if I hurt her that way, it was still better than letting her relive that horrifying experience again.

She woke, still screaming. I immediately took her into my arms, even though that had to hurt her. I stroked her hair and tried to calm her.

"Shhh, be calm," I soothed her. "I'm here. And no one else is here. You're in Paris. You're safe now." Her whole body was shaking. She was tortured by the muscle cramps. I looked in her eyes. They were dry. "Go ahead and cry," I pushed desperately. "Crying helps."

It shook her again, but she didn't cry. How could she get rid of the pain and the tension? It took a long time before I had calmed her enough that she could breathe normally. I couldn't speak to her. I laid her gently back down. I didn't want to cause her any more pain. She sank back onto the bed and moaned again – this time from the pain she felt at the moment.

Some of her wounds had split open and begun to bleed. I saw the blood seeping through the pajamas. They were shot! But that was the least of her problems. I got one of the tablets the doctor had prescribed and gave it to her. If only she could go back to sleep! I would watch over her sleep and, if I saw the slightest hint of another nightmare, wake her immediately.

She was still in agony. She looked at me, but I didn't even know if she recognized me. Then, finally, she sank moaning into sleep. I got a blanket from the next room and stayed in an armchair next to her. If this kept up, I'd soon be able to sleep better in armchairs than in beds! When I had the feeling that she was really sound asleep, I went over to the library to get myself a book.

She didn't have anything simple at all. Most of it was in French, and what she had in German wasn't exactly relaxing. I could certainly imagine that she didn't read romance novels, but not even Agatha Christie or *The Name of the Rose*? So I took Madame Bovary – why she had that, I really had to wonder – and went back to her. In school, I'd always refused to read this book in French. I would never have believed that I'd end up in a situation one day where I'd read it voluntarily.

I read, and when she moaned, I looked up at her each time. She slept a little more calmly as time passed. I became more and more absorbed in the book. After three hours, I still couldn't believe what drove Emma Bovary to love that guy.

It occurred to me that something had changed. She wasn't moaning any more. I glanced at the bed. She was watching me. I shut the book and set it aside. "You're awake?" I asked unnecessarily.

"Yes." She still had me fixed in her gaze. I began to feel uneasy. What was it now?

"Can I do anything for you?" I asked rather formally. I stood up. "I bought some soup. I think that would be good for you now." I wanted to head for the kitchen in order to escape her stare.

"Stay," she ordered before I could take a step toward the door. I stood still. I understood her. She felt absolutely wretched. But did she always have to take her bad mood out on me? *On whom else?* After all, there was no one else there.

I stood with my back to her and said resignedly, "yes?"

"Please, come over here."

I turned around and went over to her. I stood next to the bed.

"Sit down," she said.

I sat on the very edge of the bed. She lifted her arm, wincing a little. "Don't," I protested.

"Yes." She caressed my cheek gently. Then she let her arm fall, tired. She wanted to smile, but all she could manage was a pain-twisted grimace. "I've wanted to do that ever since I first regained consciousness," she said.

I wanted to kiss her, to hug her. I sighed. The most obvious was not, at the moment, possible. I looked at her. Even in this condition, she looked to me like the most beautiful woman in the world.

"I'm glad you're feeling better." I looked down at her tenderly.

"Without you, I wouldn't be," she stated earnestly.

"I'm afraid that's not all true," I replied with a sigh. "Without me, for example, you wouldn't have to take a medicinal bath this afternoon."

She didn't allow herself to be distracted. "Without you, I wouldn't be in Paris."

"Probably not," I had to admit.

She attempted to laugh at my silly embarrassment, but the pain kept her from doing so.

"You see," I came back. "if I weren't here, you could've avoided that pain just now."

"Please, make me the soup." She tried with great effort to keep from laughing. "Or else I'll have to admit that you're right."

I stood up and smiled down at her. Then I turned around and went to the kitchen.

I arranged everything on the breakfast tray again: soup, baguette, and orange juice with a straw, and brought it to her. As before, she had sat up by herself. But this time, she looked much more relaxed.

"I'm even hungry," she remarked in astonishment. What did she think, then? That her body had endless reserves?

"That's good," I joked. "They only had the soup in liter packages. There's still a lot left."

She coughed, probably to avoid laughing again, but of course, that caused her just as much pain at the moment. "Ow," she said softly.

Then she looked at me. She said nothing. She took the straw and drank her juice. Then she ate her soup cautiously. She had great difficulty holding the spoon level. It kept shaking in her hand.

"Should I help?" I asked.

She shook her head and tried the next spoonful. It all landed back in the bowl. "Well, maybe," she admitted. "But please, don't say, 'one bite for Mama, one bite for Papa . . .'"

I laughed. "Of course not!" She was truly on the way to recovery. I could have jumped for joy.

I took the spoon and fed her. When the bowl was empty, she said: "Under these circumstances, I'd rather pass on the rest of the liter. Do you mind?"

"No, not at all." I felt quite relieved. "I'm happy that you ate anything at all."

She leaned back and moaned a little.

"Does something hurt?" I asked fearfully.

"Something?" she asked back. "Everything! It feels like I've been put through a meat grinder." She looked that way, too. I wasn't going to ask, but my facial expression said everything.

"I don't want to talk about it." She closed herself off again.

"You don't have to," I reassured her. I understood. Who could ask that of her! I, too, would rather think about something else. "Would you like to sleep some more now, or would you prefer to go right for the bathtub torture?" I asked as cheerfully as if she had to choose between oysters and caviar.

She moaned – somewhat exaggeratedly. "Can't I take the bath tomorrow?" she suggested hopefully.

"If you do it today, you'll feel much better tomorrow."

She sighed. "I understand," she admitted. "Right away, then. I've already slept enough anyhow."

She'd see that differently after her bath! "I don't want to cause you any unnecessary pain," I began. "Can you stand up by yourself? I'll support you."

"Yes," she said heroically. "I'll try." She managed it, and with a little help from me, we made it to the bathroom. I turned the faucets. Water shot out in fountains.

I took off her pajamas and helped her into the tub. When the water touched her wounds, she groaned horribly. "You don't have to stay in long." I could almost feel her pain as though it were my own. "Only fifteen minutes. Can you tolerate that?"

She nodded with gritted teeth. The way it looked, I would've thought she had to tolerate a lot more than a bath.

After the bath was over and I'd put her to bed in a fresh pair of pajamas, she fell right back to sleep. And she thought she'd had enough sleep already!

She improved visibly. Her bruises changed color to all green and then to a pale yellow. Fearfully, I had determined that she also had wounds on her face. She would have scars, if not terribly large ones. But I was worried about her self-consciousness. So much for her depended on her appearance. I wondered about myself – since when would I be worried that she wouldn't be able to go back to work?

I sat in the small salon and read. Since she was doing better, I no longer needed to observe her constantly.

Unexpectedly, she appeared in the doorway. She even had her white robe on. She came in, smiling. She moved very slowly. Her graceful walk had not yet returned. With some effort, she sat down in the overstuffed chair. "Why are you sitting over there?" she asked.

I pointed to her book and her reading glasses. "That's obviously your spot," I explained.

She looked at me. Then she smiled again. It wasn't the same as before, but it was getting close. "I just wanted to see what you do while I sleep."

"You can see for yourself," I smiled. "I have wild orgies."

She seemed to find my slightly sarcastic tone a bit indecent, but she smiled anyway. "Yes, I can see that." Her gaze wandered through the room. I had the impression that she only now fully understood where she was. She took in the room and its furnishings with loving recognition. I could tell she was truly at home here. She sat up straight. "I'm going to get dressed."

"You're still too weak!" I protested with dismay. "You have to stay in bed for another couple of days."

"No," she countered solidly. "Today I'll stay home, but tomorrow I want to see for myself that I'm in Paris."

She wanted to go out? I'd gotten so used to her not going out that I'd never have thought of it on my own. But here, in Paris, that prohibition of course did not exist. She didn't have any clients here. Here, she was free. I noticed that I'd never even thought about whether she worked while in Paris. When I learned that she had an apartment here, I might've assumed automatically that she did. I really should be ashamed of myself!

"You'll overexert yourself." I was honestly worried about her. She seemed to be so hungry for life. And she was still very weak, even if she didn't want to admit it

She laughed. "You would pack me in cotton if you could!"

"Yes," I said, "I would."

"It doesn't have to be the Ritz, you know. The bistro around the corner would do as well. Would that make you feel better?"

"Yes." She hadn't really quite convinced me yet, and she knew it.

"If you really want to go to the trouble, you can accompany me everywhere I go," she suggested congenially.

I laughed. "I was planning on it. You're not going to get rid of me that easily. Not in your condition."

She smiled to herself. "To listen to you, I'd think I was about to give birth."

I looked at her with interest, imagining her in the latter stages of pregnancy. Even then, she'd look absolutely stunning.

"Tsk, tsk," she said, shaking her head. "You don't expect me to fulfill that wish, now, do you?"

"What wish?" I asked, irritated.

"Seeing me pregnant," she said, amused.

I looked away. "I think you're well enough." She'd barely gotten out of bed, and already she was making fun of me again!

She stood up laboriously. "I'm going to start getting dressed. I have to practice for tomorrow." She looked back at me. "Would you like to help me?" Impossible! She was flirting with me!

"No," I declined obstinately. "I think you can do that by yourself."

"Yes," she agreed jokingly. "But with you, I'd have a lot more fun for the pain."

"Have fun," I replied sourly.

Still smiling a little, she made her way out slowly. *Who was I, then?*

After a rather long while, she returned. Good thing I'd thought to pack loose clothing for her. She was wearing the blue shirt that I'd loved on her so much. I was sure she'd had the jeans for years. They conformed to her figure perfectly. That set a few things going inside me. I swallowed. She wasn't even halfway done recovering, and already I was thinking thoughts like that!

I eyed her face. The blue of the shirt actually brought out the changing colors of her bruises. She saw my expression. "Oh, that," she glossed over my impression, "that can be corrected with a little makeup."

Corrected with a little makeup? She looked remarkably like Frankenstein's monster. But of course, I couldn't tell her that.

"If you think so," I said, with as little doubt in my voice as possible.

"Yes," she assured me harmlessly. "I have some experience with that."

I almost fell out of my chair. Experience? With what? With makeup, or with "correcting" the marks that the "tastes" of her customers had left behind? I knew so little about her life. Except for the one time, she'd never really talked about it. She had always spared me that. I thought about the handcuffs around her wrists. Were those also marks that she normally "corrected" with makeup?

She hadn't, thank God, been watching me; instead, she'd had to devote her full attention to sitting down in her overstuffed chair. "So, here I'll stay," she announced.

I had to pull myself from my dreary thoughts. "Until tomorrow?" I tried to joke.

She was already excited about it. I could see that clearly. "If necessary. In any case, it's better than lying in bed. That was starting to get boring."

She was bored in bed? *I could fix that! Just hang in there!*

Against her strongest will, she had to admit that staying up for a long time still required too much effort for her. She excused herself. Hours later, when I went to bed, she was sleeping quietly for the first time in days. I watched her for a while, until I could feel the love welling up inside me. She didn't need to use her body at all to make me melt. She was so unendingly lovable. If only she would believe that herself!

The next morning, I woke early, but she was already up. When I went into the bathroom, I found her in the tub. I didn't know where she'd gotten this boundless energy. Three days before, she'd barely been able to lift a finger. I smiled and knelt down next to her.

"Is it still worth it for me to make coffee, or are we going right to the bistro?"

"I'm afraid it's still worth it," she stated rather remorsefully.

"It'll be a while before I'm done with all my preparations in here."

I stood up. "Okay, then I'll be in the kitchen." I went out. Much longer in there and I wouldn't have been able to resist her – despite the bubble bath!

While I drank my coffee in the kitchen, I heard her rattling around; first in the bathroom and then in her bedroom. When I was working on my second cup, she came into the kitchen. She'd really pulled it off. Her face looked like it had never been injured. The most one might have suspected is that she'd just spent a rather passionate night somewhere.

"How do I look?" she asked, displaying her work.

"Breathtaking!" I was truly impressed.

"Thank you," she replied politely, "but that isn't quite what I meant." She smiled.

Why did we have to go out at all? "I can't see anything," I assured her honestly.

She was satisfied. "I had that impression also." She looked at my cup. "Can we go?"

I nodded.

It was a pleasure to watch how she handled herself so confidently and so freely in this neighborhood. She didn't quite have her flexibility back, so she walked rather stiffly yet. Had it not been for that limitation, she would've been the embodiment of liveliness. I kept feeling like I had to put the brakes on for her. She sparkled with joy.

I just walked next to her in complete astonishment. The nearest bistro really was right around the corner. She entered casually and

greeted everyone. She was obviously a regular here. What a difference from the carefully guarded hiding I'd seen her in before!

The man behind the counter greeted her with genuine pleasure.
"Bonjour, Madame! Back in Paris again?" I could tell by looking at
him that he appreciated the gift of her beauty as much as I did.

"Bonjour, Jean," she replied cheerfully. The pleasure was visible
in her as well.

He'd already put a café noir in front of her. He looked at me politely. "Madame?" I took the same.

I was totally fascinated by the playing out of her connections with
this world. Like all regular customers – "customers," that word had
an uncomfortable aftertaste – she simply stood at the counter, stirring sugar into her coffee and conversing in brilliant French with
the barkeep. They didn't talk about anything special – the weather,
prices, the barman's children. But the whole thing held an unusual
attraction for me. Here, she was a completely normal woman;
here, she was at home.

She'd forgotten about me completely. I looked over at her and
wished that I would never experience her any other way. After a
while, it occurred to her that she hadn't come in alone. She turned
to face me.

"I'm sorry," she apologized with a guilty smile. "It's always like
this when I come here. I didn't mean to –"

I interrupted her. "You don't need to apologize. It's just wonderful here." I continued softly, with a glance at the barman, "Does he
understand German?"

She looked at me, confused. "Not a word."

"You are wonderful," I said.

If she hadn't been completely covered with a thick layer of
makeup, I would've seen how red she turned. Instead, I could only
guess. She turned back to the barman and let loose an extremely interesting torrent about the weather. He jumped in and helped her
overcome the embarrassment he hadn't even noticed.

I sat down on one of the nice barstools and observed her a little
more. This could take some time. The other regulars – so I assumed – had gathered around, and the whole thing was one big
conversation full of laughter.

I looked out the window and watched the bustling street traffic pass by. Now and then, someone else came in, greeted her and the others, conversed with them or didn't, stayed or left.

Obviously, there were differences in degree of intimacy. One greeted her with a handshake, another in the typical Roman style with a kiss right, kiss left, kiss right on the cheeks. She must've been coming here a long time.

Why didn't she just stay here? Why did she torture herself by leaving this place of love and friendship in her life to go back there?"

While I was wondering that and watching her, she caught my eye. She dodged the protests of the others charmingly, such that everyone said their friendly goodbyes, and came over to me at my table.

"I'm sorry," she said again. "I'm sure you expected this to go quite differently."

Actually, I hadn't expected anything. I just wanted to look out for her. "It's very interesting," I smiled at her reassuringly. "I love sitting in a bistro in Paris and watching you at your best. You couldn't bring me any greater joy."

She was upset again. I wanted to calm her and reached for her hand. She pulled away. Oh, boy, she didn't want that! I grinned. So that was one thing that this new environment required.

"Don't be afraid," I promised. "I'll be very good."

She was extremely uncomfortable. She fidgeted. "You have to understand . . ."

"I understand," I admitted, still grinning. "I didn't become a lesbian yesterday, you know."

She was taken aback at first. Then she broke into joyful laughter that sounded like tiny little raindrops. "Why . . .?" she asked. She started again. "Why isn't that a problem for you?"

"Because I don't have a problem with it. There are lots of things that I don't do in public, and most of them aren't even remotely related to who I sleep with."

She was still a bit taken aback. "Funny," she stated, "I've always heard differently before now."

"Do you have a problem with it?" I asked with genuine curiosity. Such things always interested me.

She considered this. "No, not really. I've just never really thought much about it before."

I understood that well. She had put so many other limitations and taboos on her life that she'd surely never gotten around to dealing with this one before. She just never had occasion to. Besides, with whom would she hold hands? With her clients?

"But somehow, it still just doesn't seem right." She tried to knit her eyebrows, but gave that up right away with a wince. She wasn't nearly as well as she portrayed herself to be.

"No," I agreed with her. "I don't think it's right either. But that's not my problem; it's the problem of those who can't stand to look when two women are being tender to one another." I shrugged. "For that, my time is too precious and life is too short. They should solve their own problems."

"I believe you're right," she pondered. "I'll have to think about that some more." She sat for a while, deep in thought.

I looked at her and noticed that she was about to fall asleep. "Don't you think we'd better go home?" I asked urgently.

She sat up a little. "Yes, I'm suddenly awfully tired. I hadn't noticed it at all before." Of course not – she'd been swimming in a sea of friendship and happiness!

"Have you paid?" I was really afraid she was about to tip over right here. She looked absolutely exhausted, despite all the makeup.

She waved that away. "We don't need to. The first cup when I come to town is always on the house."

She gathered herself up and went up to the counter once more. She marshaled the last of her strength for her goodbyes, and let her charm flow. It was obvious that everyone was captivated by her. They would have liked most to hold her, to keep her there. She declined regretfully, putting them all off to the next time.

We went back around the corner. As soon as we were out of sight, she leaned against the building. She was grey under her makeup. I was afraid for her. Why did she always have to overextend herself?

"Should I help you?" I asked. Somehow, I still had to get her home.

She shook her head. "I'll manage. Just let me rest here for a minute." She closed her eyes.

The control she exercised over her body was really unbelievable. After a minute, she opened her eyes again and said, "We can go." She still didn't look very well, but she walked along the street as if she had nothing more than a long day at work behind her. I didn't know how long her strength was going to last. I tried to stay as close to her as possible.

She made it into the apartment. On the other side of the door, she collapsed. I picked her up and helped her into the bedroom. There, she fell onto the bed and didn't make another sound. At first, I doubted that she was even still breathing. I put my ear to her mouth and was reassured. I laid her in a slightly more comfortable position, took off her shoes, pulled a blanket over her, and left her to sleep.

The next morning she'd go out again, I decided, but this time for x-rays!

—— **21** ——

O h, no!" she moaned.

"Oh, yes!" I stood my ground. "Today you're going to be x-rayed. I promised the doctor you would. If I ever run into her again and she finds out that I broke my promise, she'll lynch me."

She tried again to get out of it. "Come on, she won't be that bad."

I had to have proof that she was well. Since she had collapsed yesterday, I was more worried about her. "Yes, she is that bad. You didn't really get a chance to talk to her. I did."

She had to admit that. "Yes, that's true." She sighed in resignation. "I'm not going to get anywhere going up against the two of you. When then?"

"Right after breakfast," I replied energetically. I didn't want to give her a chance to think about it too long.

When I picked her up at the doctor's office, she informed me, "Everything is fine. I'm supposed to take it easy for another week. Are you happy now?"

"Yes," I said. "That was all I wanted to know." I looked over at her. "Did he ask you anything else?"

"Nothing special." She shrugged absently. "They always believe the story about the stairs."

My God! How often had she done this already?

Slowly, it began to seem like I'd spent my entire life up to this point in a glass box, sheltered from the evil side of the world. I took a great deal for granted. Consideration of others, for instance, and mutual respect for the idea that people shouldn't hurt each other intentionally, or that everyone had a right to self-esteem. I didn't ask her anything else. How could I question her life when I enjoyed everything so automatically that was obviously a luxury for her, which she only now and then got to experience here in Paris? Instead, it was my job to ensure that this trip was as comfortable and relaxing as possible for her.

"What would you like as your treat for being so brave?" I kidded her gently.

"Do I get to choose?" She pouted a little. "That's new."

I held her tight, wrapped an arm around her neck, pulled her down to me, and kissed her softly on the lips. "You do," I said tenderly. "Anything you want, darling."

She was too surprised to react right away, then "darling" gave her another shock. Finally, she remarked, "I thought you didn't do that in public."

I laughed. "I didn't say that I never do it on general principle. I've just never felt like it before." I eyed her carefully. "If it bothers you, I'll never do it again."

She looked at me with an unreadable expression. Then she leaned over me and kissed me very lightly. "It doesn't bother me." Her face lightened. "I even think I could start to like it." She put an arm around my waist, and we took a few steps together like that.

"So," I asked again. "What would you like to do?"

She stopped. "I'm not quite sure. I don't want to make the same mistake I made yesterday."

"That was no mistake," I said warmly. "Those people did you so much good."

"Yes," she admitted, "but it was too strenuous. Today, I don't want to see any people." Did she mean me with that as well?

I looked at her questioningly. "Do you want to stay in the apartment?"

She shook her head. "No, not that, either."

I didn't know what alternatives she was weighing in her head, so I just stood there and waited for an answer.

"Do you like the countryside?" she asked suddenly.

"That depends," I replied uncertainly. *Countryside was a rather vague description.*

"I'd really like to drive out there. Just in the general area." She looked at me doubtfully. "If you want to."

"If *you* want to," I emphasized "you" in my reply. "I don't know anything about the area around Paris. I've only ever been in the city before." I smiled invitingly at her. "Will you show me the most beautiful parts of the landscape?"

Only now did she let me see how important this trip was to her. "Yes, I'd love to," she beamed.

It really wasn't easy to fulfill a wish for her!

After I found my car again, we drove out toward the south end of the city. When we could see nothing but fields, left and right, she pointed toward a dirt road.

"You can park there. Then we can walk."

I followed her instructions, and we walked right into a small forest. It was as if the huge city of Paris no longer existed, although it was so close. She stood still and breathed it all in.

Her appearance really struck me. She fit in here just as well as she had in the bistro in Paris or in the apartment there. She filled every situation with her charm and beauty. I asked myself what I could possibly offer her. She gave me so much. And I? I could take care of her when she was sick. But she wouldn't always be sick.

Smiling, she turned to face me. "Isn't it lovely here?" She was so relaxed. Her bruises were barely visible now. Of course, she'd put makeup on again, but that couldn't account for it alone. Here, no one threatened her, and she was completely herself. My love for her pained me deep inside. As soon as I knew for sure that she was well again, I'd have to leave her.

I returned her smile. "Beautiful," I confirmed, and I didn't just mean the landscape.

"Come," she encouraged, "let's go for a little walk."

"But not too far," I warned.

She laughed at my concern. "I promise I won't collapse. I'll be careful."

We walked quietly along, side by side. She picked up a twig from the ground and smelled it. Then she bent down to investigate some flowers that were growing in the underbrush.

"You like to be out in nature," I concluded.

"Yes," she explained casually, "I grew up in the country."

"In the country – you?" I asked, totally amazed.

She looked up at me from her crouch. "You thought I was a city kid, right?"

"To be honest, yes. I never would've come to a different conclusion by myself."

Her external appearance really didn't lead one to that thought, either. A woman like her!

"I am now, actually," she said regretfully, looking around. She stood up and brushed the dirt from her hands on her jeans.

"Not entirely." I laughed and pointed at her dirty pants. "I don't think something like that would happen to a city woman." That made her even more lovable!

She looked down at herself and laughed with me. "Probably not. When I'm out here, I never think about things like that." She sighed and looked toward the edge of the woods. "Unfortunately, though, I don't get out here very often."

I went over to her and put my arms around her waist. "But you're here now." I looked up at her. "Let's enjoy it. Where are the prettiest spots?"

Her gaze wandered off to the left. She raised an arm. "There's a clearing back there, completely hidden off in the woods. Sometimes I spend the whole day there, when I have time."

I got the impression that this was a very private place for her. "But that's your space," I objected.

She smiled enchantingly at me. "I'll show it to you."

We walked over to it slowly. The soft ground sprang back under every step. One could walk around here for hours without getting tired. The asphalt of the big city suddenly seemed to me like a completely perverse sensation.

I would never have guessed where we'd find the clearing. If one didn't know exactly where to look, one could walk past it time and time again without ever noticing it was there.

"It feels like we're on the hunt for the treasures of Atlantis," I marveled. "A real adventure!"

"I felt something like that the first time I was here. I found it by pure coincidence. And I have yet to meet another person here." She pushed the last bough aside, and we stood in the middle of what felt like a little natural room.

When I looked up, I saw the treetops waving high above me in the sunshine. The rays streamed down to the ground in a thousand bands of golden light.

"I've seen things like this in photographs," I mused dreamily, "but never in nature."

She looked up as well. "It's like its own little world. Its own sun, its own light. And no people." She let her head fall again and looked over at me. "Except for you and me."

I felt the tension that had suddenly appeared and wanted to remove a little of the intimacy. "Like Eve and Eve," I joked, "without Adam." Where was this supposed to lead? She was still much too fragile.

Apparently, she thought differently. She walked toward me, and then leaned against one of the larger trees. If the snake was this seductive with Eve in Paradise, no wonder she picked the apple!

She reached out her arms. "Come," she said softly.

I couldn't resist her. I had been yearning for her the whole time. She let herself slide down the tree a little, so that she would be the same height as I was. It was as though I was hypnotized by her mouth; I let myself fall into her arms and kissed her.

At first, it was a tremendous relief to touch her at last, finally to be able to kiss her. Then I noticed that her kiss was different than usual. She was kissing me back, but with less passion than experience, and she had enough of the latter that it was hard to tell the difference. I pulled back. "You're in pain," I remarked.

"No," she insisted immediately. She tried to pull me back to her.

I braced myself against the tree trunk. "Yes," I repeated. "You usually kiss differently."

She lifted her face to mine and ran her lips softly across mine.

"It's not good?"

Oh, now I had to watch out! This was drifting in the wrong direction. But I couldn't. Her proximity made me completely defenseless. "Don't," I pleaded. She just looked at me.

I let myself sink forward and I kissed her again. I tried to be careful, but she kept probing deeper. She knew I couldn't resist her kisses. I had told her that myself.

Slowly, she let herself glide down along the tree. The soft forest floor was more comfortable than any bed. She lay next to me. I caressed her thighs, then reached her bottom and let my hand rest there. She began to undress me. When I stroked her again, she started to moan. That reminded me of something.

I pushed gently away from her. "You're acting," I stated conclusively.

"No," she argued immediately. "I want you." She slid her hands under my shirt again, trying to convince me. "Come on, let me. You want it too."

Her hand against my skin should easily have brought me to boiling, but I walled myself off from it. "I want it," I admitted. "I know that. But I can also tell that you're not in the mood."

She pulled her hand away. "That's the worst part," she explained, discouraged. "I am in the mood. But only in my head. My body doesn't feel anything."

"So you are in pain." I knew it.

"Yes," she admitted hesitantly. "But it's really not that bad." She looked at me. "You have to believe me. I really do want you."

When she looked at me that way, I would've believed anything she said! "I believe you," I said honestly, "but that's why you shouldn't put on a show for me. We'll just have to wait."

"But you don't have to wait." She caressed the skin under my shirt again. "Not on my account." Her hand wandered over to my breast. It was as if I had been struck by lightning; I moaned involuntarily. "You won't notice any difference," she assured me.

That brought me back to my senses. I grew angry. But she

couldn't help it. She just wanted to do something nice for me. I controlled myself.

I laid my hands on her shoulders and held her at a distance. "Yes, I know," I said. "You're a professional."

She looked at me with dismay.

"I don't mean that in a bad way," I pacified her. "I know that you have enough experience and skill to bring me incredible pleasure, even when you don't get anything from it yourself."

"I'd love to," she said earnestly.

I smiled at her. "Yes. But for me, it takes two." I gazed at her understandingly. "I'll wait."

"You told me how much you desired me. And I felt it." She hung her head. "I wanted you to —"

"I know," I interrupted her. "But I'll wait anyway." I laughed good-naturedly. "It'll be good practice for me!"

She got mad. "But I want you, too! It's just that this body won't let me!" She punched herself in the thigh. Immediately, she yelped in pain. She wanted to hit herself again.

I held her arm. "Stop it! What are you doing?"

She looked at me with blazing eyes. "How long do you want to wait? Perhaps I'll never be able to feel anything again!"

I gripped her arm more firmly. What was making her so angry? This was a completely natural reaction.

She tried to pull free. "It's her fault!" She yelled angrily, "It's all her fault!"

I was too surprised to think quickly enough. "Who?" I asked automatically.

"Her!" she hissed with all the rage in her being. "You saw her yourself!"

I was too upset to be ashamed at our last uncomfortable encounter. That would come later. "Her?" I asked, horrified. "She did this to you?"

She laughed bitterly. "Not alone, of course. She knew she'd never be able to do it alone." Now I couldn't hold her back anymore. It streamed out of her like a swamp of bile and vitriol. "She came that evening, unannounced again. I was actually already done for the day."

She sat up and wrapped her arms around her knees. "Heaven knows why I even opened the door." She looked over at me. "I have a client who sometimes comes at that time. Maybe I thought it was her." She stared out across her knees again. "At first, they tried to talk me into it. A special threesome – very special. I declined. Then they got more direct. They threatened me. But in my experience, there's usually nothing behind that kind of threat. I'm too tall. That scares most of them away. So at first, I didn't take it seriously. But suddenly, one of them had handcuffs in her hand. The other one held me down, and at that point there was nothing I could do."

She had to take a break. She was obviously reliving it all. She laid her head on her knees and spoke into her lap. "They did everything with me that I wouldn't do for her the last time. They beat me, they raped me." Her voice got softer and softer, until at the end it disappeared completely.

I was completely paralyzed. I'd seen her; I'd seen how she looked. But to hear it from her now and imagine this huge woman in leather before me, hitting her ... And the rape? Could that be the reason why she was completely numb now? That's why she was so angry!

I sat up and took her crumpled body in my arms. I cautiously began to rock her gently. Her body shook. I swayed with her back and forth, back and forth, like a pendulum. Slowly, the shaking got stronger. I couldn't do anything but hold her.

Suddenly, she screamed out, then, painfully whispered: "It hurt so much. It hurt so horribly much!"

I rocked her again. All at once, I felt her tears. She was crying – finally! I let her cry until nothing more would come. She was totally worn out. I lay down on the ground with her and let the warm forest floor do the rest. She fell asleep, completely exhausted.

After an hour, it got too cold to stay on the ground. I woke her carefully. It took her a moment to get her bearings. Disoriented, she looked around and then at me. Then she remembered everything. She sat up higher and leaned against the tree, away from me.

"What did I tell you?" She seemed very protective again. I couldn't blame her. She was afraid.

"Everything," I said quietly.

She covered her face with her hands. "No, not that!" she groaned, horrified.

I stood up and crouched down next to her. Then I took her wrists and pulled them gently away. She hung her head. I kissed her left wrist. The marks were still readily visible. The handcuffs had cut into her so deeply that even the best make-up couldn't disguise her wounds. They hadn't just handcuffed her. They must have tied her to something as well. I felt her agony almost physically. It wouldn't have taken much more for me to moan aloud myself.

I pulled myself together. They hadn't, after all, hit me – I didn't even want to think about the rest – she had had to live through it.

I kissed the other wrist and then the palm of her hand. "Come," I tried to encourage her gently with the tone of my voice, "I'll take you home."

She didn't look up. She held her head low against her chest. I lay down next to her and looked up from below. I saw what she was thinking. "No!" I insisted, dismayed. "You're not ashamed, are you?"

"I never should have told you about it," she mumbled gloomily.

I kneeled next to her. "But it's not your fault!" I bent over and took her in my arms. She let me, but it felt like she was a limp, lifeless doll.

"It's not your fault," I repeated. "You shouldn't be ashamed of what they did to you." How could she ever come to that conclusion?

She still didn't look up. "I am what I am," she whispered self-tormentingly. "With someone else, it wouldn't even have occurred to them to do this."

"I have to doubt that," I countered energetically. This self-defeating, self-deprecating attitude had to come to an end somewhere! "If they had something like that in mind, they would've found a victim anywhere. You or someone else."

She wouldn't let herself be convinced that easily. Her self-esteem was too low. "That's what I'm there for." She was summoning her debating skills.

"That's not what you're there for!" I stood up and yanked her up with me. She cried out in pain. "I'm sorry," I apologized, "but you have to finally wake up."

She looked at me, distraught. Her eyes were still swollen from crying.

"What you told me was absolutely awful, but you are not responsible for it!" I had spoken with great emphasis, but she stood there as if she hadn't heard me at all.

I shook her. She moaned again from pain. I couldn't stand much more of this! I felt it right down to my core. "Do you hear me?" I shouted loud and clear. "It wasn't you. They did it!"

"They did it," she repeated obediently, like a school child. It still sounded like it didn't have anything to do with her personally.

"Yes," I sighed, slightly relieved nonetheless. I took her in my arms again. "Not you. It was them."

"Them," she echoed again, tonelessly. She laid her head on my shoulder. Soon, I felt her tears again. At least she'd gotten that far – she was able to cry again.

I let her rest a little, and then said softly: "Come on, let's go."

Her apathy continued all the way back to the apartment. I sat her in the kitchen and convinced her to eat something. Then I made coffee, and we went into the little salon.

She looked exhausted again, but she didn't want to sleep. Probably, she was afraid of nightmares, now that everything was so fresh in her memory again. We sat and drank our coffee in silence.

"Don't you have to go back to work?" she asked suddenly. Did she want to get rid of me?

"I had this week free anyway," I replied readily. I watched for her reaction. There wasn't any. "If I need to stay here next week, I can call."

"You don't need to stay here." She answered with an expressionless voice, as if none of this affected her at all.

"I'll stay until you're completely healthy." I had already made that decision. Then she could do whatever she wanted!

"I am healthy," she claimed, still without expression.

"I don't believe that." It wasn't easy to make her happy, and it seemed just as difficult to argue with her stubbornness. But I could be stubborn, too! We'd see who was better!

"The doctor said . . .," she began.

I finished her sentence. "The doctor said you should take it easy for another week." If this was taking it easy, this battle with her tormenting memories, I didn't want to see what making an effort looked like!

She sat there in her armchair and looked horribly alone. She didn't respond to me; she probably considered it pointless. I went over to her. I crouched next to her and laid my hands on her knee. I looked at her face, which stared blankly and emotionlessly ahead.

"You're sweet." It was just a simple statement. Another argument seemed unlikely to get anywhere with her at this point. "Did you know that?"

Her gaze moved to me, somewhat uncomprehending. She hadn't expected that.

"Can't you imagine," I explained, "that I enjoy doing this for you?"

She couldn't. I could see that clearly. I tried to hold her attention with my voice.

"You are the most lovable woman I've ever met. You make me feel so good inside. I don't know how I'll ever be able to return the favor." While I spoke to her, I observed her face. It relaxed a little, but the uncomprehending look remained. "I love you and I desire you in a way I've never experienced before in my life." *Aha! Now she'd found a clue.*

She grabbed onto it, though she didn't yet quite understand it. "But you don't want to sleep with me as long as I don't feel anything." She looked at me honestly. This terrain was familiar to her. "Although you desire me."

It was apparent from her facial expression that my willing restraint was still incomprehensible to her. And also, that she thought of this as sufficient grounds for me to leave her.

"Is that so important to you?" How could I get her to see the situation through my eyes, to make this self-explanatory to her?

"But if you can't sleep with me . . . ," she objected uncertainly.

I had to smile. She was so used to this; she couldn't imagine it any other way. "What's left then?" I asked with intentional simplicity.

The consequences were absolute in her mind. "Well, then you can't . . ."

"Then I can't love you either?" I said it for her. "Do you think that my love for you depends on the availability of your body?"

"Yes, of course." She was convinced of that. It came out as though it had been fired from a pistol. She'd hardly said it when her professional conscience took over.

"Didn't you enjoy sleeping with me?" She was truly irresistible when she looked remorseful like that! I had to gulp. "Have I ...?" she added.

"No, you haven't done anything wrong." Defeated, I sighed. By now, I could follow her train of thought in this area perfectly. But there must be some way to convince her. "I like sleeping with you a lot." What kind of question was that? "Why shouldn't I? It's wonderful, sleeping with you. It's new and different every time."

"I have a great deal of experience," she pointed out darkly.

"Yes," I agreed. If she really wanted to go there ..., "you do." I decided to persist along these lines. I laughed in mild embarrassment when something occurred to me. "I was so jealous. I never thought to guess how many women you've already had. I imagine the number is in the hundreds."

"Hundreds." Her voice made that sound criminal.

I looked at her and took her face in my hands. Now she would have to look at me. I entreated her forcibly. "And that's exactly it. I've never felt like the hundredth, rather always like the first."

When she'd switched over to professional mode, it wasn't easy to get her back out of it. "Then I must have been very good," she persisted passionlessly.

"To argue with that would doubtlessly be a shameless lie," I capitulated cheerfully. More cheerfully than I actually felt. "Despite that." I couldn't leave it there. "Or perhaps because of it. I didn't just feel like the first, I felt like the only one." I looked into her eyes earnestly again. "I felt like the woman you love."

That was a hard blow for her. She had convinced herself that she could hide all of her true feelings behind the facade of her experience. Now they were out. Right in the spotlight.

I repeated myself. "You slept with me like with a woman you love."

"No." She denied it automatically, but it didn't quite work. "I ...,"

I provoked her even more. "Say it," I dared her. "Say that you don't love me. If you can't say the opposite, then that should be easy for you."

I let her go. I didn't want to force her into anything else. She knew that too well. But she was going to have to decide for herself how she felt about me. Only then could she understand that I felt at least as much for her and was prepared to put her needs ahead of my wishes.

She looked at me mutely. Her eyes were desperate. She was incapable of expressing what she felt, but she would've loved to do it. She said more with her silence than I would ever have thought possible.

"I can't," she explained after a long while.

I smiled and laid my head in her lap. "I love you too," I said happily.

I sat like that for a while without thinking about anything else. All of a sudden, I felt something touching my hair. She was caressing me. It was a hesitant caress, as if she'd never done it before. Perhaps that was so. I was almost positive that it had been years since she'd caressed a woman without erotic intentions. It had to be a strange feeling for her. I enjoyed it. I didn't feel one bit un-erotic. Just the opposite. But that was now my problem.

She stroked my back with her hands, down to my waist. My skin tingled like crazy, but I tried to stay still. Making great speeches and then not holding oneself to them – I wasn't going to make that mistake!

She left her hands where they were and leaned over my back with her torso. So she stayed, without moving. I felt her, I felt her everywhere, right down to the tips of my toes. It was almost unbearable. But I remembered what she had had to bear and calmed myself a little. Then it began again. I wondered if I had perhaps promised more than I could deliver. I hadn't imagined it would be this difficult.

She was breathing quietly. There was definitely no erotic intention in her movements. Even if she hadn't said so, she'd obviously believed me. Now it was up to me to protect her newly gained trust. I took a deep breath. It wasn't enough. As much as I'd enjoyed lying in her lap again, I couldn't handle it. I pulled away slowly and sat beside her. She sat up.

"I'm sorry." This time, I was the remorseful one. "I couldn't breathe anymore."

She smiled and caressed my face, again completely non-erotically. Then she leaned over and kissed me softly on the lips, again without erotic intentions – at least from her point of view!

"That was very nice," she remarked dreamily.

I stood up and shook out my legs. "They fell asleep!" I said, laughing. That was in fact true, but I knew very well that I was tingling for other reasons, as well.

I stretched my arms in the air, trying to get them back to functioning. "I think I'll go to bed," I yawned. Self-control was really strenuous! I admired her abilities even more.

She stood up as well and stretched carefully. Her muscles would surely still be causing her some discomfort. She winced a little. "Don't you want to sleep with me?" she asked innocently. "The bed is more comfortable than the chaise lounge."

"No doubt." She could be quite a temptress. "But please excuse me." *She couldn't possibly expect that of me.* "It's difficult enough to resist you. Lying next to you in bed would exceed my capacity, I'm afraid. And I really want to keep my promises."

"Oh," she said, "I didn't even think of that." She looked truly innocent.

"Yep." I went over and put my arm around her. That at least was relatively safe.

"And perhaps you also forgot that you're an incredibly attractive woman?" I looked at her inquisitively

She avoided my eyes, as if to confirm my statement. I laughed involuntarily. Most beautiful women were so occupied by their beauty that they'd never forget about it for a moment, but she? She was definitely a wonder.

I leaned against her and took in her scent, which was now mixed with so much else. But her scent was always there. I'd know it anywhere. Regretfully, I stepped away from her.

"I'm going to my chaise lounge now," I told her as casually as possibly. "Please don't be mad at me."

"I'm not mad at you," she smiled. "I'm just sorry."

"Me too." I emphasized my regret with a slightly crooked grin. At that moment, I cursed my heroic streak, which damned me to keep all my promises and, in this case, restrain myself heavily. That was all well and good. But did it have to be right now?

We walked down the hall together, and I passed her bed with deadly contempt. The room in which I slept didn't have its own door off the main hall.

She said: "Good night." I answered, "sleep well," without turning around. When she turned out the light, I shut the door between the rooms. I could make no guarantees that I wouldn't sleepwalk that night.

—— **22** ——

The next few days went by relatively quietly. I called my office and took the next week for vacation. I knew already that there would be no way I could claim she still needed me after that.

She already looked vibrant and lively. She went to the bistro every day; sometimes she even went shopping on the Metro and came back happy and well laden. She almost exclusively bought nonsense, but it was clear that she hadn't done that much before, either. She enjoyed it wholeheartedly. And every time I didn't go with her, she brought me back a little present. In this fashion, I'd already acquired a pair of silk pajamas, though I hadn't worn them except to try them on at her request.

Although I would have liked most not to let her out of my sight, I forced myself to let her go out alone more and more often. She didn't like that at all. But I had to get used to not seeing her all the time. Soon, I wouldn't be able to see her at all. I wanted to lessen the shock of that a little. She just assumed that I wanted to be alone now and then.

When we were both in the apartment, she was very tender and also very open to tenderness. She rarely left me to sit someplace in peace without coming over and caressing me or snuggling with me. She reminded me of a big, cuddly cat. My argument appeared to have convinced her entirely. She no longer felt the need to invite me to sleep with or next to her.

Once, while I was sitting in the armchair and reading – I had, meanwhile, found some lighter reading material for myself as well – she came over and sat on my lap. I tensed all of my muscles to avoid grabbing her immediately and kissing her.

"Yes?" I smiled at her. She shouldn't feel my tension.

"Am I bothering you?" *I wouldn't exactly put it that way!* She was simply indescribably sweet. The longer she was in Paris, the more she relaxed. The daily humiliations that usually kept her down did not exist here. She was a completely different person.

"No," I said with a friendly smile. "Would you like something in particular?"

"Not really." She sighed and leaned against me. I was about to go back to my reading, but she started fidgeting back and forth. "Actually, yes, I do want something," she said, smiling with an enchanting sort of uncertainty.

I raised my eyebrows in a question. "What, then?"

"I don't know if you'll like it." She acted shy and embarrassed.

"Is it that bad?" I asked teasingly.

"No, no." She shook her head energetically. "It's not at all ... Do you like to go dancing?" It burst out of her as though she'd been holding it back for a long time. She looked at me uncertainly again.

I laughed with surprise. "Dancing? Is that all?"

"Yes," she said. It seemed to be very important to her.

"You'd like to go dancing?" I asked her once again.

"Yes," she said, "very much. But only if you feel like it." She still couldn't get used to the idea of putting her own wishes first.

"Fine," I said. "When do you want to go?"

"This evening!" It came out in a blast. She'd been waiting for this. Her whole face beamed.

I gave her a kiss and pressed her to me. I was happy for her, but now she would have to get off of my lap, or else I wouldn't be able to guarantee anything.

There was no need for me to worry about that after all. She leapt up and suddenly began to concentrate on other matters. "What should I wear?"

This question was one that I'd only rarely considered in my life. It had always seemed trivial. So I asked her, "What kind of place is this, where we're going? As far as I'm concerned, you could go out just like you are."

She looked at me and laughed out loud. "Like I am?" In my eyes, she was entirely passable. But I didn't spend much time in discos, either. She laughed secretively.

"I was actually thinking more along the lines of an evening gown."

I almost fell out of my chair. "You have an evening gown?"

"Not just one," she said. She reached out her hand. "Come on, I'll show you."

She led me to her bedroom and opened one of the huge, built-in closets. It was true. She didn't just have one evening gown.

I was completely knocked out by the billowing fabrics and colors.

"Heavens!" I said. "When do you wear them all?"

She sighed. "Unfortunately, much too seldom." She rifled through the rustling silk – what else? – and chose a dress. She held it up to herself. Instantly, I could barely recognize her. And she didn't even have it on yet!

"What do you think?" she asked doubtfully.

"It's gorgeous," I stuttered. I cleared my throat, "Just ..., I'm wondering what I should wear. I didn't expect we'd be going to a ball."

She sighed again. "You're right. We're not, either. I'm afraid the idea of the evening gown wasn't such a good one." She hung it back in the closet and ran her hand over it once more, regretfully. "I would've loved to put one of these on again."

"You must look fantastic all dressed up." I was still wondering at the large selection. "I've never known a woman before who wore evening gowns."

She smiled. "It's an exciting feeling. Too bad that there aren't many occasions for it these days." She grinned a little. "Maybe you should try it once?"

"Me?" I protested ardently. "I don't think that's right for me. I'd feel like I was wearing a costume."

She laughed. "Perhaps you're right."

I looked at her lovingly. I was sure it suited her outstandingly.

"I'm convinced that you'd look stunning in an evening gown. I hope very much that I get the chance to see that someday."

She looked at me and said nothing. Then she shut the closet and turned around. "That's that," she sighed. "And so now we're back to the same question we started with."

An hour later, she had managed to decide what to wear. As always, she looked quite impressive, but I gathered that her clothing was selected so that I wouldn't look too bad. I could still never compete with her. She had put on a little more make-up than usual, but that was nearly all. I was very curious to see what awaited me.

When we entered the place, I was still surprised. In contrast to all similar bars with which I was familiar, I got a sense of dealing with privilege. The Frenchwomen were very well-dressed, and the place had a distinctly feminine flavor. At the front of the room, there was a long bar at which a number of women sat on barstools. There were hardly any open seats. Beyond the bar, there was a deep space set up with tables and small booths. Past that was the dance floor. The whole thing was quite grandiose, but somehow intimate at the same time. Outside the dance floor, the lighting was quite low.

As would likely occur in practically every lesbian bar in the world, all eyes were on us when we first entered the establishment. Although most of the women in the room were expensively dressed and well groomed, she stood out here as well. First it was based on her height, which seemed even more unusual here in France, and then again because of her beauty and her posture. I felt their eyes on my back as we walked past the bar and into the back half of the room.

I'd wondered on the way over whether she'd know many women at this place well, and if so, then how. I simply couldn't shake that thought. My knowledge of her life in Paris was still even more limited than that of her "workplace."

She walked to the back, completely unaffected by the stares, and found a booth. "We're lucky tonight," she laughed. "I wouldn't have liked to stand all evening."

A waitress came over to our table to ask what we would like. She seemed rather scantily clad to me. We ordered something to drink. When the drinks came, I leaned back and watched the women on the dance floor.

The music seemed to fit the surroundings. At the moment, they were playing songs from the fifties – first some rock 'n' roll, then a slow song. The women all appeared to be excellent dancers. That, too, was different from the places I knew.

I was so fascinated by the gliding and swinging, the movements of the dancers, that I almost didn't notice when another woman came up to our table and greeted her. It looked as though they knew each other. The other woman was obviously glad to see her. For a moment, the thought that this could be a client of hers flashed through my head, but her behavior indicated otherwise.

She shook her head, laughing, friendly, but firm. The other woman shrugged her shoulders regretfully, then caressed her cheek with the back of one hand. The local woman turned, begged my pardon, said goodbye, and left.

I sat there, somewhat perplexed. She looked at me and began to laugh softly. "I know I probably look pretty stupid." That's exactly how I felt, anyhow. "But why did she ask for my pardon?"

She laughed, just as amused. "Because she touched me without your permission," she explained knowledgeably.

"Without my permission? What do I have the right to permit?" The connection was not at all clear to me.

"I'm obviously your companion," she stated, as if that would explain everything.

"Yes," I agreed, still irritated, "and I'm yours." I'd never seen anything like this before.

"No," she corrected. "That's not quite true. You take me out, not the other way around."

That didn't mesh with the facts of the situation at all! I must've looked very confused.

She laughed, pleased. "You have the right to decide with which women your companion may dance, and who may touch her, as always."

"I have the right? You've got to be kidding! You're an adult." I was totally outraged.

She enjoyed my indignation visibly. "Been one for some time now," she confirmed. "But that's the custom here."

"Custom!" This didn't bother her? Just the opposite. "You seem to get a kick out of it, somehow!" I scolded some more.

"More out of you," she replied. She had to try hard to keep from laughing. "Because you're so excited about it."

"Don't you find anything wrong with it?" I blazed.

She curbed her laughter a bit. "More than that," she whispered. "I think it's sweet." She gave me a long look. "I think you're sweet." My helpless embarrassment was obviously amusing her royally. "She only touched me at all because she already knew me. Otherwise, she would've asked you first." With pretend innocence, she looked at me and awaited my reaction.

This was all too much for me. The fact that she was clearly having a good time and at the same time making a fool of me didn't seem funny to me at all. I was truly glad for her good mood, but I would rather have enjoyed it with her than have it come at my expense. I declined to respond. However, I would have liked to know how well she knew this woman. Quick as she was, she noticed this.

"I only danced with her," she explained, unsolicited. "Nothing else."

"I didn't want to know that," I replied in annoyance.

"Oh no?" she asked, giggling. She was in the best of moods.

Another woman came over to our table, and this time she adhered strictly to the convention that ruled here. She asked me if she might dance with her.

I almost exploded, but I didn't want to start a fight. Certainly not in French. "Please tell her that she should ask you if she wants to dance with you," I hissed through gritted teeth. The woman looked irritated. She didn't know what my reaction was supposed to mean.

My companion leaned saucily over the table and asked, "Would you mind if I danced with her?"

"No," I hissed, dangerously quiet.

She laughed like satin. That melted me inside immediately, but I'd be damned if I was going to let her see that. "I was actually saving the first dance for you," she remarked lovingly

"I can't dance anyway," I replied, somewhat calmer.

"I don't believe that." She smiled and stood up. The woman who wanted to dance with her was still standing next to us, looking annoyed. "I don't want to be rude, so I'll dance with her now. But the next dance, it's your turn."

"No," I disagreed.

"Yes," she said firmly. Then she offered the poor woman who'd been waiting so long for her an enchanting smile and said something to her.

The woman went with her to the dance floor, pleased.

I observed her. I should've known already but when I watched her now, I was completely bowled over. She danced outstandingly well. Since she was so tall, I would've thought that she would lead. She didn't, though. She followed her dance partner so well that the height difference was barely even noticeable. I asked myself how she did that. They looked like they were the same height.

Her movements were more graceful than ever. She must not have any more pain at all. When the dance ended, her partner wanted to talk her into another. At least that's how it looked. But she declined. Nevertheless, she didn't return to the table alone; instead, the woman who'd taken her out brought her back to me. That was the feeling I had, and it brought my indignation back to the surface.

"That's unbelievable!" I scolded after the woman left.

"She couldn't do otherwise," she explained, grinning conspicuously.

"Yeah, yeah, because that's the custom here," I snarled angrily.

"That too." She winked mischievously at me. "But I also told her you don't like to be crossed." Now she laughed out loud. "And what you'd do if she did."

"You . . .!" I really didn't know what to do with her. This could turn into an interesting evening!

"Come on," she requested, when the music started again. It was a slow song.

"I told you, I can't dance." I could see several women looking in her direction already. She would have no shortage of dance partners. "There are enough women here who would just love to ask you to dance with them."

"I'm not particularly interested in that at the moment," she decided, refusing to indulge me. "I want to dance with you."

"But that won't get you anywhere," I argued with my most sensible voice. "Why do you want to spoil your fun? You're such an incredible dancer."

"Then you can try it for yourself." She tried to talk me into it gently. "I'll show you how it goes."

I raised my hands in defense. "I can't follow a lead! I tried once and failed terribly."

"Then you can lead." She stood next to me and put her hands on my shoulders.

Just the touch by itself softened me, but I still didn't want to give in. "I . . ."

"Come," she ordered me with such a commanding tone of voice that my defenses collapsed. I stood up and followed her blindly.

On the dance floor, I felt completely lost. She took one of my arms and put it around her waist, then raised the other to the height of her shoulders. Then she put her free hand on my shoulder. This looked all right as a dance position, but what was I supposed to do with it now?

She simply began to move. She went backwards, and I had to follow her. It looked like I was leading her, but that wasn't anything close to the truth. During the first few steps, I stumbled a little, but then I realized that she was moving in just such a way as to make things easiest for me. I tried a step in the other direction. She was there right away, as if she had expected it ahead of time.

I listened to the music. With such a slow song, even I could figure out what would come next. Slowly, I got braver. She actually let me lead, even though she could do it a thousand times better. She stood, supple and excited, in my arms. She leaned into me. I felt her whole body against mine. I began to feel warmer than the slow dancing itself could account for. When the dance came to an end, I stepped away quickly.

"Didn't I tell you?" she triumphed, beaming.

The heat let up a little. "Yes," I remarked, still astonished. "It really worked."

The next song began. This time, I led from the beginning. She fit me so well that I felt as if I'd never done anything in my life but danced with her. Even though I couldn't dance at all. However, I could tell that I wasn't going to make it through another dance with her. My whole body was one singular desire. Because of that, I stood firm when she wanted to dance some more.

I pretended to be worn out. "I can't," I claimed. "I'm not used to this."

When it became clear that I wasn't going to dance with her anymore, my replacements appeared everywhere. They practically fought over her. I turned her over to the next woman and went back to the table.

Now she danced to rock 'n' roll. She was boisterous and wild. Several of the women on the dance floor clapped to the rhythm. That song was hardly over when the next one began. Did she have the stamina for this yet? How long would she last? But she looked unbelievably fit. As if her body hadn't experienced the past two weeks at all.

She was going to find out now. I enjoyed seeing her like this and tried not to worry. The women were enchanted by her. There was no break. To rest, there was a waltz. This time, she led. She swept across the dance floor with her partner as if she weren't even touching the ground. Now, she seemed as tall as she actually was.

Afterwards, she excused herself from amidst her admirers and came back to the table. She was a little warm, but that made her even more desirable. From a distance, I'd been able to control my arousal, but when she got this close, my desire flared up with unstoppable strength.

She sat down next to me. Now that too! "In a minute, I'm going to dance with you again," she predicted, overflowing with energy.

"Leave me here," I begged her. "I'd much rather watch you. That's a bigger treat for me." She was conflicted for a moment, but then her desire to fulfill my wishes kicked in.

"All right, then," she said. She leaned over and put her arms around me. She snuggled a little. I tried to ignore the growing heat between my legs and throughout the rest of my body. She stopped again. I took a deep breath, which I hoped she wouldn't notice. It didn't take long before someone came and asked her to dance again. I didn't resist the ritual this time. I just said yes.

While I watched her, I didn't notice at all how the time flew by. Now and then, she talked me into a waltz, and I felt as though I were being swept across the floor exactly as the other woman had looked. Why had I always had trouble following a lead before? With her, it was pure pleasure and completely self-explanatory.

I was constantly afraid that she was going to overdo it, so I kept trying to convince her to take little breaks. I never got her to sit out more than one song in a row, though. She became restless right away. Then I let her go again. The other women kept giving me looks that indicated without a doubt that they considered me to be a spoilsport.

Eventually, I started to get tired. My eyes kept closing, even though her movements on the dance floor made me want to keep them open. She came to the table.

"The closing tango," she stated regretfully. She smiled invitingly. "You have to dance this one with me."

"I'm so tired!" I protested lamely.

She just pulled me up. "No excuses. This is the last dance. You can't refuse me this one."

I'd never danced a tango before, not even in play. But with her, it was again as if I'd never done anything else.

When she bent me back almost to the floor and looked down at me with seductively parted lips, I understood why the tango was such an erotic dance. I wanted her. Here. Now. Immediately. And I couldn't have her.

She stood me up again and laughed. "Too bad," she said sadly, "we have to go now." That would've sounded like a nice idea if it hadn't been for my promise and the cause of her numbness.

The fluorescent lights finally drove us out of the bar. When we reached the door, I realized that it was already dawn. The Parisian streets lay under a grey veil, and a handful of retiring night owls met with the early risers who were already on their way to work.

The street-sweeping trucks from the sanitation department were spraying Paris with water, washing away the dirt of the city. We had to jump over a few small rivers flowing down the gutters as we made our way to the taxi stand. She jumped excitedly from one puddle to the next, and pulled me with her. I could barely keep up. She squealed like a child when she stepped in the water, and kissed me in between on the mouth. She was doing well.

I wasn't so well. I was really tired. That would help when we got back to the apartment. She was still rather wound up. She didn't seem to know the meaning of sleepiness. Though I wanted to go straight to my bedroom when we got back to the apartment, I didn't make it.

"Please dance with me one more time." Her eyelashes batted at me. How could I resist that? She led me into the large parlor. We'd never really used it since I'd been there, but the parquetry floor was of course perfectly suited to dancing.

"But only a waltz or something," I qualified. "I'm really too tired for anything faster."

"No problem." She put on a CD. The sound of a waltz filled the room. She went to the door. "I'll be right back."

I acknowledged her weakly with my hand. I sat in one of the Louis XV chairs and stretched out my legs. When she came back, I would tell her I was going to bed. I was really dog-tired. It took a while before she returned. I was just about to give up and go to bed. If only I hadn't promised her the dance!

I heard a rustling sound, and she stood in the doorway. In an evening gown! No scene from a film could have been more breathtaking. And certainly nowhere in the world an actress who knew how to wear an evening gown as perfectly as she did. I hoped I wasn't staring at her with an open mouth. I certainly couldn't have moved at that moment.

What an idea, to bring out her evening gown now! She came over to me gracefully. Her bare shoulders were perfect. Her walk was seduction itself.

I had to run to bed before the fire that had been building in me all evening burst out. If I broke my promise to her, I'd never be able to look myself in the eye again. Was that possible – a world without mirrors?

My thoughts were all jumbled together in one big heap. The eroticism of the dance, my exhaustion, and now seeing her in this dress that seemed to have been made for seduction . . ., I stood up quickly, before she had quite reached me. It was a good thing that the room was so large.

She stood still and smiled. "Do you like it?"

I had to tear my eyes from her shoulders and her low-cut neckline. I wondered at the fact that dresses like this were legal to wear in public. It seemed to me that many less harmful things were forbidden.

I smiled at her. "You've knocked me unconscious with this dress. I have to gather my wits again. You look simply . . .," I couldn't imagine a word that would convey the overwhelming impression she made on me, "fantastic."

"Thank you." She accepted the compliment in her usual polite manner.

"Then it was worth it for me to change clothes."

"It was." I was still having trouble with my grasp of language.

She came closer. "Would it bother you to lead? In this dress . . ."

I understood. It just didn't fit. She wanted to savor the feeling. I made a joke to hide my insecurity. "If you don't mind running into the furniture."

She laughed her satiny laugh. "I trust you." The next waltz began. This time, she did nothing. She left everything to me. I took her in my arms and had to take a deep breath. No more barriers between us! I wasn't used to the dress. I began to dance with her, and as always, she followed perfectly. The dress swung around her and emphasized her movements. My mind crumbled. I couldn't dance with her like this anymore! It could only lead to one thing. But I couldn't let go of her, either. One dance – just one dance! I swung her around, and she followed willingly. I really did lead her right by the furniture, despite the size of the room. Now I understood why the ballrooms in old mansions were so enormous. With these dresses, that was the absolute minimum.

I enjoyed it more and more. The silk was thin, although it rustled so much. I felt her thigh clearly against mine. It was an exciting feeling, just like she'd said. I had always thought that dresses like this were, except for the plunging necklines, quite conservative. I could no longer claim that. On the contrary, they offered just the right combination of hidden nakedness, of secretive borders between cloth and skin, indirect and for that reason doubly erotic.

I couldn't stop when the music changed. I swept into it with her – I was fully aware that this was more her decision than mine – and wished that I'd never have to let go of her, except for one reason: to help her out of the dress. The closeness of her body and the way we moved together as we danced increased my arousal even more. If I didn't stop now, I was going to carry her off to bed soon, with or without the dress!

The waltz ended, and I spun her around where we stood. She leapt into the air in enthusiasm. I caught her, breathing heavily, and then let go of her when her feet were solidly back on the ground.

She gasped a bit for air herself, and then looked at me, beaming with joy.

"What was it you said: you can't dance?"

I demurred. "You know very well that you did most of the work. That's why it was so easy for me."

She laughed freely. "Yes, sometimes it was a little difficult for me to follow you. You make that little half-step with which I'm not familiar."

"You see," I let out a humble sigh, "and I didn't even notice that."

She looked me right in the eyes. "I enjoy letting you lead me." Oh, boy! There was something lurking in there! Her eyes glittered seductively.

"I won't do it," I tried to convince myself.

She acted as though she hadn't understood me. "What won't you do?"

"I won't sleep with you as long as you don't get anything from it." If she really had to hear it again!

"Who told you it's like that?" She bent over and kissed me. Passionately. Aroused.

But I wasn't sure. She'd betrayed herself once before. She never made the same mistake twice. Certainly not in her job.

She pulled back a little and looked at me. She was breathing heavily. The dress emphasized that even more. I could see how her breasts rose and fell.

I rested my hands on her bare shoulders. "Please," I begged her.

"Don't take revenge on me for this evening. Not like this."

She looked at me without comprehension. Then she understood. "Is that what you think?" She didn't seem annoyed.

"I don't know," I stopped, uncertain, and hesitated, "I only know that I couldn't take it if you acted something out for me."

"And if that's not what I'm doing?" She ran her lips gently over my cheek.

"That's what I'm not sure about," I replied honestly, although her touch was sending lightning through my whole body. "You come up with the strangest ideas when you want to thank me for something."

Now she stopped. She laughed softly. "Strange?"

"Well, yeah." She knew exactly what I meant. I looked at her helplessly. "I don't want you to do it for me. Please . . ."

She said nothing. She looked at my face. I couldn't read her expression. Slowly, she bent forward. Her lips came closer and closer. She kissed me very lovingly. Her tongue entered my mouth tenderly. She stroked the tip of my tongue with hers and I began to moan. She caressed my lips from the inside once more, and then she pulled back.

"You want it too," she concluded happily.

My knees were shaking. "Of course." I gasped for breath and was completely confused. "That's not the question." *This was all up to her!*

"Yes," she contradicted, "it was for me. You've been very reserved for a while now."

"I promised you I would," I replied, not quite understanding what she was after.

She laughed tenderly. "The fact that you always keep your promises has started to get just a little irritating."

"Why? What else are promises for?" And it had been difficult enough for me as well!

She pressed her cheek against mine and sighed. "How clear that is to you. I'm just not used to it. I thought you didn't want me anymore. You never reacted. Not even this evening. Until now."

I laughed, amazed. "I didn't want you? I wanted nothing else the whole time. But I won't do anything if you don't get anything from it." I looked at her probingly "You can seduce me any time you want. You should know that. I can only resist you when I keep my distance." I had to laugh. I held one hand up between us. "Not at this distance, anyhow!" I took the hand away again and wrapped my arms around her shoulders. I pulled her close to me. "I want you. I want you so much," I whispered in her ear.

The dress rustled. I'd never heard a more erotic sound in my life.

She pressed her whole body against mine and stood that way. "I want you too!" Her voice had suddenly taken on a desperate tone. "If only I could convince you of that! I yearn for you. It really hurts. But you always think I'm acting."

I loved her so much. And I wanted so much to believe her. I kissed her shoulders and let my mouth wander to her neck. I felt her pulse beating against my lips. I changed direction and glided down toward her breasts. Her breathing grew heavier. The edge of the dress stopped me. I turned back up and sought her mouth. She was more than ready. I leaned my head against the wall. She pushed inside with her tongue and kissed me with more desperation than before. She dug her fingers into my hair. "Believe me, please!" she whispered into my mouth.

I couldn't think about anything other than the fact that I desired her. I needed her touch, her kisses, her body, her devotion, which was so sweet. What should I do with all my love if I couldn't give it to her? I didn't want to have any more doubts about that; I didn't want to know it anymore. I wanted to give myself to her, to entrust myself to her experienced hands that could bring out every feeling I could wish for. I capitulated.

"Convince me." *How could I resist my own desire any longer?*

"I will, if you let me." She entered my mouth again and kissed me with such passion that it would've overcome any resistance I could possibly have offered. Her hands ran down along my body. I moaned. I wanted her to undress me. She didn't.

I caressed her shoulders. She shivered. I ran my hands across her naked back. Now, she moaned.

When I reached the edge of the dress, I wondered why jeans had ever come into fashion. The transition from her skin to the silk of the dress was the most erotic thing I'd ever felt. I searched for a zipper. She laughed quietly into my shoulder. "It doesn't have one."

The surprise brought back my capacity for logic. "How do you put it on, then?"

"It has hooks," she explained.

I sought them with my fingers and found them. They were innumerable.

"Oh, my goodness!" This could take hours!

She laughed softly again. "You only have to undo a few of them, not all of them."

It wasn't very easy to figure out the mechanism of the things. Once I had it, I began to open one after the other. I reached under the cloth with my hand and caressed her. She moaned again. Actually, I didn't want to remove the dress too quickly It was exciting to keep switching back and forth from the cloth to her skin. The similarities and differences became more and more apparent. Her warmth and the coolness of the silk, her softness and the flowing firmness of the dress. I didn't want to stop. Her moan became deeper and deeper. I undid nearly all of the hooks and caressed the skin on her back from her neck to her waist.

"I never should have put it on." Her voice sounded a little forced.

I stopped caressing her, surprised. "Why?"

She gasped for breath, now that she was free of the stimulation for a moment. "I should have remembered. You have a silk fetish."

"Me?" *Who was the one who slept in silk pajamas on silk sheets?*

"Yes, you," she repeated, calmly and without moving. "Without my bathrobe, I never would've had a chance with you."

She had me! I laughed. "Before I met you, I hardly even knew what silk felt like. Especially against the skin of a woman."

She leaned back in my arms and looked at my face. "Wouldn't you like to know what the woman under the silk feels like, too?" Before I could answer, she took an elegant step backwards. The dress fell to the floor.

"Do you ever wear anything underneath?" I asked saucily, remembering the beginning of our relationship.

She remembered it as well, of course. "With you?" She laughed seductively. "That would be pointless, now wouldn't it!"

When she saw the wild look on my face, she took off running toward the bedroom. I chased after her. I caught her right in front of the bed and tackled her. We landed together in the middle of the mattress.

I looked at her. There was nothing lascivious about her naked-ness. Her beauty overcame me anew. "Aphrodite herself could never compare with you." I felt almost helpless in her presence.

"Now!" she denied with firmness, "you're really exaggerating things!"

"There are no exaggerations in love," I explained earnestly. "And I love you."

That was again the point at which she could say nothing more. She looked at me briefly; then she turned away.

I rolled over next to her and took her in my arms. I snuggled up against her. "I don't require anything of you for that," I told her, "only that you accept it."

"I can't do that," she replied, expressionless.

"I hope that will change someday." I turned her carefully onto her back. "I love you," I repeated. I wanted to kiss her gently, but she wouldn't allow me to. Instead, she threw her arms around my neck and pulled me down on top of her. Her kiss wanted proof that my words were true. I gave it. I no longer had any doubt that she want-ed me. And I wanted her.

The full strength of the passion that had been dammed up for the previous hours broke loose. She sighed in my mouth. We rolled from one side to the other across the bed, sometimes coming very close to the edges. I was still dressed, but that obviously didn't bother her. It did bother me a little. But she didn't give me a se-cond free.

Her wild passion aroused me incredibly. I held her tightly and took her nipples between my lips. They were so hard my tongue could play with them like little marbles. I ran back and forth across them. She writhed in ecstasy beneath me. I caressed her down to her stomach with my hands. She moaned loudly and thrust her hips against me. I left her breasts and let my mouth follow the path my hands had made. She was practically screaming with lust. I ran my lips along the inside of her thigh. She dug her fingers into my hair and pressed my head between her legs. She let go and lay very still for a moment. All I heard from her was heavy breathing.

"Please …," it was very weak. I touched her clit with the tip of my tongue, very gently. She jerked. "Please," she whispered even more desperately. "Don't make me wait any longer."

I let my tongue circle her center. She was well beyond simple arousal. At every touch, she thrust high into the air and collapsed again. Then, at last, she cried out her lust and lay, still; exhausted.

I propped myself up slowly and regarded her. I covered her up. Then I stood up and took off my clothes. I slid under the blanket and could finally savor her warmth against my bare skin. When I snuggled up against her, I felt her even breathing. She was asleep. Soon after, so was I.

I awoke to something tickling me. She was caressing me with a feather.

"Ooh." Pleasant tingles coursed through me.

"Does that tickle too much?" she asked attentively.

"I'll tell you after you've done it for a while," I answered with relish. She continued.

Laughing softly, she asked some time later, "Doesn't it tickle yet?"

"Mmm," I answered like a true connoisseur.

"Not here, either?" She tickled me boldly between the legs.

I twisted around and tried to escape her. "Yes, right there," I giggled.

"Wonderful." The result seemed to please her. I'd gotten an entirely different impression of the situation. Expectantly, I watched her movements. She caressed me some more, now switching back and forth from her hand to the feather. I always reached for the hand and tried to avoid the feather. Every time, she increased the level of stimulation. My skin prickled; the heat inside me had reached the boiling point. I moaned.

"What are you doing to me?" She touched me with the feather. I jerked again.

She set the feather aside and entered me. I let out a throaty sound. She left her fingers where they were and rose to kiss me. She caressed me inside. Both together drove me forcefully to a climax. I exploded without warning.

She observed me and smiled lovingly. When I lay still, satisfied, she remarked, "It's too bad that you can't see yourself doing that. You're beautiful."

I didn't know what to say to that. "Every woman is beautiful at that moment," I replied.

She laughed. "Certainly not!" I could hardly contradict her there, given her experience. She kissed me softly on the lips. "But you are," she said tenderly.

"Thank you," I said – this time it was my turn to be polite. Nothing else at all occurred to me.

"I think it comes from within," she mused.

I looked at her. *I think it comes from the fact that you love me*, I thought, but I didn't say it aloud. Sometime she was going to have to deal with that. If I was still there.

—— **23** ——

Unable to sleep from my love for her, I lay awake. I watched her sleep next to me. The nearer our goodbyes came, the worse it got.

Lost in thought, I watched the moonlight play across her face. It would still caress her long after she'd forgotten me. Very carefully, I stroked her hair. She blinked.

"I didn't want to wake you." I spoke softly. Perhaps she wasn't all the way awake and could go right back to sleep.

"Hm." It sounded like a confirmation.

It looked as if her eyes were tiny, deep lakes reflecting the light of the moon. Why did love have to hurt so much? I turned over onto my back and tried to put up walls against my emotions.

"What is it?" She wasn't quite awake. Her voice sounded sleepy.

I did everything I could not to show my feelings. "Nothing. I'm sorry I woke you. Go on back to sleep."

"You were caressing me," she remarked, much more clearly.

"Yes," I admitted remorsefully. I thought she had been sleeping much more deeply. I repeated, "I'm sorry."

"You're sorry that you caressed me?"

"No, that I woke you." Why couldn't she just go back to sleep?

"Something's up with you." Amazing how quickly she became alert and coherent when she woke up. Apparently, she didn't only do that in the morning, but in the middle of the night as well. I'd never understand how she did that.

"I'm going back tomorrow." She rolled over onto her back and put her hands behind her head. "That had to happen eventually," she said quietly.

"Yes, sure." Her unexpectedly calm reaction threw me for a loop, since I'd been preparing myself for something completely different. But if she could stay calm, so could I. Maybe it wasn't such a big deal to her as it was to me. After these days of tenderness and love – even if she refused to call it that – I had anticipated something else, but she was still a mystery to me in so many ways. Her feelings were her deepest secret, which she didn't like to share. For that reason, I could rarely tell how she really felt. I only hoped that it was the same thing I would feel in that situation, or at least something similar. She lay there, still saying nothing. I at least wanted to know one thing. "Do you want to . . ., are you going to stay here?"

"Yes," she answered immediately, "for a few more days, most likely."

I looked over at her. The moonlight made her face glow. Strong contours made themselves visible: her forehead, her nose, her mouth. That wonderfully curved mouth that could kiss so perfectly! It captivated me magically.

A paralyzing fear struck me suddenly. What would the situation be now? She couldn't possibly just go back to work! The danger of something like this happening again, as it had happened already, was too great.

And she would simply refuse to take that danger into account. She was so good at repressing and minimizing everything, especially when it came to her person. That hurt. My body tensed. I would be there, but I couldn't protect her. And the next time could be even worse than the last.

"No!" I'd spoken out loud from the sheer tension.

She turned her head. "What, no?"

I could no longer hold it in. "I'm afraid. I'm worried about you," I explained laboriously.

"Worried? Why?"

I knew this would draw her wrath, but now that it was out, I had to take the opportunity and run with it. "Do you want to go back to work?"

She turned her head away. I saw her profile turn to a stony mask. "I knew you would get around to that eventually." Her controlled voice indicated that she was absolutely furious.

"Not how you think," I corrected quickly, even if that wasn't quite the whole truth. "I don't want to stop you, only . . ."

She stared straight up at the ceiling. "Only?" It sounded completely uninterested. But I knew that that couldn't be the case.

"Only . . . I'm horribly afraid for you." I gulped. "That something like this could happen again." After all, she couldn't deny the facts of what had already happened.

Her eyes continued to stare at precisely the same spot. "It won't." She minimized the event exactly as I had predicted she would. "That doesn't happen every day."

Not every day – heavens! "But the danger is there," I insisted. How could she live with the thought, how could she imagine opening the door and not knowing what awaited her?

"Then I couldn't go back to my profession at all," she concluded calmly.

Yes. Please! I would gladly have implored her to do so, if I'd seen any sense in it whatsoever. But now . . .? I said nothing.

"You'd love that, wouldn't you?" She spoke my thoughts aloud, completely without expression.

"You know that as well as I do," I said softly.

"Yes. I know that." Her calmness was frightening. "I knew from the moment I first saw you that you'd never be able to live with it."

I propped myself up on one elbow and looked at her face, to the extent that I could see it. "I wish so much that I could." My desperation grew "I love you so much." That was precisely the reason! "I don't know how I'll live without you." Now I'd said it.

But she'd been expecting that already. "You don't want to see me anymore." That statement would've sounded harsh anyway, but her voice made it even worse. She was relentless.

"No!" It was almost a shout. "I want to see you. Every day, every minute, every second. And that is exactly the problem."

"You can't have me all to yourself," she stated, still horribly calmly. It was more awful than anything I'd imagined. She said everything aloud that I'd feared the whole time.

I let myself fall back into the bed. "I know."

"So you'd rather not have me at all." Her voice hovered tonelessly in space.

If only I could claim that wasn't true! That I wanted her under any circumstances. But I couldn't do that. "If only things were different! If we could change places . . ."

She let out a hollow, resigned laugh. "Hardly."

I wanted to touch her, to hold her, to forget that this would be the last time. I leaned over her and brushed her shoulder.

She turned her head and looked at me. "I . . .," she stopped.

I could've bet she wanted to say I love you, but she couldn't. That was her flaw.

Mine was my jealousy, but hers hindered her just as much from doing what she wanted.

She turned her body, bathed in moonlight, slightly toward me. That movement alone made me crazy with longing. I sought her mouth and kissed her. Her lips responded immediately. She had the same wish as I: to forget everything and enjoy our last moments together. I caressed her breast. She moaned. The nipple was hard in my hand. I stroked her skin all the way down to her thighs. She writhed passionately.

"Lie on top of me," she whispered throatily, "I want to feel all of you."

I pushed myself on top of her, until I could feel her everywhere. Her skin was hot and dry. She moved her hips beneath me, as though I were almost weightless. I felt the heat between her legs.

I pressed hard against her, out of anger at myself, out of desperation. Why? I cried inside. *Why couldn't I just take her as she was, with everything that went with that? Was this really love? Love doesn't ask questions, does it?* I didn't know anything anymore. My thrusts grew harder.

She put her hands on my hips. "Please," she said softly. "You're hurting me."

I stopped abruptly and laid my head heavily on the pillow next to hers. I breathed her in. Yes, it was love, I knew it. I loved her and I wanted her, but still . . .

"You can't fuck it out of me," she remarked sensibly.

I was ashamed of myself. She'd caught me. Then I had to grin against my will. "I didn't know you knew words like that." I qualified that, "Privately, I mean."

She was obviously happy that we were back to our old selves for the moment. "I don't," she joked back, "that must've slipped through." She let her hands wander from my hips to my back. I shivered. My persisting shame made room for another feeling.

"Although," I said lightly into her ear, "there's something to it. It makes me sort of . . ."

She laughed understandingly. At the same time, she began to circle her hips slowly below me. ". . . horny?" she completed my sentence.

Oh, boy, where was she going with this? That didn't sound like her private side at all! "Yes," I said distastefully. "That's the word. But we should stop this now."

"We don't have to," she offered obligingly and professionally. "I can say anything you'd like to hear."

Would I ever get her off of this trip? I lifted myself up high and let my entire weight fall on top of her. The wind was knocked out of her, and she panted. "Was that necessary?" She at least allowed herself a hint of indignant protest.

"I was about to ask you the same thing."

"Oh!" She was upset.

"Mm-hmm," I confirmed.

"I'm sorry." She sounded unsure.

I looked down at her. "It was my fault. I never should've started with that."

She began to turn under me again, but this time I had the feeling that she really wanted it. She snapped at my lips and nibbled on them. "At the moment, I really just want to be the woman of your wishes." She came very close to my mouth with her lips again. "All of your wishes." She kissed me. Her kiss was so fiery, I wished it would never stop.

When she finally let me go again, I gasped for air.

"That was my revenge," she said, grinning. She seemed to be her private self again.

Why did we have to break up? Why was that? I had to chase those thoughts away. I looked at her earnestly. "You are everything I've ever wished for. You're my dream woman."

She tried to turn away, but I was lying on top of her and so she couldn't. She had to look at me.

"Never say that again," she hissed.

"How can I not say it?" The prospect of a future without her saddened me deeply. "We're never going to see each other again."

That brought back the desire in her and in me. We were both at the ends of our ropes. My head was too heavy to hold up. I let it fall back on the pillow next to her.

"Why does it have to be like this?" I asked quietly.

She ran her hands along my back. "Fate," she concluded dejectedly, "we can't help it." Her hands glided down to my bottom and pressed me against her. Her heat was there once more. "I don't want to think about that anymore." She breathed heavily. "I just want you."

My arousal sprung right back up. She did something very special with her movements beneath me. I could hardly hold myself up above her. I let one leg slide between hers. The sensations she caused with her passion became unbearable, and I began to move in synch with her rhythm. She stroked my back again. My skin prickled as if it were stuck by needles.

She found my mouth again and kissed me. Her tongue drove me higher with every caress. I moaned out loud. I felt the heat climbing inside. *Almost* . . . She stopped kissing me and suddenly lay very still.

"What . . .?" I gasped, confused.

"Not so fast," she teased me.

I propped myself up next to her. "Are you insane?" I was still having a hard time breathing. The heat was subsiding very slowly. "I was almost there!"

"Yes, I noticed that." She laughed softly. Then she let the smile fade slowly from her face. "I want to turn over." Her voice was suddenly raw and excited.

I didn't understand. "Turn over how? On your stomach?" That wasn't exactly her favorite position! I wondered what was going on.

"No," she remarked impatiently. "But you have to let me up first." She laid her hands on my shoulders and pushed me away a little. I let myself slide off of her.

She really did turn over, but not like I'd thought. She traced a path across my stomach with her mouth. At the same moment, her navel appeared before my eyes. An unusually attractive navel, as I'd noticed many times before – though perhaps not quite from this angle.

I stretched out next to her and nibbled at the skin above her triangle with my lips. She was already a bit further along. I felt her between my legs. Along the inside of my thigh, she traced her tongue down to the back of my knee. When she reached it, I almost went wild. I moaned. "I had no idea my knees were such erogenous zones." Aroused to my limit, I could only pant.

"Most people don't know that." She laughed sensually.

I concentrated on her navel again. First, I traced its edge with my tongue; then, I wandered slowly inside.

She shuddered. "That's not exactly un-erotic, either," she gasped.

"In this position, everything is erotic." One could certainly say that.

She sighed with satisfaction and dove into the backs of my knees once more before working her way back up my inner thighs. I held her hips tightly so she couldn't slip too far up. I wanted her most sensitive places well within reach of my tongue. I felt her coming nearer and nearer to my favorite spot. I let my lips wander across her mound. She moaned and tried to escape my mouth. I held her still.

"You needn't . . .," she objected nervously.

"Mm-hmm," I murmured with my mouth already halfway between her legs. Then I pulled away for one last moment. "I always do a 69 so that only one partner gets anything out of it."

"I just meant that . . ." *Always such a discussion when she was afraid she might get something out of it!*

I pushed my tongue over her mound of Venus. "Come on," I

whispered excitedly, "don't talk so much."

Her bottom tensed, as I got closer to her center. She did the same to me. I tried to hold my legs still, but I couldn't. She couldn't control her hips any longer, either. I felt the tip of her tongue at my gate. We entered one another at the same time. I felt how her moaning reverberated through my whole body. She must have felt the same thing. I wasn't exactly quiet myself.

Her tongue inside of me was at least as arousing as it was to taste her at the same time. I concentrated on her. After a while, I couldn't any longer. I had to concentrate on myself. She halted her caresses. "Not again!" I moaned torturously.

"No." She laughed softly. Her sensuous voice drove me up another level. She entered me again. This time, she stroked deeper with her tongue. I could barely even move anymore, I was so completely aroused. I couldn't get enough air. Suddenly, a flood of feelings overcame me. I didn't even feel them coming. I didn't have enough breath left to cry out, but I had to. I couldn't take it anymore. She caressed me with her tongue, refusing to let me rest. "Stop," I groaned. "I can't take anymore."

She stopped long enough to say something. I collapsed. "I'll stop at two dozen. Understood?"

She began to suck on my clit. I exploded immediately. "Oh, no!"

"Oh, yes," she replied, laughing. "You're halfway there already."

I surrendered. When she wanted to, she could really be more than demanding. I moaned again. As long as the exertion felt like this . . .!

I didn't count, but eventually I reached two dozen or she was otherwise satisfied. I collapsed as if I'd just run a marathon. She lay still and snuggled her head between my legs. It still tickled sweetly.

There was one thing I definitely wasn't going to do for her now: fall asleep! I rested for a minute, and then remembered her belly in front of my face. I ran my lips over it.

She jumped. "What are you doing down there?"

"Guess," I replied cheekily.

"You're exhausted." Her voice sounded sweetly concerned.

"You'd like that, eh?" She couldn't have expected that, after her treatment, I would only be able to move my tongue. But I could! I didn't even wait for her to recover from her surprise. I pushed my tongue between her legs and listened to her moan. "How many would you like?" Revenge is sweet! "Three dozen?"

"No!" She dug into my thigh.

"We'll see." I played around with the idea of never letting her come down from her orgasm. At first, it seemed that she wanted me to try to talk her into it at least, but then she parted her legs and gave herself over to me. She moaned without interruption. I couldn't have counted even if I'd wanted to. She seemed to be up on a plateau the whole time.

"Let me ... please ...," she beseeched me. Her voice was barely audible. I stopped soon after. She thought it was over. I waited a few moments. Then I entered her again and stroked her back to the top with my tongue.

She moaned. "Darling!" That's what I wanted to hear! I let her go and snuggled up to her lap, like she had done with me. We fell asleep just like that.

—— **24** ——

I packed my things. She stood in the doorway, leaning against the doorframe, arms crossed and watching me, expressionless. I wished with everything I had that I were already on the road. At the same time, I wanted to put off the separation as long as possible.

Finally, I was finished. I looked at her. I could've bawled. There was no reason for this. We both wanted each other. Nonetheless, we had no choice. Despite her motionless face, I could feel the tension in her as though it were my own.

I went to the door. I didn't dare touch her anymore. That would push me over the edge. I opened the door. She came after me, first hesitantly, then with long, fast steps. She took me in her arms. I stood there, desiring nothing else.

"Stay with me," she whispered, choking on her tears.

I let my suitcase fall and hugged her back. I pressed myself against her, wanting to feel her one last time. "I can't." I spoke into her shoulder. I smelled her. I could almost taste her. I wanted her more than anything in the world. I tore myself away, grabbed my bag, and ran down the stairs. Tears poured down my face. I didn't look back.

The drive home went by as though I were in a trance. I pulled onto the turnpike, paid the toll, and drove on. I grew calmer with every mile I put between us.

I'd found the love of my life and lost her again. *No big deal, right? Happens to everyone.* I couldn't kid myself. I knew I'd never experience anything like this again. It would always be my happiest, and at the same time my saddest, memory. After I arrived home, the first thing I did was unplug my telephone. I didn't want to see or speak to anyone. I unpacked my bag, put my laundry in the washing machine, and gathered up the mail that had already begun to overflow from my mailbox onto the landing. The ordinariness of these activities allowed me a few minutes of rest.

I drew myself a bath and lay in the hot water. That had always been relaxing and calming for me. One of my favorite activities. The physical relaxation did come. But when I tried to empty my head, as usual, I found far too many thoughts. No, there was only one thought: her.

I remembered how she'd lain in the bathtub in Paris. About how I'd felt seeing her there. In addition to the heat of the water warming me from the outside, I began to feel a new heat growing inside. That would pass. In time . . . I would get to know other women, I'd sleep with them; they'd chase the memories away. Maybe I'd live with one of them. That was my future, not a future with her. Perhaps I'd remain alone instead. That situation seemed the most desirable to me at the moment. If I couldn't have her, the difference didn't seem that great.

And sex? You, my nasty little sex drive, can't you just leave me in peace? Do you think that all your wishes just come true, like that?

No. No, of course not. But what could follow her? Sex with her was an unbelievable experience. I couldn't get that memory out of my mind. I imagined I was feeling her hands against my skin. I sighed. The stirring in my belly was so real, as was the tingling of my skin. I rubbed the spot with my hand to make it go away. I shouldn't have done that!

The gentle caresses of the warm bathwater increased my sensitivity a little more. I needed it even more. I saw her face before me, her lips parting slowly. I yearned for her to come to me. I pretended she was there, her hands gliding through the water between my legs. I closed my eyes. I knew it wasn't her, but I summoned up all of my fantasies to imagine that it was a different hand – hers – that stroked me. I moaned as the sensations flowed over me.

I didn't need to command my hands. They worked by themselves. They danced across my breasts. In the water, my nipples stood up quickly. A red-hot arrow of desire shot up between my legs. I let one hand glide downward. I saw her bending over me. As I touched myself, she touched me. I moaned her name. I couldn't stop. I wanted to summon her presence somehow. I slid deeper down in the tub and writhed with arousal. Water splashed over the sides. My strokes grew faster. I tightened and moaned aloud. "My darling." I let my hand lie between my legs, savoring the feeling a little. I lay deep in the water. I almost fell asleep. I opened my eyes. I pulled my hand away. With my eyes open, it was only my hand. And this was nothing more than masturbation.

Was this it? Was this my future? It had never bothered me before. I'd always enjoyed it, when I was alone and had the inclination. It didn't matter if I had a girlfriend at the time or not. But now the prospect seemed entirely shallow.

I would just have to get used to it.

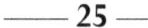

— **25** —

I became a hermit again for a while, compensating for my frustration with work. But this time it was different. I knew it was over. There was no going back. I wasn't angry with her or with myself. We hadn't broken up due to a fight. I was simply numb.

I plugged my telephone back in. I laughed when someone told me a joke. I scolded my colleagues when they made poor management decisions. I swore out loud when a project didn't turn out as I'd planned. But really, none of that affected me. My emotions seemed to be locked up in a little box. Between the outside world and me there was an unscalable, impenetrable wall. Perhaps not such a bad thing. My head and my body felt like they were packed in Styrofoam most of the time.

Evenings, when I came home, I cleaned my apartment automatically. It had never been so neat. Everything was in its place. No book lay askew; I had no dirty laundry; no CD was left out of its case or in the player.

I didn't read. I didn't listen to music. When I'd put away my groceries and my dust cloth, I just sat there until I got sleepy. Then I went to bed and slept without dreaming. I had no doubt that I would go on like this forever, but I didn't even feel the need to wish for something better. Life was simply dreary. Hadn't it always been that way?

A few days after my return, I thought about her suddenly. Would she be back by now? The probability seemed great. But what did that mean? I let that thought fall into a black pit and bolted the door behind it. Another few days later, I was sitting in my office, grumbling over a project report. The telephone rang. I picked it up and said absently, "Yes?"

"I can't do this anymore," she said.

I sat up stick-straight in my chair. "Don't!" I whispered defensively.

Her voice sounded choked. "I long for you so much. I can't sleep. And I can't ..., I have to see you!"

"That's not possible," I said. "That would only make it worse." I felt it already. My wall had collapsed with one blow

"It can't be any worse than it already is," she said tiredly.

"Yes, it can," I squeaked with iron will. I would have liked most to rush over to her. "Please, don't call me again. We're only tormenting each other this way." I hung up without waiting for her reply.

I took a long time to recover from that phone call. The afternoon passed me by. Toward evening, I had convinced myself that everything was all right again. She wouldn't call me anymore. That wasn't her style. She would have to live with it just as I did.

I went shopping and then home. When I arrived there, I saw her sitting on the steps in front of my apartment. I wanted to turn around, groceries in one hand and keys in the other, but where was I supposed to go? I climbed the last flight of stairs. She stood up. Two steps above me, she was more than half a body's length taller.

I looked up at her. "There's no point to this," I told her feebly.

"Please." She didn't speak, she begged.

I walked past her and unlocked the door. She didn't move. I turned around and looked at her. "Come in," I sighed, "at your own risk."

She followed me in and shut the door behind her. I went into the kitchen. "Would you like a cup of coffee?" I called back into the hall as I put the kettle on. "Now that you're already here."

She came over and stood in the entryway to the kitchen. The doorway framed her like a portrait. She didn't seem to want to answer.

I indicated the rocking chair. "Please, have a seat. I can't stand to have you milling around like that." My nerves were already exposed. I held my equilibrium by a thread, maintaining it only through the mundane task of making coffee.

She did what I told her. I tried to act as though this were a completely normal visit. I sat across from her, with the table between us. I could already tell that this distance would not suffice for long. Her charm was already putting a spell on me.

"Where is this supposed to lead?" I asked, as calmly as I could manage.

She hung her head, and her voice was barely audible. "I don't know."

She looked up. For a moment, I thought I saw tears in her eyes, they were so red and blurry. "I only know that I need you." Need, not love. Even now, she was incapable of speaking it aloud.

I propped my chin up with my hands. "You know that won't work. We'd drive each other insane."

"And what are we doing now?" She had a strong point, although her voice still sounded weak.

We had certainly come to the same conclusion in our estimations of the situation. I had to agree with her there. "Yes, you're right. But that will pass. We just have to give it time."

"How long, do you think?"

Was she trying to convince me, or herself? How long would it take until we were so numb that we no longer felt any desire? Until, perhaps, we felt nothing at all?

"How should I know?" Abysmal desperation overcame me.

"I've missed you so much." The tenderness in her voice rendered me defenseless.

I buried my head deeper in my hands. "Please," I begged her, "don't do this!"

She got up and came over to me.

"No," I said. She stood behind my chair and leaned forward. Her hands slid over my arms. On my back, I could feel her breasts. She sighed.

"It's so nice to feel you," she whispered in my ear.

I pushed my yearning back. "We mustn't do this. Then everything will start over again from the beginning."

"Not from the beginning," she corrected, "from now."

"What's the difference?" I asked, resigned.

She said nothing. Her hands glided over my belly and unbuttoned my pants. I leaned back. "Don't," I pleaded. "Be practical."

"I am being practical," she whispered. "What's impractical about this?" She kissed me on the neck.

I moaned. "Everything. Absolutely everything about this is impractical."

She kissed me again. Her tongue traced the hollow between my neck and collarbone. I almost melted. I wanted to; I wanted her so much!

"I don't want to!" I leapt up. "I don't want to go through all of that again!"

I'd thrown her backwards by jumping up like that. She had to fight for her balance. I turned away from her. She came back to me and hugged me from behind. I stiffened my body, trying to resist her. But that was useless.

She caressed me with her voice, as she could so wonderfully well.

"Don't think so much." She talked to me like to a sick animal. "Just let go." Now she began to caress me with her hands as well. She unzipped my pants.

I let her do it. "What are you doing down there?" I whispered with the last of my strength.

She laughed softly. "What do you think?" Her hand caressed my belly under the cloth.

I melted. "Please," I pleaded, however. "Think about this first!" I leaned against her. I couldn't say anything more. She pulled my pants down over my hips with both hands. When that obstacle was out of the way, she put her hands on my thighs and began to work her way toward the center. I thrust my hips toward her. She shoved both hands between my legs. My knees went weak. I raised my arms and wrapped them around her neck. My body was strung like a bow. I could tell I wasn't going to last like this very long. "I can't," I gasped with great effort. "Not standing up like this."

She didn't bother herself with my objections. "I'll hold you up." Her gentle reassurance lulled me momentarily into a sense of security. Her one hand stayed where it was; the other climbed up my thigh and between my legs from behind. She began to stroke me from both sides.

I moaned. "Holy heaven!" She didn't let that disturb her. Why did I have to bear this standing up? There had to be more comfortable alternatives! Her caresses would have robbed me of my senses in any case. I moaned again. While she continued in front, she entered between my legs from behind. I didn't find that particularly comfortable.

"Stop it," I commanded. "I don't like that."

"You will," she stated confidently. She reached deeper inside me. Even she couldn't have fingers that long! She stretched me wider and wider.

"You're going to hurt me," I worried nervously. "I'm too narrow."

She continued what she was doing. "No, you're not," she whispered excitedly. "Just wait."

She was going to rip me apart soon. This couldn't turn out well! I felt something touch me deep inside. I'd never felt anything there before. It felt like she was touching the inside of my belly. I cried out as the explosion overcame me. The tension in my groin increased the sensations to the point that they became unbearable. That was no orgasm; that was a volcanic eruption.

She pulled out slowly. I collapsed. She held me up. As children, we'd played a trust game a little like that. I had turned myself over to her hands.

"Fantastic!" I gasped, exhausted.

"And? Did it hurt?"

"At first it was . . . a little uncomfortable," I admitted truthfully. "But then . . . simply unbelievable!"

"I shouldn't have done that," she said suddenly.

Why not? Now it was all over, and she had my approval.

"I've never done that to a woman who's never been with men before."

Ah, true, I'd told her that. I became mistrustful. "Those were just your fingers, weren't they?"

"No, it was my hand." She seemed self-conscious.

"Oh, no!" My eyes flew open in surprise. "If I'd known that!"

"Then you would've tensed up." She took her hands away carefully, then hugged me. "It was only part of my hand, not the whole thing," she explained soothingly. She let me go slowly.

I felt so pleased and worn out, I could only imagine one place I wanted to be with her. I wrapped my hands around her waist and laid my head on her shoulder. "Come on, let's go to bed."

"No." Her posture suddenly became defensive. "That won't change anything either." She tried to work herself free from my hug.

"Won't change what?"

"The fact that I used you." It was almost as if she'd admitted that against her will.

"Used me? What for?" I had no idea what she was talking about.

"For what I just did with you."

I hadn't actually felt like I was being used — more like satisfied.

"I told you, it was fantastic." I tried to make a joke out of the whole thing. "You can use me that way as often as you like."

"That's not funny!" She was annoyed.

"So tell me what's so terribly sad about it." How was I supposed to know that? I couldn't identify any direct source.

She straightened and stared off to the right, through the window and at the nearby rooftops. Her chin made an almost perfect right angle with her neck. I saw her jaw biting the insides of her cheeks.

"I came back a week ago."

So she hadn't lasted much longer in Paris.

"I went back to work immediately."

She hadn't really needed to tell me that; I would've assumed it anyway.

"The first few days, everything went fine. I wasn't too busy, so my clients all got everything they could ask for. But obviously, it still wasn't enough." She laughed self-consciously.

"Once a pro, always a pro!"

I had never doubted her capabilities in this area, either. After the last few days in Paris, during which she had been such a completely different person, I felt doubly pained by the life she led back here, by the damage it did to her self-respect.

She continued. "Until yesterday, I thought I could go on that way."

Just like me!

I suddenly became afraid. "What happened yesterday?"

I looked down at her arms. She didn't look like she'd been beaten. My frightened tone of voice rattled her a little.

"Not what you think," she reassured me.

I exhaled.

She went on. "Yesterday, two women came over, a couple. I've known them for a long time. They come in now and then, not very often. I really like them. And they're always very nice to me."

Well, at least she had a couple of clients who were nice to her! I imagined what it might've been like if Karin and I had come to her as a couple. That must be odd. I never would've thought of it on my own. But I was sure there was a lot that I'd never tried before. I almost blushed. I remembered what she had just done with me. But that wasn't the issue at hand.

"And it was precisely because they were so nice to me that it was so awful." She spoke of it like something out of a dream. "With the others, I could shut it all out, I was just there, not really present, but with those two . . ."

Her shoulders trembled a little. I saw them – saw how tender they were with one another. I almost had to run away. Then they wanted me to join in, as usual." She shuddered again. "They touched me gently. They tried to get me into it. I always used to like that, even though they're clients. But this time . . . I couldn't. And I couldn't give it to them, either, even though I wanted to." She was silent for a moment. I thought that was all, but then she began to speak again. "I sent them away. I asked them to forgive me, and refused to let them pay, even though they wanted to. I thought it was just because they were a couple. I couldn't bear to see their tenderness with each other."

I could easily imagine that!

"But that wasn't it." There was more. "With the next client, I could barely concentrate. I could hardly force myself to touch her. She complained about the bad service."

What a way of putting it!

Now she laughed, cheered up a bit by the memory. "I threw her out. I never did like her, anyway. But still, I'd never done that before."

That was definite progress!

"Then, a few hours later, I had another appointment. With that particular woman, I'd really never had any problems. She was fairly neutral to me. So I thought I could do it." She broke off. Then she said violently, "But I couldn't do it! I just couldn't do it."

She was more surprised than dismayed. It scratched at her professional consciousness, at her work ethic.

"I complimented her and begged her pardon. She was very understanding." What other choice did she have?

"And then . . ." *What, yet another one? Hadn't she made enough attempts already?*

"Then I had to think about you. I couldn't do anything else." She laughed, somewhat dismayed. "The espresso machine ran all night."

She was unbelievably sweet.

"I drank coffee by the gallon. "The rest you know," she concluded quietly. "I called you."

I had to think about my reaction with shame. "I . . ."

She interrupted me. "You couldn't do otherwise. I knew that. But I absolutely had to see *you*. That's why I came here." Now, she straightened her back, and her face became hard. "And then I used you to see if I was even still capable of bringing a woman to orgasm."

That was absolutely the last thing I was going to believe!

"Mm-hmm." I behaved as though I would seriously consider the possibility that that was how it had happened. "And you only came here to fuck me." Perhaps stating it brutally would bring her to her senses. That wasn't really my style.

"Yes." She acted hard and unmoving. "Just for that."

"You didn't think about anything else?" I recalled how she'd sat in front of my door in a miserable heap. How she'd spoken of yearning.

That had been believable. This wasn't.

"No." She didn't want to admit it.

"Tell that to your grandmother," I replied carelessly.

"I don't have a . . .," she stopped short. "What do you mean by that?"

"Exactly what I said. As far as I'm concerned, you can tell it to my grandmother. I have one. But even she wouldn't believe it." That was short and clear. I was sick of beating around the bush.

She'd turned to face me again. "Why don't you believe me?" She was irritated.

I sighed. "I hate having to repeat myself like this, but if you insist . . ." I ticked off the reasons. "First: I love you. – Stay here!" I grabbed her by the sleeve when she tried to run away. "Second: You love me too, even if you continually refuse to admit it." She shook her head, lips pressed together tightly. I didn't bother myself with that. "Third: That's why you can't sleep with other women anymore. Fourth: You want to sleep with me for the same reasons. That's more than normal. *Quod erat demonstrandum?* That stupid high school Latin class had finally proved useful for something! I took advantage of her confusion.

"So come to bed now," I told her. I took her hand and led her off to the bedroom.

She stopped in front of the bed when I let go of her, and looked down at it as though she'd never seen one before in her life. I had to laugh. "That is my bed," I pointed out, "do you remember it?"

She said nothing. I brushed gently against her arm. "Go on, get undressed. I'll give you a massage. That'll make you feel better." I turned around. "I'll get the hot water bottle and the oil."

Although she still seemed rather skeptical, she began to unbutton her shirt. One could've ordered her to do that when she was fast asleep, and she would've done so immediately. Like almost everything her clients demanded of her. How could this continue?

At the moment, in any case, with a massage! I went to the bathroom and retrieved the necessary supplies. I filled the water bottle with hot water. Then I went back to the bedroom. She was still standing in exactly the same position by the bed in which I'd left her, with the one difference that she was now naked.

Had I really made the right decision with this massage idea? Didn't I really want something else instead? I savored the view of her naked beauty for a moment. I walked up behind her and kissed her between the shoulder blades without kissing her anywhere else. She yelped with surprise. Then I saw her shiver from head to toe, and a relief of tiny dots covered her skin. She laid her head back. Otherwise, she didn't move. "More," she whispered.

It was a good thing my hands were otherwise occupied, or I might not have been able to control myself! I swallowed my desire. "Soon. First the massage." She stood exactly as she was. "Please, lie down." I'd never imagined I would have to order her to do that. "On your belly." Maybe that would cool her off!

But she seemed not to fear that position quite so much anymore, at least not with me. She lay down on the bed with complete self-assurance and stretched out expectantly. I stuck the hot water bottle under the blanket. She was warm enough already!

I took the oil and rubbed a little of it into my hands.

"Hmm, that smells good," she remarked dreamily.

"Cinnamon and cloves."

"And a hint of musk," she stated knowledgeably.

I smiled. "I think that's probably your perfume."

"Could be," she replied, "but they mix so well. I hardly smell that anymore otherwise."

That made her smell even better! Her scent drifted over to me. The combination was really stunning. I had to begin.

I started by massaging her heels, very slowly and gently, for several minutes. Then I pressed my fingers carefully into the middle of her soles. I moved softly up to the backs of her knees and rubbed them gently. From there, I caressed the lengths of her calves down to her ankles. I stopped for a moment in order to climb into bed next to her.

"That's quite different from the last time." Somewhat bemused, she realized the difference.

"Yes," I confirmed. I knew what she was feeling, and she was going to feel even more of it soon. I traced her spine from her neck to the tops of her thighs, then once again to the base of her back. There, I pressed down a little with my flat hand.

"What are you doing up there?" She was moving her hips back and forth restlessly. I felt the blood rushing through her veins beneath my hand. She must have been feeling the same thing in her groin.

Her reaction confirmed this. "May I turn over now?" she asked impatiently.

"Yes," I consented.

When she lay on her back, she said to me with a husky voice, "My breasts are burning." She glanced excitedly into my eyes. "I want you to touch them."

There was nothing I would rather have done. But I didn't touch her breasts. "Later," I promised her.

She moaned with disappointment. I began to massage her again. I placed my hands flat on her hips and pressed them into the sheets. She threw her head about. I massaged her legs again, down to her ankles. She moaned. "I want to kiss you. Please . . ."

"Not yet." It took an iron will on my part to deny her this request. I took her middle finger in my mouth and sucked on it. I ran over the base of her nail with my tongue. She dug her other hand in my hair. I freed myself from her hands and began to stroke upwards from her ankles once more, along the insides of her legs, up to her thighs. No farther. I repeated that about a dozen times. Then I ran along the very tops of her inner thighs, massaging her there as well.

She moaned aloud at every gentle touch and began to breathe in short, excited gasps.

I couldn't make her wait any longer. I stroked her pearl very softly and tenderly with my fingertips. She came in seconds with an intensity that mirrored the strength of her arousal. When she had calmed down again, I undressed myself and lay down next to her.

She turned her head toward me. She smiled. "That was no massage."

"Yes it was," I protested. "It was an erotic massage."

"I noticed that. I've used some of those spots before myself. But I had no idea how intense that is." That meant she'd done something for her clients of which she knew nothing, or at least only in theory. She shook her head a little. "My belly feels wonderfully warm and soft. As if the tension just melted away."

"So it should be." I was, for the moment, completely satisfied. I snuggled up to her and pulled the blanket over us, which had been warmed perfectly by the hot water bottle.

She slid her arm under my head and pulled me closer to her. "When you stroked the length of my leg the thousandth time, and stopped right before you got to the best part, I wanted to kill you!" she laughed.

"Not a thousand. Twelve at the most," I corrected.

"That was plenty for me. I do that with my clients three times at most. And that is sometimes too much." She spoke casually and relaxed.

I looked at her. At the moment, we could talk about anything. That was wonderful. But I didn't just want to talk. I leaned over and kissed her. She kissed me back in a new way. It was erotic, yes, but also trusting, as if we'd known each other for years and no longer required any other means of communication.

The telephone rang. I was so comfortable lying next to her, why should I pick it up? I let it ring. She stopped kissing me.

"Don't you want to answer that?" she asked.

"Why should I?" I answered in high spirits. "It can't be you. You're already here."

She smiled. "Perhaps there are other people you want to talk to now and then "

"Not at the moment." I continued to ignore the phone and sought her lips again. But she dodged me.

"I'm sorry," she said, "but that's making me nervous." She started to get up. Her phone rang for only one reason. I understood why she was nervous.

I hardly realized that she almost had the receiver in her hand. "No!" I called. She gave me a hurt look. "It could be my mother," I explained. "And she always gets so irritated when strange women answer my phone." She shook her head, picked up the receiver, and handed it to me.

"Oh, Karin!" I was admittedly relieved when I heard who was there. I didn't think I could've handled an hour-long conversation with my mother just then.

"I hear you've been back for a while. And you haven't called me!" As my best friend, she had every right to complain about my silence. The reproach in her voice was genuine, but I could be sure that she wasn't really mad at me for it.

"I've only been back for eight days." I knew that that was no excuse, certainly not in Karin's eyes.

"Ten," she said softly from the background. I spun around quickly and gestured violently for her to be quiet.

"That's no excuse," Karin scolded as expected. "After all, a lot of things can happen in eight days."

"That's true," I admitted. I squealed. She'd kissed me on the butt. I turned around indignantly.

"What is it?" Karin asked, a bit concerned. Our last telephone conversation had, after all, been of a serious nature.

"Nothing," I asserted quickly. "I got my finger caught in the phone."

"In the phone?" Karin was a little irritated.

I couldn't say anything at that moment. She was kissing the nape of my neck and caressing my stomach at the same time. She was only doing that to annoy me!

"Yes." Breathless, I tried to continue. "I have a new one with all the bells and whistles." She didn't stop. Now she was stroking my thighs. I gasped for breath.

Karin laughed. "Now I understand. You're not alone."

"No," I confirmed. I was incapable of anything more. She was teasing my breast with her lips.

"Is she there?" Karin asked, interested. Apparently, she wanted to continue the conversation.

"Yes." I could only gasp the answer. She had one of my nipples in her mouth now, and was running her tongue back and forth across it.

Karin chuckled. "And you don't seem to be fighting at the moment!"

"Not at all," I said to Karin. "But soon!" I hissed in her direction.

She raised her eyebrows innocently, let go of my breast for a second, and waited.

"The reason I'm calling . . .," Karin continued harmlessly. At the same moment, she took my other nipple in her mouth and began to suck it. I moaned out loud.

Karin asked, "You're doing well, aren't you?" She knew precisely how I was. She was obviously getting heathenish enjoyment out of this.

"You two are just the same," I squeaked between gritted teeth.

Karin chuckled again. "I wanted to ask you if we can meet at the pub this evening." She was clearly repressing a giggle. "You can bring her along. When you're both dressed."

"Karin!"

Karin acted entirely innocent. "Well, you always got undressed for it before. Don't you do that anymore?"

"Stop it!" I said, directed at both of them. Her hand glided between my legs. I couldn't take it anymore. "We'll come to the pub." All I could do was agree. I was completely gone.

"At eight," Karin specified. She laughed. "And have fun in the meantime!" She hung up.

I let the receiver fall and collapsed onto the bed. She pulled her hand away and laughed. She laughed freely and high-spiritedly, as though she'd just learned it was a snow day off from school.

"That was mean!" I fumed.

"Yes, that's true." She was still laughing, but she tried to control herself. "But it was so much fun!"

"For you!" I scolded. "For both of you!"

"She noticed?" she asked, smiling to herself.

"Of course!" I snarled. "She knows me well enough from before."

"Oh, yes," she remarked smoothly. "I'm convinced she can interpret all of your noises." She raised her hands in front of her face to protect herself from the pillow I threw at her.

I turned my back to her. I felt her crawling carefully up behind me. She wrapped her arms around me. "Please don't be mad at me," she whispered in my ear. "You looked so seductively busy."

"You've got a thing for that, eh? Driving me insane while I'm talking on the phone." I scolded her like a naughty pet.

"I only just discovered it with you. And you do it really well!" She laughed teasingly.

"And what do I get out of it?" I tried to sound annoyed, but I had really already forgiven her.

She leaned against me. "I hope a lot." If ever a voice could be called seductive, it was hers. Her hands began to wander over my body. A short time later, I had to admit she was right. I seemed to get a lot out of it.

As evening approached, I realized that she still knew nothing of Karin's invitation. And I had simply accepted. Understandable under the circumstances, but we weren't in Paris anymore. I didn't know if I could convince her to come along.

We were lying together in bed, occupied with nothing other than rest and recuperation. I turned to her and caressed her cheek. She turned her pretty face toward me. I could barely look at her. She knocked me out every time. She smiled. I ran my fingers through her hair.

"You're so beautiful," I remarked for the I-don't-know-how-many-eth time since I'd met her.

"That doesn't help, either," she replied. She wasn't exactly sad, just realistic. She laughed. "And it's a fault that age will remove."

I felt my tenderness for her well up inside. "You'll still be beautiful when you're eighty."

She raised her eyebrows. "If I live that long, we can test your prediction," she joked.

I played with her hair some more. "Do you have any plans for this evening?" I asked harmlessly.

She looked at me with astonishment. "What made you think of that?"

"It could happen." I shrugged my shoulders.

"You mean: appointments?" She looked annoyed. Her face indicated she was shutting down.

I always got off on the wrong foot!

"No," I corrected quickly. "I actually hadn't assumed that. It's about something else." She still looked closed.

I sighed. "Karin asked me earlier if we could meet her down at the pub this evening." The diplomatic route was not in my cards! I would be damned to directness my whole life.

"We?" She'd picked out the deciding factor right away.

"Yes," I replied, as though it were completely self-evident. "And I said yes." She started to shake her head. I followed quickly, "You're not exactly innocent in this. At that point in time, I was unable to think at all."

She remembered and had to smile. That was something! "Still . . ." She was cautious. Her expression became serious again.

Her thoughts were the same as the last time I'd asked her out to dinner; that I could imagine. And they weren't exactly unfounded, as I'd seen for myself.

"You won't meet anyone you know at this pub," I explained reassuringly.

"How do you know that for sure?" she countered defensively.

I laughed. "The people there can barely afford their pizza." Dammit, what had I been thinking? *Nothing,* that was the problem. And the expected reaction came right away.

"You mean the women there can't afford me?" I wasn't about to convince her to go this way!

"Please forgive me," I pleaded softly. "I wasn't thinking again. I didn't mean it that way."

She wasn't quite ready to be calmed.

"You're probably right," she snapped harshly.

I pushed myself closer to her and touched her cheek. She just let it happen. She didn't seem to feel anything at all. "Please. Let's not have this discussion now. I know I made a mistake. But I don't want to ruin the evening that way."

She refused to soften. Her face remained motionless. I just bent over and kissed her softly on lips, which were so cool and reserved. "Can't you forgive me one more time?" I whispered against her mouth. "I'll behave myself better. I promise."

The corners of her mouth twitched a little. "But only this once." *I had her — thank God!*

I hugged her and rolled around the bed with her. Now she lay on top of me. I kneaded her butt cheeks. I would have liked most to pull all of her inside me. "Will you come?" I asked casually.

"No."

I squeezed her bottom tighter and pressed her against me. "Really?" I asked again.

"No." She persisted.

I let one leg slide between hers and lifted it gently. At the same time, I pressed her more tightly against me and began to move beneath her.

"You'll regret it," I warned.

"I already do," she said. When I reached a hand between her legs from behind, she moaned. It almost sounded like she was enjoying it against her will.

"Please, say yes," I begged her. "Karin will be very disappointed if you don't come."

"You just want to show me off," she countered laboriously. Her hips had begun to follow my movements.

"Yes, there's some truth to that," I admitted. "I do want to show you off. I don't know a single other woman who can match you."

"In what area?" she asked mistrustfully. Her voice already sounded very forced.

"All of them." I lay still. "I don't want to force you into anything," I explained softly. "I want you to do it willingly."

She lay still as well. Her breathing was still rather heavy. "Willingly," she repeated, as though she had to think about what that word meant. I waited. She changed the word a little. "Of my own free will," she then said. I caressed her back. She relaxed on top of me. "That must be nice," she philosophized, completely absorbed in the thought. "To do something of your own free will."

She almost made me cry with the thoughts she spoke aloud.

Finally, she decided. "I think I'll do it. Of my own free will," she continued with special emphasis.

I pulled her head down to me and kissed her. "I'm so glad."

—— 26 ——

Karin came through the saloon doors into the pub. She saw me and came over to our table. Before she even greeted me, she looked my companion over. "So this is the woman." Karin gave me a reproachful look. "Why have you been hiding her?"

I looked back questioningly. *What did she mean?*

"Venus would die of jealousy," she added. If I hadn't known Karin so well, I would've assumed she was merely flirting. But I knew if she'd ever meant anything seriously in her life, this was it. "You are the most beautiful woman I've ever seen." It was a genuine compliment.

I saw a defensive motion next to me. Karin saw it as well and sat down. She reached for the hand that lay next to mine on the table. As she had done back in the bistro, her first reaction was to pull away. Karin wouldn't let her.

"No, no," she insisted gently, "you're among family here." She glanced around wildly. "And anyone else can just dare say something against it!" She grew more serious.

"I'm glad you're feeling better. After what Aunt Hildegard hinted at – she couldn't tell me any details, of course, because of doctor-patient confidentiality – I was afraid there might be long-term effects." She indicated the small scar on her pretty face, the one that refused to be hidden by her makeup. "Is that all?"

My companion swallowed. "Yes," she said. She let Karin hold her hand now. "Aunt Hildegard?" I asked, completely shocked. "The doctor is your aunt?"

"Well, sort of; I call her my aunt. We used to live in the same building when I was a kid. She was the loony, the workaholic that no one quite knew what to do with. Not married and so forth. She was always too engaged in her profession. For a while, she treated prostitutes almost exclusively, usually at no cost."

At the word prostitute, she twitched next to me. Then she spat quietly: "That's why you sent her to me."

Karin was wholly unaffected. "No, that's not why. I wouldn't have known of anyone else. Because of Aunt Hildegard, I almost became a doctor myself. But I thought it was impossible to make a living that way, because I had her as a role model." She laughed. "What a mistake!"

Next to me, a beautiful face still stared blankly ahead.

Karin took the hand she'd been holding all along in both hands now. "I know what you are," she said. "And it's completely irrelevant to me. Couldn't you just perhaps forget about it for the evening?" Karin's facial expression changed. "Something else here is much worse," she asserted jokingly.

"What?" I asked, although I already had a good idea what it was.

"You're her girlfriend." She looked at her and pointed her thumb at me. "And that wouldn't be the case if I'd met you first!"

"Karin!" I snapped in warning.

"Keep a close eye on her." Karin's eyes twinkled. "You know I'm not monogamous."

"Only too well," I sighed theatrically'.

Karin leaned over and gave me a friendly kiss.

The object of our playful competition had backed away from me somewhat, and looked back and forth at the two of us as if she were watching a tennis match. "May I have some say in this as well?" she asked, rather indignant.

"No!" we forbade her simultaneously, as though from one mouth.

She blushed slightly, took her hand decisively away from Karin, and stood up. "I'll come back when the duel is over," she told us. "In the meantime, I'm going to powder my nose." She took a few steps, then turned back toward us. "I'll take the winner." She seemed satisfied again, so she granted us a charming smile before going.

"My God," whistled Karin, "she's a knock-out. How do you stand it?"

"Not at all." I blotted my forehead. I was sure I looked like a wet poodle.

Karin looked at me sympathetically. "Are you two still having the same problems?"

"I don't know." I really couldn't answer that at the moment. "I don't think she's going to go back to work for a while." *At least that's how it had sounded earlier that afternoon.*

"For a while?" Karin raised her eyebrows a little. I liked how the gesture suited her also, but it was something entirely different.

"We haven't discussed it."

"Mm-hmm," Karin resumed, "you don't want to tell me anything about the reasons." *She knew me better than I knew myself.*

"I can't," I protested. "It's her business."

Karin nodded knowingly. "So you have found out a thing or two."

"I think so," I had to admit. I was surprised myself at the sudden realization. Karin said nothing and just looked at me.

"I love her so much!" It broke out of me. With a desperate look in my eyes, I added, "I can't live without her any longer!"

Karin smiled. "I can well understand that." She took my hand. "She's a wonderful woman." She shook her head. "I can hardly believe she . . ."

"That she's a whore?" I followed bitterly.

"Yes." Karin shook her head. "I've never met a woman who looks less like one than she does. "

"That's for sure," I confirmed with a sigh. "But that doesn't change the facts."

"Maybe it does." Karin expressed her doubts in her usual, logical manner. "If her innermost being disagrees so strongly with external things, like her profession, then she'll have to make a choice one day."

There was something to that. "And if not?" This possibility existed too, after all.

Karin shrugged. "Then that would certainly be very bad for her."

"And for me." I continued Karin's thought. "I don't know which one of us would go crazy first."

Karin smiled encouragingly. "I don't think it will come to that." She smiled again. "You two make a lovely couple."

I hung my head in order to hide my embarrassment. "She's lovely," I tried to correct her.

"Oh?" remarked Karin, teasingly. She wouldn't fall for something like that. "And you're ugly?"

I fidgeted. "No," I admitted, "but compared with her . . ."

"She is stunningly beautiful," Karin stated. "That's true." She squeezed my hand energetically. "But your beauty together comes from something else entirely. You really love each other."

I tried to pull my hand free. She wouldn't let it go any more than she would with the other woman.

"She's never said it to me," I replied uncertainly.

"She will." Karin was convinced of that. I wasn't. "Considering the circumstances, I can understand that it's difficult for her to say those words."

"You mean, considering her profession?"

"Yes," said Karin. "It has a different meaning for her than for us. And the danger is greater for her."

"What danger?" I asked obtusely. Actually, I knew the answer already.

"The danger of getting into a situation of dependency from which she cannot escape. The danger of extortion. Whatever you like. The consequences could be deadly to her." Karin could see much more than I could from her distance.

"Her occupation could be deadly to her," I confirmed urgently.

Karin looked at me. "Are you afraid that something like that might happen again?" she asked.

"And how!" I was really desperate. "I can't just ignore that danger." I nodded in the direction in which she'd disappeared. "She can."

Karin shook her head. "I don't believe that. At most, she's convinced you of that."

I sighed in resignation. "As long as she doesn't practice her trade, I don't have to worry about it. But then . . .?"

"You're going to have to talk to her about that." Karin merely spoke out loud what I already knew, but I still hadn't thought of a useful solution to the problem.

"I've tried that already," I explained. "She minimizes the whole thing. She says it doesn't happen every day."

"She's no doubt right about that." Karin nodded.

"Now you're agreeing with her denial!" I raged.

"No, I'm not," Karin corrected me. "I'm just not as biased as you are." She took my hand and kissed my fingers. "Anyhow, we're not going to solve the problem by talking about it with each other. You two have to work that out between yourselves." She let go of my hand. "Did you have a good time in bed after I called earlier?" she asked suddenly, batting her eyes innocently.

I gulped with surprise. "That's none of your business," I mumbled.

Then I had to smile in spite of myself. "But if you really must know, it was very nice."

She grinned impishly. "Her job has its advantages, doesn't it?"

"And disadvantages you couldn't imagine," I added. "Precisely, in bed." This was a topic I'd always had a hard time getting her to drop.

"I bet the advantages in bed outweigh them," she probed further.

I let her fidget. "If you think so," I said, grinning.

"Come on already," she insisted. "Tell me a little."

I tossed her a crumb. "She's simply fantastic," I needled her. "What can I tell you?"

"You've always had a sadistic streak." She was really being unfair there. "But I'll get it out of you eventually!" She slouched in pretend frustration.

I had to laugh out loud. This was one of the few instances in which I'd won a battle with her.

The topic of conversation returned to the table. "You seem to have an awful lot of fun when I'm not around," she remarked as she sat down next to me. I would have liked to greet her with a kiss.

"We weren't talking about you." I tried to deny.

"Yes we were." Karin didn't want to drop the thread. Greatly pleased with herself, she winked at me, provocatively.

"What were you talking about, then?" the woman at my side asked innocently.

"I'll tell you later." I really wanted to talk about something else. I was already embarrassed enough.

"In bed." Karin couldn't keep herself from making every insinuating remark that came to her mind.

"If you don't stop that right now, you're going to regret it!" I hissed at her.

Karin made a face, as if she hadn't done anything at all. While we were glaring at each other, my companion leaned against my shoulder and laughed. "You two were talking about your telephone conversation!" It would've been a miracle if she hadn't caught on to at least part of the theme, given her expertise. Thank God it was the benign portion.

I gave Karin a threatening look. Finally, she went along with my strategy. "Yes, exactly. We were talking about that phone call." She grinned again. "I thought I was hearing things!"

"But you didn't hang up, either!" I grumbled, still a little annoyed.

"Oh, please!" Karin reacted as though I'd insulted her honor. "Was I supposed to let such an opportunity pass me by? "Besides . . .," she scooted away from me a little. "Besides, it's been a long time since I heard that kind of sound coming from you." For safety's sake, she had already prepared herself for my reaction. Otherwise, my fist would've landed right in her stomach.

"Should I perhaps leave you two alone? I hate to interfere with courting rituals." The way the corners of her mouth crept upwards with amusement indicated that she was enjoying the situation much more than I was.

"Courting?" I retorted indignantly. "I think you're misinterpreting the situation!"

"No." She was certain about these things. No one could pull the wool over her eyes in this area. "You like each other very much."

Karin looked at her and then me. "That's true," she confirmed, and added, "I like both of you very much." She observed us. "You belong together," she asserted with an air of certainty. Giving my companion a final examination, she concluded, "I'm glad she finally found you." She was pointing to me. "She's been searching for you for a long time."

It was a situation I couldn't cope with much longer. "You're terrible, dear Karin," I said, close to tears. "Would you be mad if we left now?"

"No." Karin was quite satisfied. "I understand completely." She smiled. "I wasn't sure you were going to come at all."

We left the pub. On the sidewalk, we walked along next to one other silently for some time. We reached the fork that divided her way home from mine. "My place or yours?" I asked.

She looked at me. I. couldn't decipher what she was thinking. "I'll go to my place and you go to yours," she answered in an un- readable way.

Had the evening with Karin brought up uncomfortable thoughts for her after all? Had we reminded her of her work with our insinu- ations?

She saw that I was standing around uncertainly and went on. "It doesn't have anything to do with you," she explained. "I would love to be with you tonight, but I have to think about some things." She hesitated. "I'm going home now." Her words sounded regretful.

"But not alone." My interjection came quite suddenly.

She wanted to protest. "I told you . . ."

"I'll just walk you to your door," I insisted unrelentingly. "As it should be."

She remembered. "Oh, yes, that's right," she said. "You're so well brought-up." She smiled. "I'd sooner say gallant, but you don't like that." She hesitated nevertheless. "Well, ok," she said giving in. She added cautiously, "But really just to my door!"

I put my hand over my heart. "But of course!" I emphasized the chivalrous gesture with a slightly mocking bow. "I give you my word, my lady!"

"Then I'm relieved." She agreed, amused.

I put my arm around her waist, and we set off in the direction of her apartment. Unfortunately, it wasn't very far. When we had ar- rived, I let her go regretfully. I didn't want to leave. I couldn't tear myself away from her. "Well, then," I remarked hesitantly.

"Until tomorrow," she said. "I'll call you."

Well, that was new! "But not at my office again, please." Playful- ly, I rolled my eyes back into my head. "I'd never survive that." .

"Neither would I." Her voice sounded raw. She stepped toward me and took me in her arms. She kissed me. Her tongue sent me reeling. She shoved her thigh between my legs and pressed me against the doorframe. Her hand reached down and grabbed my behind. "I wish so much that you could stay," she whispered into my mouth, "but I really need to be alone." She kissed me passionately once more, then let me go and stepped back.

I stayed there, leaning against the doorway, my eyes closed. I could still feel her tongue in my mouth and her thigh between my legs. The blood raced through my veins.

She touched me gently on the shoulder. "Wake up." She laughed softly.

I kept my eyes closed. "How can you ask that of me?" I asked dreamily. "I'm in the land of your kisses."

"Really?" she teased. "I've never been there."

"No wonder," I remarked, still dreamy. "You don't kiss yourself, you know."

"Come on," she decided, "come up with me." She unlocked the door.

Now I opened my eyes. "I gave you my word." Apparently, she'd forgotten that.

"I invited you," she answered. She seemed not to have anticipated a refusal from me. She was surprised.

"That doesn't make any difference." I stepped forward and kissed her on the cheek. "Good night." She stood in the doorway lit beautifully from behind, and watched me in amazement. I waved at her and left.

—— **27**—

The next day, she called me at work anyway. "Have you gone insane?" she asked in greeting.

I acted like I didn't know what she was talking about. "No," I said innocently. "Why?"

"Then what are fifty red roses doing in my apartment? They must've cost a fortune!" She was absolutely indignant.

"Oh?" I replied, still innocently. "Somebody sent you fifty red roses?"

"Not somebody. You!" she raged on. "Quit denying it!" It was lovely, how she got so excited. Her voice sounded like it was turning cartwheels.

I laughed. "I'm not denying it," I said cheerfully. I loved her! She was so dashingly temperamental.

"So you have gone insane!" It sounded genuinely triumphant.

"I love you," I said softly. "If that's insane, then I'll be happy to be crazy my whole life."

For a moment, the line was silent. "They're beautiful," she replied then, just as softly.

"I hope so. I picked out every one myself."

"Every single one?" She was dumbfounded.

"Of course. How could I have left that to someone else?" Her voice was already waking the desire in me. And it was still such a long time until evening.

"You are crazy," she asserted tenderly.

"We'd better stop," I requested as sensibly as possible. "This is already heading in the direction of phone sex." "Will you come see me today?" she asked without transition.

"If you want." I still wasn't sure what that meant.

"I do," she confirmed quickly. She was determination itself – extremely unusual. Was she going to make that her routine now? She'd carried it through since yesterday, anyway. "When are you finished?"

"Around seven." Shivering with desire for her, my feelings rebelled, but I had to acknowledge the reality of the head-high stack of paperwork on my desk.

"You can't be serious," she protested.

"I am." I had to hold my ground this time. I couldn't just keep dropping everything whenever she turned up, much as I wanted to. My work was piling up and deadlines were drawing near. I tried to explain that to her. "You should see my desk sometime."

Obviously, that didn't interest her in the slightest. "Then I'll come there," she announced enthusiastically.

"Not again!" I almost raised my hands in an instinctive defense reaction, but I needed at least one of them to hold onto the receiver. I tried to reason with her again. "You know that's not possible."

"No, no," she persisted. "This time, I won't be put off. Either you're on my doormat by four o'clock, or I'm at your office." She sounded absolutely determined.

"Here in my office on the doormat?" I couldn't help imagining that and teasing her with it. "That would be a new one."

She laughed. "Now you're starting the phone sex."

I admitted it. "I'll come earlier," I promised. "But I don't know if I'll make it by four o'clock."

"Don't come too late," she whispered sensuously. "I'll be waiting for you."

"My God," I sighed. "I wish I were there already."

"So do I." I could feel her impatience pressing through the receiver.

"Until then. I'll water the roses in the meantime." She paused. "I'm thinking of you." She hung up.

I kissed the telephone receiver and said," I'm thinking of you, too." Then I put it back in its cradle. I seemed pitiful to myself as I stared at the plastic handle.

I held out until five. When I entered her apartment, she greeted me with a long kiss. My knees went weak. Astonishingly, however, she let me go. She pushed me away from her.

"Sit down." It wasn't a request – more like an order given in a polite tone. "I'll make you some coffee."

She seemed decidedly housewife-like. "Have you got a pair of felt slippers for me as well?" I asked, irritated.

She looked back over her shoulder. "Not yet," she said. "But I can get you some, if you'd like." She appeared to mean it seriously.

"For heaven's sake!" I was stunned. This reception didn't quite match my expectations. "What's up with you?"

She switched on the espresso machine and came back to me. I was still standing there in a daze. She poked me in the nose with her finger. "I like it when you come home from work tired and I can take care of you. I've never had the chance to do that," she explained in answer to my question.

She pushed me onto the couch. I let myself fall. "Just don't let this become a habit," I objected. "I'm so lazy; we'll end up spending our evenings cozily in front of the TV if they start off this way."

She leaned across me and caressed my cheek sensually with her lips. Then she sought out my mouth and kissed me anew. "I know how to prevent that," she said, laughing softly. She stood up. "Besides, I don't have a television, and neither do you as far as I know."

"Yes I do. In the basement," I contradicted.

"And there it shall stay." She laughed again. "At least as long as I'm in charge of the program." She was definitely doing that. I had no idea what this was all supposed to mean.

She went back into the kitchen and brought me my coffee. She sat next to me on the sofa, like the first time I had come to her. She crossed her legs exactly as she had back then. Only today, she was dressed. Despite that, I could feel my desire for her. I took the coffee cup and drank. Over the rim, I watched her. Her arms lay casually on the back of the sofa. She returned the stare and caught my eye.

"Should I change clothes?" she asked. She laughed when she saw my dismayed expression. "I mean so you can enjoy the situation as much as you did then." She knew exactly what she was doing!

"Stop that," I pleaded uneasily. "You know I don't like that."

"But you remembered it." Unlike me, she obviously felt comfortable enough to be amused by this.

"You were unbearably sweet." She positively reveled in the memory. "I knew right away that you were in love with me."

"I must've stared at you like an idiot." I was still deeply embarrassed by the memory.

"Stared, yes. Like an idiot, no," she corrected.

She controlled the situation with sovereignty. I almost felt like I had then. "I didn't like it very much, by the way."

The thought of it alone drove me to react with a measure of annoyance.

"It was terrible."

"Being my client?" She was serious now.

Where was she going with this? She never brought this topic up herself.

She bent over and took a rose from the vase, which she'd placed on the coffee table. She smelled it. "I didn't have these then." She looked at me. "I've hardly ever gotten red roses before." She laughed, overwhelmed. "And never this many!"

I couldn't possibly imagine that. During the course of her adult life, there must have been masses of people who fell in love with her, men as well as women!

"The first time I got red roses, I was seventeen," she explained unexpectedly, her attention still absorbed in the flower in her hand. "From a man." She laughed contemptuously. "And of course he wanted something in return!"

She didn't say if she'd given him what he wanted. I really didn't want to know, either. She looked at me again. "Then I didn't get any for a very long time. Until a couple of years ago." This time, she didn't say from whom. She continued, "And now from you."

That was really very few occasions for a woman like her!

She stretched out her arm and tickled my cheek with the rose petals. She stroked me up to my ear and then back down to my lips. She caressed them as well. The scent of the rose under my nose was intoxicating, although the whole room was filled with it. The rose petals were soft and satiny on my mouth. I plucked one with my lips and held it tight. She kept the rose in her hand, leaned over, and laid her arm across my shoulders. She tickled the nape of my neck with the rose. She leaned into me. She put her lips on the opposite side of the rose petal. Our lips touched very lightly. Barely a whisper. I moaned nonetheless. She pulled the petal and, at the same time, my mouth in with her lips until she could kiss me. Our tongues played with the petal. She pushed it into my mouth and I passed it back until I could no longer bear the stimulation. It appeared to go the same way for her. She pushed me back onto the sofa and lay down on top of me.

She set the rose down next to us and removed the petal from my mouth. "We won't be needing that anymore," she breathed, softly and erotically.

I reached my hands down to her waist and began to undress her. When I felt her bare skin, I pushed my fingers around to the front and unbuttoned her pants. She moaned deeply. I stroked her belly between us.

"Wait," she commanded. I didn't move. She straddled my thigh and rubbed against me. She came fast and furious.

I hugged her when she collapsed back on top of me. "I'm sorry," she remarked after taking a moment to catch her breath, "that wasn't what I wanted to do."

"Was it good for you?" I asked tenderly.

"Yes." As usual, she admitted it only reluctantly. "But . . ."

"Then everything is fine." I squeezed her tighter. "Everything is fine," I repeated soothingly.

"You're going to make me cry." She had her head next to me on the couch cushion so I couldn't see her face.

I rubbed her back. "Then do it. It won't hurt anything."

"Yes it will!" she argued with unexpected violence. She leapt up sharply, stuffed her shirt back in her pants, and pulled up the zipper. "And nothing is fine!" She was having a hard time with the button. She let her hands drop and looked at me in utter desperation. "I can't even get my pants on right!" She was ever so close to tears, but her pants were definitely not the reason.

I sat up. "Come here," I told her. She came over, and I fastened the button. I pulled her down onto my lap. "So what's the matter?"

"I can't do my job anymore," she explained. I had thought this might have something to do with that. "At least temporarily," she qualified immediately.

I would have to see if this was temporary!

She turned slightly in my lap and looked at me. "You're happy about that, of course," she threw at me angrily.

I could hardly contest that. "Yes, on the one hand," I answered truthfully. "But on the other hand, I'm sad because you're sad."

"I'm not sad!" She almost jumped out of my lap in protest. "I'm not sad at all. But in the foreseeable future, I don't know how I'm going to make a living!"

I had a brainstorm. "You could marry me," I joked.

"Oh, yeah!" Now she was really mad, "and buy you felt slippers!"

"I didn't mean it quite that literally." I tried helplessly to calm her down a little. I still felt like this was a piece in which I had a role to play but didn't know the script.

"What?" She reacted even more angrily than before. "You don't really want to marry me at all? Why did you propose, then?"

Now I was completely baffled. "No," I contradicted, absolutely confused. "I would marry you right away if I could and if you wanted. But until the activists and lawyers battle that one out, I'm afraid we'll just have to live in sin."

She calmed down a little. "I see," she said. She must really be turned inside out!

"But I earn enough money for two." If she wanted to discuss this topic, we could certainly list off the alternatives. *Why not?* I looked around. "Although I couldn't offer such luxury."

"You don't need to." She seemed absent. "I'll sell the apartment." She got up from my lap and paced across the room with long steps, back and forth, back and forth. "Or I could always sell the apartment in Paris," she thought out loud. "I could certainly live off that for a while."

She owned two apartments and she was worried about her future? "I think I should quit work and marry you instead." I was dazed enough to do it.

She looked at me, deep in thought. "This apartment won't fetch much."

She spoke like a bookkeeper. "It's not even all the way paid for."

It pained me already to think that she might have to give up the Parisian apartment, but I asked anyway. The apartment in Paris must be worth a fortune."

"Yes, probably," she remarked without paying much attention to me. "I don't know exactly."

"You don't know? But didn't you buy it?" I was more than astonished.

"No," she answered absently, as though she were somewhere else in her thoughts and didn't wish to stop concentrating on it. "I inherited it."

"Inherited?" Was her brilliant French, then, perhaps her mother tongue? "Are you French?"

"No." She looked at me more clearly now and stopped her pacing. "No, unfortunately not. A client left it to me." She set off again, more slowly this time.

"A client?" Perhaps I'd chosen the wrong career after all! "What . . . how . . .?" I didn't know how to ask.

She understood right away what I meant. "She died two years ago and left it to me."

Just like that? Any old client? A luxury apartment in Paris? I couldn't imagine that. Then something else occurred to me. "Two years ago," I mused thoughtfully.

She stopped abruptly. "You notice everything, don't you."

That didn't sound especially flattering.

"Yes, you're right. She was the last woman before you, with whom I . . ." She broke off, as though she'd already said too much. She turned away from me and stood there. She propped one arm up with the other and held her forehead in her hand. Something about that bothered her dreadfully.

Just a client? I knew that couldn't be true. With a client, she never would have let herself fall that far. "You were a couple," I concluded suddenly.

"No!" She raged. Love seemed to be just about the worst thing one could accuse her of. "She was only a client." I could see that she was fighting hard for control.

"She must have been more to you than that," I argued, convinced. "If she left you an apartment."

"She paid me. So she was a client." She was obstinate.

There had to be something to my claim. Otherwise, she wouldn't have felt such a strong need to deny it. "How long were you together?" I asked, undiscouraged.

"We weren't together!" Now she finally exploded. "I always had my own apartment."

With that, she involuntarily confirmed my original assumption. The more vehemently she denied it, the more I was convinced it was so. "She must have loved you very much."

"Yes, yes!" Her unwilling protest became more and more strongly defensive. "She probably thought it was love."

"And you didn't love her?" In any case, she certainly wouldn't have told her, the way I knew her.

A long silence indicated that she still wasn't sure about it, or didn't want to be. "No," she said finally.

"What happened?" The silence continued for a while. I could do nothing but wait until she told the story.

"She was older than I was – much older. She went and fell in love with me." That was easy! She turned halfway toward me and folded her arms across her chest.

"She couldn't stand it any more than you can for me to do my job. But I didn't want to be dependent on her. She begged me, pleaded with me, more than once. To live with her. She had enough money, she said, to last more than one lifetime." She shook her head. "But it wasn't enough for her life. All the money in the world couldn't stop the disease in her body."

That was the cause of many of her reactions! She was completely buried in her own mind, as she had been once before.

"I didn't know anything about that. She kept it a secret from me." She turned more toward the wall and stared at a picture. "By the end, she'd convinced me not to see any other women. She gave me money – more than enough to make up for my lost wages. Just so I wouldn't sleep with other women. She was my only client for two years. And I thought, if she didn't have a better use for her money, why shouldn't I take it?"

She threw her hands in front of her face. "And then she went away. To a spa, she said. She was supposed to return in two weeks. She didn't tell me where it was." She let her hands fall slowly. "I didn't hear anything from her the whole time. After two weeks, she didn't come back. I waited a few days. I thought she'd left me. I was angry and hurt. I slept with the very first woman who was ready to pay. I resumed the life I'd led before."

Slowly, she crossed the room, stopped in front of the kitchen counter, and sought consolation in the espresso machine. She spoke again. "Then – after six weeks – a letter came from an attorney in France. She had died in a special hospital in Switzerland. She'd left me the apartment in Paris."

That must have been a horrible shock for her. She was still shaken by it.

She sighed in resignation. Her voice sounded almost uninterested as she continued. "I said I was her daughter and spoke with the doctor who'd treated her at the end. He said if she'd come sooner, he might have been able to do something for her. With long-term, intensive treatments and stays in a nursing home. But she had always refused that. There was a person whom she couldn't or wouldn't leave alone. She'd hinted at something like that."

Her head sank lower and lower toward her chest as she spoke. Now, she turned toward me and looked up with tearless, empty eyes. "She refused treatment because of me." She made the statement even harsher. "She died because of me."

I wanted to comfort her, but I knew she wouldn't allow that now. In a certain way, she was right, and she had to get rid of her guilt somehow; but on one issue, she was definitely wrong. "And although you believe that – which I do not – you still call her a client?"

"She paid me. She even set up a bank account for me. And it was always well-filled." She just didn't want to accept the truth!

"Yes, of course. Because she didn't want to lose you." I could easily understand that!

That word finally brought her to a boil. "Lose? Didn't want to lose me?" She looked at me with extreme aggression. "Do you all believe you can own me?" She turned away from me again with a jerk. "You pay me, and for that, you think you can treat me like an object. Buy and use. Own and lose." She laughed contemptuously.

I could not and would not allow myself to be drawn into that discussion. I knew that much of this could be attributed to pure anger. I stayed calm. "Who is 'you'?" I asked.

She turned around so quickly, she almost tripped. "Well, you," she shouted. "My . . .," she stopped as quickly as she had begun.

"I'm not a client," I said. I tried to answer calmly. "I don't pay you, and I don't want to own you either. I love you." It was very hard for me to say that so calmly. I felt the fear climbing up my throat. She seemed to have lost all connection to and all feeling for me. Could I get through to her at all? She was still standing there, mute.

I had to say something, or else I would break into tears in desperation. "I'm convinced that she felt the same way." She didn't appear to hear me, or at least didn't comprehend what I was saying. "And I feel exactly as she did. I don't want to lose you." I didn't know how much of that was getting through to her. I hoped she would answer.

She didn't react right away. It seemed to me like an eternity before she spoke again, very quietly.

"I don't want to lose you, either."

For the first moment, I felt like I'd been struck by lightning. I hadn't expected that. What was going on inside her? Was this just a temporary glitch, or did she really mean what she said? Did she even realize that this was the first time she had confessed her true feelings to me since we had met?

I went slowly to her and stood before her. I didn't touch her. She stood there, unmoving, staring blankly past me. She obviously no longer saw me or anything else that existed in the present. The images that played before her ghostly eyes had long since been burned into her consciousness. I waited.

"She was so good to me. And I needed her so much." If any voice could be called toneless, it was hers. "And then she left me."

I reached out my hand and touched her arm. Very softly, I began to speak. "She stayed with you as long as she could. She never would have left voluntarily, you know that."

"No, she went voluntarily!" She obviously heard my words, but they had a different meaning to her. "She just left me in the lurch!" Her rage seemed real, but it was still directed against a bygone reality.

I held her arm tighter. "No, you know that that's not true. She thought of you right up to the end. She gave you the apartment, so you'd be taken care of." Actually, I knew that it was pointless to discuss anything with her in this condition, but I didn't want her to fall deeper into these absurd thoughts. That couldn't be good for her.

"Gave? She never gave me anything! She just left." Whoa, something didn't fit here. She had just told me something entirely different. And it had sounded very believable. What was the truth?

"Without a word. From one day to the next. Without a word." She sounded like a broken record. "I don't know what to do." The record went on, and she was obviously immersed completely in the past now. I could only guess what sort of horrible disappointment she was talking about now, but I began to suspect something. Could it be that she spoke of two different people? And two different times?

Maybe I could make a cautious attempt to find out what exactly she was talking about. I didn't move and spoke very softly. "What happened?"

It seemed to me that she wasn't even aware of my presence. She was talking to herself. "Gone. She's gone. How can she do something like this? I have no one but her. We've known each other since we were fifteen. I love her!" Her voice had a painful, almost whining, undertone, like a child who's been hurt and doesn't understand why.

She spoke of a woman she'd known since she was fifteen years old. That couldn't be the same woman who'd left her the apartment. But who was it then? In any case, she had left deep scars behind. Such deep scars that she did not appear today, so much later, to be over them.

"I love her so." She repeated what she had just said, this time with the most despair I'd ever imagined. It stung me. Desperation over one and then the other ... Yes, I had to admit that I was jealous of them. I was ashamed to feel that way, but I knew I couldn't change it. Then she could still say it. She'd probably said it to her hundreds of times. And because of her, she could no longer say it. Vengeance filled me. Then I pulled myself together.

That wasn't important now. What was important was to bring her back into the present, if possible, without falling apart completely. I smiled soothingly at her, even if she couldn't see me.

"Love is so fragile," I explained, "but the memories remain. The bad ones with the good. Time makes the bad ones pale, and you remember the good ones your whole life. Don't you think?" I hoped to help her recall a more positive experience with this kind of gentle suggestion, but I had my doubts.

She laid her head to the side a bit and looked down at me, although I could've sworn she was talking to a ghost. "I was looking forward to this evening so much. And now ...? What should I do now? The apartment is empty. She's gone. She can't have just left. Without saying anything to me." She sniffled, but I could see no tears. Then she repeated softly and disbelievingly, "Without saying anything ..."

I felt so much sympathy for her that the tears almost came to me that wouldn't come to her, even though I didn't know exactly what was going on. Her voice had such a different sound from the one I knew, a sound that shook me at least as much as the whimpering in the clearing in Paris, when she'd told me the most frightful of stories. The recollection of that scene brought me back to reason. There was no sense in letting her languish in this state any longer. It didn't serve either one of us, her even less than me, and gentle coaxing from the outside seemed not to reach her, or worse seemed to make the journey into the past even worse. I looked at her. Her eyes were still blurred, not necessarily in the same kind of pain as back in the clearing, but she was obviously not there.

I reached out a hand and touched her arm. Dazed, she looked down at me. Then a smile began to lighten her face.

"You're here!" She came up to me and hugged me forcefully – not passionately, but more like a young, strong teenager who doesn't yet know her own strength and expresses her joy at seeing you again. I gasped for breath. It was clear to me now that she wasn't hugging me.

And at that moment, jealousy caught me completely unprepared. I reacted automatically. I raised my hand and smacked her. I really got her. Totally shocked, I stared at my hand, which still hung in the air, and at her face, which was beginning to redden. I'd never done anything like that before, for as long as I could remember. I began to stutter: "I-I-I'm sorry. I . . ."

She stared back, at least as shocked. Our gazes met in the air and didn't seem to be able to decide to whom they should return. We were both paralyzed for a second. Then – all of a sudden – she began to laugh. It was more than a hysterical giggle. It grew a little, then stopped as suddenly as it had begun. I was relieved. Completely irrationally, I'd gotten the idea that one had to give hysterical people a good slap in order to return them to their senses. And I was by no means capable of repeating that at the moment.

She stood there and looked at me seriously now. Her eyes appeared to be clear again.

"You hit me," she stated calmly.

I squirmed. My God, what could I do to make up for that? "I don't know what to say." My stuttering returned. "I d-don't know how that c-could have h-h-happened. I'm – I'm so sorry." I could only repeat myself, so I remained silent. This was really a hopeless situation. It seemed that there were never two free minutes in which we could just be together calmly and happily. Every time, something unpredictable happened.

This time also. She laughed, as if I'd said something humorous. "Do you know what's funny about that?"

I shook my head. I couldn't imagine that in my wildest dreams!

"That I thought, in the first moment, that she was really here. She did that often."

The astonishment must have been written across my face. "Hit you?" I couldn't believe it.

"Yes," she said plainly, and turned around. She went to the sofa and sat down. Expectantly, she looked up at me. "I'm glad you did it," she remarked, very calmly again.

I was amazed. This calm, this sudden change in her behavior. It had only been a couple of minutes since . . .

Nonetheless, I still couldn't agree with her. "I'm not," I replied sadly. "I hate violence. It's not me." I looked at her and awaited her reaction.

"I know that," she said. She smiled gently. "Come here."

I shook my head. I wanted to go to her, but I didn't want all of this to be swept back under the rug. If she just wanted to celebrate our reconciliation again . . .

She smiled again. "Come," she repeated. "You've brought me back to my senses; now let's talk about it. You want that, don't you?" Her expression took my answer for granted.

"Yes." I agreed, but although it was my wish to learn as much about her as possible, I hated the thought of being forced back into the role of voyeur. Until now, that had always come to a very unhappy ending. I asked myself if it was worth it. To satisfy my curiosity. She was still looking calmly up at me. The danger did not seem too great, but still . . . "You don't have to tell me."

Her head moved slightly, as if she couldn't decide whether to accept the offer of freedom. Then she fixed her gaze on me again. "I've already told you so much . . . ," she hesitated a little.

Did she think it was too much? She sat up straight on the sofa. Her shoulders were even.

"Would you like to hear it ...?" She looked at me questioningly again, but she didn't look upset. Should I risk it?

I came to a decision. "Yes," I nodded briefly, "I'd like that." Was it just my curiosity taking over, or was it something else? I didn't know for sure. But shouldn't I also understand and be accountable for all of my actions? Everything I learned about her could help me to understand her better. And that was, in the end, what I wanted. I went slowly over to the sofa and sat next to her. This piece of furniture belonged in a museum. All the things that had happened here ...

"You're dismayed at what I showed you, right?" She looked down at the floor in front of her, although I was sitting right next to her. For her, this was all probably quite normal, but in my world – I corrected myself: before I got to know her; since then, a lot about the world I claimed as my own had changed – it certainly wasn't.

"Well, yeah." I tried to speak as carefully as possible. She recognized immediately what I was thinking about.

"You don't have to make such an effort at being tolerant." She turned her head and looked at me. "It is awful."

I sighed. "Yes, you're probably right." I didn't exactly think it was a question of tolerance. More of the capacity of my imagination. Mine was sometimes overloaded by what she offered. It was unimaginable. At least for me, who had so obviously led such a "harmless" life. Even if that had not been clear to me until recently.

I looked into her face, and a question forced its way out of me. "You were talking about two different people just now, weren't you? The woman from whom you inherited the apartment wasn't the same one who ..."

"Who hit me, do you mean? No, she wasn't." Her face softened again. "Maria was a wonderful woman. She would never have done anything like that." She got up and positioned herself opposite me behind a chair. "That only now became clear to me." She looked right at me. "After you insisted on it so much."

I shrugged my shoulders slightly. Had I had the right to do that? I didn't know anything about this woman.

"And you were right." She propped herself up with both arms against the back of the chair and bent forward. "She was no client."

I could've been proud of my victory, but I wasn't.

"I've always tried to convince myself that she was. Especially then. Then, when she didn't come back and I was firmly convinced that she'd left me. It was easier for me that way. I could place all of the blame on her." She turned around, so she didn't have to look at me anymore, and leaned her back against the chair. "Although I knew it could only be my fault." She went silent.

I stood up. "That's not true either! Does everything always have to be black and white?" She was making me angry again. I didn't want that. I went over to her, but stopped behind her. I spoke to her back. "Was anyone at fault for anything? She was sick. You couldn't help that, and neither could she. Can't you understand that?"

She turned around. There were tears in her eyes now.

"Yes," she said softly. "Yes, I understand it now."

That probably made her miss her even more. I wasn't particularly happy with my role. I wasn't exactly playing the devil's advocate but that's what it felt like. I laid a hand on her arm. "I think I would've liked her a lot, your Maria."

For a moment, she looked at me calmly, and I was afraid the whole river was going to burst out of her. There wasn't a sound to be heard anywhere in the room. Then the corners of her mouth twitched a little.

"Maybe," she said. "You have some things in common." The pull on her mouth grew stronger. "But with your jealousy ..." She frowned a bit unhappily.

I wanted to protest, because I felt, despite her sadness, that she was picking on me a bit; but I let it be. She was probably right.

She hugged me. It was like a goodbye – but not to me. Now Maria could rest in peace. In her and in her heart. She pulled away from me and went back to the sofa. She sat down with one leg under her body; then she looked up. "That was one of them."

A shudder ran down my spine. I'd almost forgotten that there was another one. And I was convinced I'd already heard the less painful part. Maria was the good; now came the evil. Everything tensed inside me. I didn't know how evil. When I thought about the day outside Paris ... I wasn't at all sure that I even wanted to hear it. I caught her eye as I went back to the sofa. But she was obviously prepared to tell me. It was so obvious that I didn't dare say no.

"The other one was my first great love – my first woman. Did I tell you that already?"

I shook my head slightly. I'd only guessed at that from the confused phrases she'd thrown at me earlier. She leaned back a little. I sat next to her and waited.

"She was a school friend. We'd known each other for quite some time. Really, since we were little kids. But then, we hadn't had much to do with one another." She looked at me briefly. Her eyes were clear and unclouded. Almost a little introverted. Nonetheless, she was completely there.

"So, it started when we were thirteen or fourteen. That's when we got closer. I don't even remember why. Suddenly, we did everything together. And everything meant going dancing, drinking, smoking: anything to avoid being 'good.' I think that's still reasonably normal." She looked at me inquisitively, as if we were on a TV talk show and she'd just made a statement that required my support.

I nodded in agreement. That had surely just been the usual teenage rebellion. I had some of that behind me as well.

"At fifteen, we slept together for the first time." It came out quickly and briefly. That didn't require any confirmation. It was simply a fact. "That is to say, she slept with me, not the other way around. And so it went on. I was barely allowed to touch her, never to enter her. She only did that to me."

I had to swallow hard. It wasn't easy to listen to a description of the things she'd done with other people. Somehow, that always felt like it should be our own private territory. Despite her occupation and despite all jealousy. And our relationship was different. She was describing the conventional butch-femme relationship, very conventional. Two women who played the man-woman game. Every relationship contained some of that. Even my own had had it. But not in this extreme form. That was strange to me.

I had been staring ahead, musing, while she said nothing. When I looked around, I noticed her eyes. She was waiting for my reaction. She was trying to guess how much she could tell me, how much I wanted to hear. I couldn't say anything, but at least my expression had told her that I wasn't terribly shocked.

"I thought it had to be like that. I couldn't imagine any other way. I only knew her." She laughed briefly. "Then again, that's not very different from the little straight couples at that age, is it?"

She looked at me. I nodded. She was definitely right about that.

"She began to talk about it more and more often, that she'd rather be a man. But I didn't find that particularly odd, either. She was always a very masculine sort."

I looked down at myself involuntarily. She punctuated that with another bit of laughter, though more cheerful than before. "No, there's no comparison to you. You don't need to worry about that." She smiled to herself a little. "She had tattoos. A lot."

I wrinkled my face in a hint of disgust. She leaned over me. "In case it makes you feel any better, I find you very feminine." She kissed me on the nose and gave me a playful little look. "Although maybe a little . . . ," she made a dramatic pause. ". . . tomboyish?"

She acted as though she were really considering it seriously. I groaned. I really couldn't stand that word! She laughed when she saw that she'd hit the nail on the head. I didn't think that there was any doubt that she would. With her sensitivity to those things . . . Then she got serious again and brushed my cheek with her hand. She touched me briefly and then leaned back into the corner. "The interesting thing about it is that today, she really is a man."

"What?" She said it so naturally, as though one was the automatic consequence of the other.

"She had an operation. But that was much later. By then, I was no longer in contact with her. Anyway, she'd already – back then, when she was still a woman – behaved along that vein. She had a group of girls, for instance, who were panhandling and turning tricks around the bus station. She lived that way for a while herself. And on drugs, but I didn't find that out until much later. She spared me that for quite some time. I don't know why. I'm sure it would've been easy. I would've done anything she wanted then." She looked at me again with that clear expression that seemed to say: you can go any time you want to. I wondered what she expected of me.

"Privately, anyhow ... Well, like I said, I didn't know anything else. Even when it got harder and harder."

I really didn't know whether I should allow her to continue. I remembered our first encounter, her fear in bed. I tried to look in the other direction. She leaned over and placed a finger on my chin. She turned my face around to her. "You remember, don't you?"

I raised my arm and placed my hand gently on top of hers. "Yes," I confirmed quietly. "You don't have to tell me the rest if you don't want to."

She slipped her fingers into mine and let them stay there. "I want to. It's always been very painful for me, and I've always repressed it. Perhaps this is my last chance to become clear about who I really am and why." She became more distant again and turned away. "Why I am what you so despise," she said softly, in the direction of the couch cushions.

I raged. I'd heard that statement from her once before and disagreed vehemently. If she still thought that, I must not have been very convincing. I took her in my arms from behind and rested my head against her back. "Do you really believe that?"

She made a hollow sound. "If not now, then later. I haven't told you everything yet."

"Then tell me everything, so I can prove to you that the opposite is true," I grumbled ill-naturedly. My impatience began to bother me again. That was hardly called for in this situation.

She turned around, so that I had to let go of her. "I'm sure you can already imagine most of it." She pressed her hands together as if to pray and said nothing. She looked over my shoulder and into a distant past. "In the beginning, she only hit me sometimes. Just to increase the arousal, she said. Pains of lust, she called it. But I didn't feel much lust with it. Only once, and that embarrassed me. When I told her that, she hit me again. So I just let it happen and didn't say anything else. Then one day, instead of her hands, she used a belt. My parents had never hit me. I had no idea what that meant. I screamed — so she put a gag in my mouth and hit harder. I bled where the buckle hit. But she did it very carefully. The places weren't visible when I was dressed. I was surprised and ashamed. Ashamed that I let someone do that to me, but I didn't dare try to stop it.

The fact that she was ashamed of something someone else did to her was nothing new. I didn't wonder about anything else. It all seemed to follow simply.

"She said it was a sign of my love for her. Every scar a symbol. How could I defend myself?"

She looked at me trustingly. I could barely stand it anymore. This calm expectation! I could've screamed.

She continued. "The next time it was a whip. And then handcuffs. The gag. The shackles." She had begun to speak more softly, also. Maybe I should stop her, after all. How much worse could it get? "That was the worst part. Having my hands and feet shackled. On my stomach, until I couldn't breathe and begged her for mercy. And she just laughed and hit me again. Again and again and again." She started beating a pillow. It was like an unstoppable flow. "And again . . .," I held her hands back.

"Come," I soothed her, "stop. It's over." She let me hold her. But her arms still jerked.

"And then – one day – she was gone. Just like that." She still said it with wonder.

"But . . .?" I couldn't see that as anything other than a great stroke of luck. "Weren't you happy that she was gone?"

"Happy?" No, she obviously didn't see it that way.

"Yes, since you were free from her then." I would've thanked everything I believed in.

She repeated one of my words. "Free?" She changed her position on the sofa. Now she sat a little farther away from me. "I was horribly lonely," she explained sadly. "She was all I had. And I loved her."

I trembled visibly. This word out of her mouth, and in such a clear state of mind, told me everything.

"Well, then . . .," I sank back into the sofa. That was then, and it was over. She would never say that to anyone again. Not even to me. I suddenly seemed horribly old and alone.

She realized what she had said. Perhaps that was what drove her to say more, to explain to herself and to me why things were as they were. "The loneliness was the worst." Her tone leveled again. "I couldn't be alone anymore. She had been with me every night. I was used to that."

"To everything?" I asked. My voice must have sounded a little harsh. She looked up, startled. "Pardon me," I followed quickly. "I have no right . . .," I was tired. It was her life, not mine. And the future looked more and more that separation would always exist.

"Yes, you do," she said, suddenly gentle. "Yes, I had gotten used to almost everything. But it wasn't like that every day. She didn't hit me or shackle me everyday. But she slept with me everyday. It was like a ritual. It didn't matter what we had done before, when we went to bed, we had to sleep together. And sometimes the rest." She fell silent.

I was unsettled again. "How old were you when she – left?" I asked carefully.

"Nineteen," she said. "But I didn't feel that way. I still felt like I was fifteen. It was as if I hadn't matured at all since I'd met her. My peers all seemed older." She laughed again unhappily. "Maybe that was the attractive thing about me. In any case, I could hardly escape all the offers."

I could well imagine how that had proceeded. She needed someone to care about her.

"I was so inexperienced," she explained. "Except for the one thing. I noticed that very quickly. That which was already second nature to me was still relatively new to the others. And they thought that what they experienced of me in the one area must carry over into the others. I behaved in such a way that they would have to believe it."

"You mean they paid you from the beginning?" The idea would never have occurred to me while practicing with a lover. I must really be naive.

"Well, no, they didn't exactly pay me in the beginning, but I received gifts. Expensive gifts. And I was usually the second woman. The one for the bed." She said it very disparagingly. And I couldn't blame her, as much as it horrified me as well.

She let out a resigned sigh. "Anyhow, they didn't make it difficult for me to live that way. And at some point, I got used to it. I didn't expect anything more."

"Until Maria came," I said clairvoyantly. That must have been a mild shock for her.

She looked me in the eyes. "Yes," she confirmed, "and then you."

I couldn't take it. That was all in the past. She'd used up her love on others, wasted it on her torturers. There was nothing left for me.

I made a dismissive gesture. "I'm not that important." I wanted to get up off the sofa. How did that go in Casablanca? *We'll always have Paris.* That fit here perfectly. We were only missing the airplane into which I could disappear, flying away to leave the evil behind me.

She grabbed my arm. "Where are you going?" She could still sound like fifteen when she wanted to. Sweet and innocent. And somewhere – it seemed to me – she was just that. But I wasn't.

"Home. I need to get some sleep. Tomorrow is going to be another long day." How the clichés poured from my mouth! I couldn't believe it myself.

I looked at her, and I loved her so. But I couldn't give her what she already knew of in so many ways, I would only disappoint her. I felt empty and burned out. Dejected, I knelt in front of her. I could only tell the truth.

"I love you. But that's all I can give you. You've earned much more. You'll find someone better easily." I sounded hollow.

I wanted to stand up, but she held me down. "Tell me, are you completely out of your mind?" This wasn't the same calm tone of voice I'd heard before. "If you don't stop that nonsense right now, I'll really throw you out." She thought about it for a moment. "Oh, no, that's what you want. So I'll keep you here." Her words were full of energy. She took me wholly by surprise.

"But . . .," I stammered, still entirely confused.

"But what?" She slid off the sofa and lay suddenly on top of me. She looked down at me from above like a tiger with its prey. "What do you think? How many people have I told what I just told you?"

I tried to think about it. It was difficult. I knew so little about her relationships. "Well, Maria for instance, and . . ."

She interrupted me angrily. "Not even Maria. Don't even consider 'and.' You're the only one. And why do you think that is?"

I couldn't imagine why, not by my best effort. I fell silent.

"I ought to thrash you," she whispered. Then she spoke again at a normal volume, "and that's not because of my occupation and not because of my past. That's just a normal reaction, as obtuse as you're being."

I didn't think so at all, but if she did . . . She was heavier, she was stronger, and she was on top of me. It didn't seem like an opportune time to argue with her. "Mother of heaven!" She groaned loudly. "You want to hear those three words. You've fixated yourself on them so much that you won't take anything else seriously. Dammit already!" She swore. That was something new. "Don't you understand? I just confessed everything to you that there is to confess." She shot me an icy look. "Something I can't say about you, by the way. And your only reaction is that you're not good enough for me? I ought to have a thing or two to say about that, don't you think?"

"Yes. No." I didn't know what to say.

She looked lovingly down at me again. "So remember this: the time where I let myself be controlled by my shame and guilt is over. And you're not exactly free of responsibility for that." I couldn't really argue with that. "My self-esteem has recovered somewhat. And a certain person has definitely had something to do with that. Right?" She stared wildly into my face, but the tenderness glowing in her eyes took away any hint of danger. I nodded to the degree that I could, given that I was pinned to the floor. "And why do you want to leave now?" She propped herself up with her arms and increased the space between us so that I could breathe a little better.

I had to answer her, I knew that, but I didn't know how. And I told her that as well. "I don't know." Softly, I added a few seconds later, "I feel so small."

"Aha!" She let herself roll off and lay next to me. She talked to the ceiling. "How about if we talk about that sensibly? What works in one place might work in another. Did you ever think of that?"

To be honest, I hadn't. And that didn't make me any bigger. More the opposite. Everything I'd demanded of her, I hadn't even thought to question in myself. Big adjustment!

She propped herself up on one elbow and watched me curiously. "What kind of woman are you, really? Have you ever let me look inside like I let you?"

She pushed me into embarrassed confusion.

"Or is that not compatible with the sublime ethos of the knight in shining armor?"

She was so right! But what I most wanted to do was flee. She noticed that immediately.

"I won't really hold you against your will, you know that." She laughed softly. I felt horribly transparent. "And you won't really go." Now she looked earnestly into my face again. "So, why don't we discuss what we really want to do?"

Yes, why not? I was angry. "How am I supposed to know that? You want your profession . . ."

"Here goes the broken record," she sighed. "I should've known it." But this time, she was less angry than any other time we'd discussed that issue. In actuality, she didn't seem angry at all. And not even so uncertain. "You know that that's not an issue at the moment. Nothing has changed about that."

"Yes, at the moment . . .," I emphasized.

"Yes, at the moment," she repeated decisively. "Leave it at that. Do you want to force a decision that I can't make right now? What do you expect to accomplish that way? Even a decision would only be temporary in a case like that."

She was doubtlessly right about that. But what was the alternative?

"You see everything in black and white, too. You accused me of exactly the same thing. How about if we both try to get away from that?" I barely recognized her anymore. What had happened? She reached one logical conclusion after the other. She laughed when she saw my baffled expression. "Sometimes I can think, too," she smiled to herself. "I've just been distracted by your presence most of the time." She leaned over and kissed me. Nice distraction! More of that . . . She stopped and I opened my eyes again.

That loving look, that tender mouth. What kind of creature was she really?

She rolled on top of me again. Her lips brushed delicately against my cheek. "We have so much time," she whispered.

I believed everything she told me. At that moment, a light came on. Could it be that my own stubbornness had caused just as many problems as it had helped to solve? And what would happen if I told her so now? I could barely imagine the consequences.

I cleared my throat. "Can you imagine us still being together in ten years?" I asked her. Her lips froze right on the spot they were kissing.

"Who knows?" she answered honestly. At least the idea didn't horrify her; I could tell that much. She continued her thought. "I don't think it'll be much different for us than it is for any couple." She was calling us a couple – it kept getting better! "But what do you say we start with the next three months first?" She smiled down at me.

Those eyes, how they caressed me just by looking. How could I have refused that willingly? I must have been crazy!

She was still smiling. "You were already my taxi to Paris once. Do you want to try it again?"

At first, I didn't quite understand her correctly, but then I knew what she meant. Her lips neared my mouth.

"Yes," I said, right before she kissed me.

THE END

An excerpt from

Forbidden Passion
by
Ruth Gogoll

The small letters danced across the monitor before Kim's eyes.
She gently massaged her eyelids. Working with the computer for
hours was none too relaxing. However, when the exhaustion grew
too great, there was this particular website on the Internet she had
a habit of visiting to ease her sore eyes. It was a website full of stories; she enjoyed reading them. They were very special stories. Stories by women for women.

Slowly, Kim slid into the narrative. The woman with the chest-
nut-colored hair let herself fall gently onto the sofa, the other
woman bent over her –

"Ms. Wolff?"

Kim spun round. Her boss stood in the door. Her chestnut-
colored hair caressed her shoulders, sleek and seductive. Kim
gulped.

"Is there something urgent you're working on?" her boss asked
her. "Or could you spare a minute to come with me?"

"I . . . I can come," Kim stuttered arduously. And it was true. She
probably could have come along with her right away.

Sonja Kantner, the department chief, and the main protagonist of
Kim's fantasies of sleepless nights, gazed at the monitor. But she
was too far away, the screen stood too slanted and the letters were
too small. Kim thanked all goddesses in heaven for that.

"I'll just save this," Kim said, feeling hot all over. Hopefully she
hadn't turned red as a tomato. But in reality she never did. She was
lucky that way. Certainly it was lucky at this very moment.

"You do that," Sonja Kantner said, nodding, and turning to leave.

Kim watched her luscious bottom leave the room. Why was this
woman so attractive? It was pure torture every day.

Six weeks earlier

The first time Kim had seen her new boss – at a meeting in the conference room – she had nearly fainted. She immediately created a plan to relocate the department chief's office from its strategically convenient place next to her own office to the end of the corridor – or to another floor. Best of all, to another building.

"Why don't you introduce yourself to us, Mrs. Kantner," the head manager said, after offering an oral curriculum vitae of his new department chief, himself.

He retreated and Sonja Kantner stepped forward. She briefly repeated what he had already said about her, but that didn't interest Kim much. What interested her was said right at the beginning: married, without children.

"Not yet, that is," she had added with a charming smile.

The guess couldn't have been better. Kim almost sighed at the confirmation of what she had actually known already. Sonja Kantner was straight, very straight. But would it have changed anything if it hadn't been that way? Kim began stewing over her plan of having the woman relocated to another building. Weren't there foreign branch offices, too? Couldn't Sonja Kantner work there?

Kim knew one thing for sure: she wouldn't last long having Sonja Kantner right next to her, every day, nearly every minute. What was the solution? Perhaps Kim could get used to her; perhaps her desires would deaden? Kim eyed Sonja Kantner's body from top to bottom once again while she spoke. No. No, that was not going to happen. The opposite was more probable.

The meeting came to an end; Kim was on the verge of leaving when the highest-ranking manager waved to her. "Ms. Wolff? Do you have a second or two to spare?"

Kim took a deep breath and straightened her shoulders. Now she had to be brave. She walked toward the two and he introduced her with a smile. "Mrs. Kantner, this is Ms. Wolff. She's going to be your closest coworker."

Sonja Kantner smiled, too, and shook Kim's hand. Kim would have preferred not touching the woman's hand at all, but she couldn't very well refuse. Sonja Kantner's palm felt soft and warm. Kim didn't ever want to let go, but Mrs. Kantner withdrew it herself after the appropriate amount of time that proper manners dictated.

"I'm glad to meet you, Ms. Wolff," she said. "I hope we'll both profit from working together."

Working together? Kim repeated that silently, but she said what was expected of her: "I hope so too. I'm looking forward to it very much." She smiled sanguinely and hoped it seemed genuine. The tingling sensation spreading from her hand through her entire body prevented her from having full control of her own reactions.

"You'll take Mrs. Kantner for a walk through the firm and show her around, won't you, Ms. Wolff?" her boss assumed. His tone was a friendly command.

Kim tried not to gulp. "Yes, certainly," she replied, desperately composed; her voice was very quiet. "Of course. I'll show her around." If only that had been possible! There was so much Kim would have loved to show this woman . . .!

Sonja Kantner laughed. "We'll save that for tomorrow. Today is my walk-through of the executive floor."

The boss melted in reaction to her charming smile, his reaction as strong as Kim's; yet only he was allowed to show it openly. Kim was not. *A day's grace! At least something positive!*

"I'll see you tomorrow, then," Sonja Kantner said to Kim. "What time will you be here in the morning?"

"No later than eight," Kim muttered.

"Fine," Mrs. Kantner said with a smile. "I'll be here at seven."

℥℥

"**O**h, this really wasn't necessary, Ms. Wolff," Mrs. Kantner said, beaming.

In such a good mood so early in the morning – what was to become of that! When had she gotten out of bed? Kim had been perfectly on time but Mrs. Kantner was already sitting at her desk as

Kim entered the office.

She made her way toward Kim to shake hands. "Good morning," she said. There was an irresistible gleam in her eyes; Kim could have sunk into them and drowned in their depths.

She probably had no idea how that affected Kim ... how *she* affected Kim.

"You could have come at eight on the dot," Mrs. Kantner continued. "I know it gets on everyone's nerves, but I'm in the habit of catching up on work in peace and quiet in the morning. You know, before everyone else arrives. You don't get any of that done otherwise." Her laugh was unbelievably pleasant.

She had barely begun. What work did she have to catch up on? Kim forced an understanding smile to her lips and withdrew the hand Mrs. Kantner was still holding. "You're absolutely right," she agreed. "I prefer doing that in the evening after everyone's left for the day."

Sonja Kantner laughed again and returned to her desk. "We all have preferences of our very own, don't we?" she said. She turned around to face Kim. "How long are you usually in the office after working hours, then?" she asked.

"Sometimes until ten, but in the morning, I usually arrive at –" She stopped in mid-sentence. Perhaps it was better her boss didn't know exactly when she used to arrive in the morning.

Sonja Kantner smiled. She was too intelligent a woman to be tricked that easily. "You're not here at seven or eight, are you?"

Kim sighed. "Well, no," she said. "But I'll change that, of course," she added hastily. "If you're here by seven, I'll be here too."

"Oh, no; that's not necessary, really," replied Sonja Kantner. "As I said: I know I get on everyone's nerves starting work so early, but I don't expect the same of anybody else." She smiled again. "I'm usually in bed by ten in the evening, though. We should strive to find a time in between."

In bed? Kim eyed her over. She was already attractive in daylight – how seductive must she look lying in her bed? She was sure to have wonderful lingerie for the nights ... or perhaps she actually wore nothing at all ...?

"What time could you be here by ... at the earliest?" Sonja Kantner asked, turning the pages of a document file her predecessor had left behind.

Kim had to put an abrupt end to her thoughts first. "Half past eight, perhaps?" she suggested. She'd be able to make that. Barely.

Sonja Kantner looked up. "Fine," she finally said. Then she smiled an unbelievably likeable, almost loving smile. "And I won't say a word if that occasionally turns into nine. I guess that was what you actually wanted to suggest, wasn't it?"

She must have gone through a vast number of leadership seminars to have reached this level. "Yes," Kim admitted.

"We'll manage together somehow!" Sonja Kantner said, a laugh in her voice. "Well, will you give me that tour of the company, now?"

Together – what a nice thing to imagine, Kim mused, as Sonja Kantner proceeded out of the office ahead of her.

An excerpt from
The L Jungle
by
Ruth Gogoll

At Sappho

"**Y**ou're not serious!" Sabrina's eyes flew open. "She was there when you got home?"

"She's got a lot of nerve," said Carolin.

"I . . ." Anita wrung her hands and looked at the floor. "I can't just send her away."

"Why not?" Sabrina shook her head. "After all the liberties she's taken with you, I thought you'd finally figured this out."

"She . . . she needs me," Anita said softly. "She said so."

"Is that a new record, or has it been playing for awhile now?" Carolin sighed.

"One cappuccino, one latte, and one fresh-squeezed vitamin bomb," Melly smiled as she set down their order.

"What would you say, Melly?" Carolin asked. "Marlene showed up at Anita's place again . . . after not being around for a week."

"Right, she hasn't been around here, either." Even though Melly nodded as she spoke, she didn't appear particularly interested.

"We have to do something," Carolin said.

"About Marlene?" Melly laughed. "She's not all that bad. You just have to let her know the score."

Sabrina raised an eyebrow. Melly headed back to the counter. Sabrina got up and walked after her. "You had something with Marlene, too?" she asked.

Melly shrugged. "When I first came to the café, a long time ago," she said.

Sabrina involuntarily glanced at Melly's ample breasts, clearly visible under her tight, sleeveless top.

Melly laughed. "Yes, that's what she's into." She glanced over at the table. "Of course I can't compete with Anita."

"Why . . ." Sabrina frowned. "Why would you take up with her?"

"Oh, she has a certain . . . robust charm," Melly replied with a laugh.

"Charm? Marlene?" Sabrina looked dumbfounded.

"I don't think she was as unhappy then as she is now. She was still working as a truck driver, so she only came in now and then."

"Chris told me that she used to drive trucks."

"That was her dream job. Ever since they took away her driver's license, though, she's stuck in an office. I think that's what makes her so short-tempered," Melly offered.

"Why did they take away her driver's license?"

"What do you think?" Melly rolled her eyes.

"Alcohol?"

"Yes, of course. She drinks way too much." Melly took a couple of bottles out of the refrigerator and began to mix a cocktail. "I told her as much, too, but she listens to no one when it comes to that subject."

"I don't think you can get her to listen when it comes to any subject," Sabrina said. She glanced over at Anita, who was talking with Carolin.

"I wouldn't say that." Melly filled the cocktail shaker with ice. "You just have to find the right starting point with her."

Sabrina laughed skeptically. "And how do you find that? Maybe I can give Anita some sort of tip."

"Anita . . ." Melly looked over at the table. "There's no sense in that. Women like Anita are deadly for Marlene. They bring out the worst in her."

Sabrina stared at her, speechless, for a moment. "You're telling me it's Anita's fault?" she finally managed in stunned disbelief.

"No one is at fault; that's not what I said," Melly countered. She decorated the cocktail and delivered it to a table.

Still mulling things over, Sabrina returned to Carolin and Anita.

"Take the key away from her," she heard Carolin say.

"I can't do that." Anita's forehead was furrowed with concern.

"You have to." Carolin appeared outraged. "She can't just come and go as she pleases. In your apartment."

"Don't get yourself worked up, Carolin," Sabrina said. "Anita has to decide these things for herself."

Carolin looked at her aghast.

"What is it you like so much about Marlene?" Sabrina asked Anita. "Carolin and I obviously can't comprehend it, but something about her must appeal to you."

"She's so . . . ," a ready smile spread across Anita's face, "strong."

"Does she hit you?" Carolin blurted out, before Sabrina could stop her.

Anita's eyes widened. "No," she said. "She's never hit me."

"But others have?" asked Sabrina. "Other women you were with?"

Anita lowered her gaze.

"So it's true?" Carolin pressed.

"No." Anita's voice was barely a breath.

Carolin looked at Sabrina. Sabrina shook her head. "Did you see there's a reading coming up at the alternative bookstore?" Sabrina asked, being sure to sound relaxed. "I'd love to go. Rumor has it the author is the new Rita Mae Brown."

"I hate Rita Mae Brown," Carolin said. "You couldn't pay me to read her books!"

"So that means I'll have to manage without you," Sabrina sighed. "How about you, Anita?"

Anita lifted her head. "I'd love to go," she smiled shyly.

"Everyone having fun?" Chris gave Sabrina a kiss in greeting, and sat down with them. "I just ran into Rick. They ought to be here any second."

"They?" Carolin looked at her in surprise.

Just then, the door opened and Rick and Thea walked in.

Chris grinned. "Yes, 'they'," she said.

Carolin raised an eyebrow in interest and regarded Thea thoroughly.

"Hello people," said Rick. She pulled up a chair and sat down across from Chris.

"Aren't you going to offer your girlfriend a seat?" Sabrina asked, smiling.

Rick looked up and stood again. "Oh, sorry," she said to Thea. "Have a seat."

Thea smiled at her and sat down. Rick dragged over another chair.

"And you're not planning to introduce your girlfriend to us, either," Carolin added with a grin.

"My name is Thea," the woman said, smiling. Rick appeared both confused and exhausted. "I'm a journalist."

"Ah, so you interviewed Rick . . . in that capacity?" Carolin asked.

"Y-yes. Yes, you could call it that," replied Thea with an even wider smile.

Carolin and Sabrina grinned. "How was your day, honey?" Sabrina asked Chris, running her hand lovingly along her leg. "Hard?"

"It was okay." Chris leaned back.

Melly came to their table, glanced briefly at Rick, and then nodded at Chris. "What would you like to drink?"

"A champagne cocktail!" Chris laughed. "No, bring me a Proud Mary, please."

"Coffee," Thea said. "I'm totally wiped out. A quadruple espresso or something." She reattached herself to Rick and cuddled up to her.

"I could offer you two doubles," Melly responded.

"Ricky, don't you want something?" Thea caressed Rick's cheek.

"Umm . . . a beer," Rick replied quickly.

"I think coffee would be more appropriate," said Thea. "Beer makes you tired, and I'd like it better if you stayed a little frisky." She nibbled tenderly on Rick's earlobe and looked up at Melly. "Cancel the beer and bring her the same as me."

Melly started to raise her eyebrows, but quickly caught herself. "All right," she said, and went back to the counter.

"Thea," said Sabrina thoughtfully. "Thea Funk?" Thea nodded. "I know your show," Sabrina continued. "I listen to it sometimes."

"And? Do you like it?" she asked, briefly releasing Rick.

"Very amusing," Sabrina said.

"That means you don't like it?"

"When you have guests in the studio that you're interviewing I find it very interesting," said Sabrina. "I like the live atmosphere."

"That's when it's the most exciting, too," said Thea. "Usually I cut together several interviews before the broadcast and just play them back; that can be kind of boring. But when I have live guests, something unexpected could happen at anytime." She let her hand glide across Rick's shirt, opened a button, and slid it inside. Rick didn't seem to appreciate it, but said nothing.

"Have you known Rick for long?" Chris asked, feigning innocence. She knew differently, as she'd spoken to Rick a week ago, and there hadn't been any Thea mentioned.

"Forever!" Thea laughed. "It seems like it, anyway. Isn't that so, darling?" She stroked Rick's breast under her shirt, as everyone could clearly see.

"A week," Rick said laboriously.

Chris could barely suppress a grin. "And you're just now introducing her to us?" she asked.

"We were . . . busy," Rick said, as she sat up, causing Thea's hand to slide out of her shirt, which she was quick to button back up.

"Oh, yes . . ." Thea confirmed, smiling. "Rick has qualities that people don't see at first glance."

Rick gave her a chastising look. "Would you please stop that," she said.

"But darling." Rick leaned forward and Thea snuggled up against her back. "We've had so much fun. Aren't your friends allowed to know that?"

Melly produced two large cups filled with a pitch black liquid. "Quadruple," she said placing them down and handing Chris her cocktail.

Rick suddenly reached for Thea and kissed her deeply and passionately running her hands up and down along Thea's body.

Melly turned around and walked quickly toward the kitchen.

Sabrina put her lips to Chris's ear. "Oh, man, here we go," she whispered merrily. "Who do you think is going to win this one?"

An excerpt from
Ruth Gogoll's Christmas Carol
By
Ruth Gogoll

It was late when Michaela headed home that evening. The streets were deserted. She entered her apartment where everything looked exactly as it always did. There were no Christmas decorations, no burning candles. Michaela missed none of it. What was all that humbug for anyway?

The apartment had only sparse furnishing; there was nothing unnecessary. Michaela's idea of superfluous included a coffee machine, a refrigerator and a television. She had none of those.

She had moved into the apartment with the few pieces of furniture remaining from the previous tenant. She had been forced to sell her family's house after she had inherited the company and discovered that she was nearly bankrupt. Her father had needed only a few months to ruin what had taken her grandfather decades and a lot of effort to build. At that moment, she had taken a solemn oath never to become like her father. Yes, he had always been everybody's darling. However, Michaela was not after that. Popularity had no value. Money was the only thing that counted, never having to rely on anybody.

She crossed her apartment in the weak light streaming through the window from a street lamp. Why should she turn on a light? She knew where everything was. There was hardly any furniture, so there was not much opportunity to run into anything. She did not have to pay for the street lamp – although, that was not entirely true either, her taxes paid for it, much to her annoyance.

She just wanted to change out of her clothes, brush her teeth and fall into her bed. She had no use for Christmas. She did not notice that the light through the window seemed to be brighter that night because the street lamp was supported by the many colored lights shining out from the surrounding windows. Had she noticed, she would not have cared. At worst, she would have gotten upset about people's wastefulness. Those people somehow felt the need to illuminate the street, which was a waste if they were inside.

She yawned and went to bed, shivering when her body hit the cold sheets. There was no heat in her bedroom. It would get warm under the blanket in a moment, as always. She was still waiting for all of her toes to adjust to the surrounding temperature when she started to drift off.

She had a strange dream. What was even stranger: She usually did not dream at all. While she was dreaming, she was not aware of that, of course.

She was running through a long corridor, searching for something, though she would not have been able to say what exactly she was looking for. She opened every door, of which there were incredibly many on the seemingly endless corridor, and looked inside. She found herself in front of storage rooms, bricked-up doors and windows, never finding what she was searching for. Once there seemed to be a room flooded with light behind one door, but when she wanted to look inside to see what kind of room it was, the door closed, and she was back in the dimly lit corridor. She noticed she was starting to panic. She knew, she had to find it ... it ... it ... whatever it was.

"Mike ... Mike ..." A voice drifted through her dream. "Mike ..."

She opened her eyes and peered into the darkness. Her bedroom faced the courtyard; not even the street lamps could cast a glow here. Still, her eyes adjusted quickly to the absence of light, and it was as if shadows populated the room, formless, faceless shadows.

"Mike ..."

It sounded like an echo, a faraway echo without any substance, as if coming from nowhere, as if it had no origin.

Michaela set up straight in her bed. It could not be that she was just imagining this! She had never had nightmares. There had to be some real cause. A burglar maybe?

She scanned the room – as much as she could see. She was not prepared for a situation like this. To be honest, she had always thought there was nothing to steal in her apartment – which was probably true – and that she could neglect any kind of security. She had an ordinary lock on her front door. That was it. She had no weapons, neither for defense nor for offense. She knew her grandfather had had a pistol, a souvenir from the war, and she knew that pistol still had to be somewhere. But, even if she were to find it, it was not likely that it would still fire.

A flashlight on her bedside table would have been very useful now. It would have provided light, and she could have used it as a weapon. Unfortunately, Michaela had thought that investment was unnecessary too.

She lay down again and tried to calm herself. She could hear the sound of her own breathing and her rapidly pounding heart. With difficulty, she tried to get both into a slower rhythm.

A rustle. She held her breath. She knew there had to be something in the room.

She stared into the darkness, unable to move. The little bit of light in the room seemed to change, as if suddenly a street lamp was switched on outside. This could not have been, after all, there were no street lamps in the courtyard.

No, the light did not come from outside, it came from inside. Michaela sat up again; and this time she got out of bed. If there was something there, she wanted to face it upright. The air was freezing, but she did not feel it, even though her feet tried to call her attention to it.

"Mike . . ." One of the formless shadows glided towards her.

Michaela shrank back, startled, but then stopped. She was hallucinating; that was all.

The shadow hovered in the air in front of her and then suddenly took shape – a female shape. A face peeled itself out of the darkness, strangely familiar and unfamiliar at the same time. Suddenly Michaela recognized something very familiar. "Karina?"

The shadow with Karina's shape smiled.

Michaela took a deep breath. What was that woman thinking? "Did you use your key again, even though I told you not to?" she asked with irritation in her voice. Then she scowled. Had she not taken the key from Karina?

With an unusual expression on her face, rather angelically innocent and a small halo around her head, Karina answered, "I didn't need to. Not this time." She smiled a shadowy smile.

Michaela wanted to say something but shut her mouth again right away. She was confused, because Karina was so different. She did not know her like this. "Why are you here, in the middle of the night?" she asked when the shadow did not seem to want to move.

"It is a very special night," Karina whispered, the angelic smile still on her face.

"It is a very cold night!" Michaela snapped. Suddenly she became aware of the frostbite threatening her bare feet standing on the bare floor. She fumbled for her slippers and put them on. Unfortunately, they were also cold.

"It's as cold a night as it has to be," Karina said. "As it always is."

"Why are you out and about then? Don't you have a bed at home?" A knowing smile spread over Michaela's face. "Or is your bed empty? Are you alone and looking for company?" Now she knew what was up. She recalled that Karina could not stand being alone. Her bed was rarely empty. And today – on Christmas – all of her lovers were busy elsewhere – all except Michaela. So Karina had come over.

"You are the one looking for something, not I," said Karina.

Michaela remembered her dream. "How do you –?" She started to feel spooked.

"I know everything," Karina replied, "but there's a lot that you don't know yet – or no longer. That's why you will have visitors tonight."

"What? More visitors? Do you want to have an orgy?" Michaela laughed.

"You just don't understand," Karina said. "I'm not the one you think I am. I'm just a messenger."

"I rather think you're a bad dream caused by my upset stomach," Michaela replied. "Or you're playing a trick on me." She waved her hand dismissively. "Leave me alone. I have to sleep. It'll be morning soon, and I have to go to work." She crawled into her bed and pulled the blanket up over her shoulders. My god, that was cold!

"Tomorrow can wait," Karina said, "but you might not."

"Don't talk in riddles!" Michaela got upset. "That's not your style." Indeed, Karina was the most direct person she knew. She never hid what she wanted. Why was she doing it now?

"You are capable of making even an apparition like me sigh," Karina said. "You don't believe in what you see. You walk through the world with your eyes shut, without looking around you. Do you never stop?"

"Stop and smell the roses, you mean?" Michaela laughed with chattering teeth as she shivered under her blanket. "Are you Satan offering me a single moment that's so beautiful I'd want it to last forever in exchange for the world?" She propped herself up. "All right, make me an offer. I'll think about it."

"I'm not the devil." Karina glided away. "Like I said, I'm just a messenger. The others will come. Be ready."

"The others? What others?" Michaela stared confused into the darkness that started to spread out again. The light coming from Karina's shape waned. "What others?" Michaela yelled into the silence that followed the darkness.

But there was no reply.

Check out these exciting books and more at

www.elles-books.com